A LETTER HOME

Dear Mummy,

We had a murder last night. Miss Springer, the gym mistress. It happened in the middle of the night and the police came and this morning they're asking everybody questions.

Miss Chadwick told us not to talk to anybody about it but I thought you'd like to know.

With love,
Jennifer

When what looks like an amorous assignation turns out to be an assignation of quite a different sort, a globetrotting murderer leads Hercule Poirot on a breathless chase from a revolution-torn Arab sheikdom to a *very* respectable English school for young ladies.

**"AN HONEST-TO-BETSY
CHRISTIE TWISTER"**
—Saturday Review

Books by Agatha Christie

Published by POCKET BOOKS

Agatha Christie

Cat
Among
the Pigeons

A KANGAROO BOOK

PUBLISHED BY POCKET BOOKS NEW YORK

**POCKET BOOKS, a Simon & Schuster division of
GULF & WESTERN CORPORATION
1230 Avenue of the Americas, New York, N.Y. 10020**

Copyright © 1959 by Agatha Christie, Ltd.

Published by arrangement with Dodd, Mead & Company

ISBN: 0-671-82077-X

First Pocket Books printing March, 1961

10th printing

Trademarks registered in the United States and other countries.

Printed in the U.S.A.

TO
STELLA
AND
LARRY KIRWAN

Contents

Cast of Characters

PROLOGUE

Summer Term

IT WAS THE opening day of the summer term at Meadowbank school. The late afternoon sun shone down on the broad gravel sweep in front of the house. The front door was flung hospitably wide and, just within it, admirably suited to its Georgian proportions, stood Miss Vansittart, every hair in place, wearing an impeccably cut coat and skirt.

Some parents who knew no better had taken her for the great Miss Bulstrode herself, not knowing that it was Miss Bulstrode's custom to retire to a kind of holy of holies to which only a selected and privileged few were taken.

To one side of Miss Vansittart, operating on a slightly different plane, was Miss Chadwick, comfortable, knowledgeable, and so much a part of Meadowbank that it would have been impossible to imagine Meadowbank without her. It never had been without her. Miss Bulstrode and Miss Chadwick had started Meadowbank school together. Miss Chadwick wore pince-nez, stooped, was dowdily dressed, amiably vague in speech, and happened to be a brilliant mathematician.

Various welcoming words and phrases, uttered graciously by Miss Vansittart, floated through the house.

"How do you do, Mrs. Arnold? Well, Lydia, did you enjoy your Hellenic cruise? What a wonderful opportunity! Did you get some good photographs?

"Yes, Lady Garnett, Miss Bulstrode had your letter about the art classes and everything's been arranged.

"How are you, Mrs. Bird? Well? I don't think Miss Bulstrode will have time today to discuss the point. Miss Rowan is somewhere about if you'd like to talk to her about it.

"We've moved your bedroom, Pamela. You're in the far wing by the apple tree . . .

"Yes, indeed, Lady Violet, the weather has been terrible so far this spring. Is this your youngest? What is his name? Hector? What a nice aeroplane you have, Hector.

"Très heureuse de vous voir, madame. Ah, je regrette, ce ne serait pas possible, cette après-midi. Mademoiselle Bulstrode est tellement occupée.

"Good afternoon, Professor. Have you been digging up some more interesting things?"

ii.

In a small room on the first floor, Ann Shapland, Miss Bulstrode's secretary, was typing with speed and efficiency. Ann was a nice-looking young woman of thirty-five, with hair that fitted her like a black satin cap. She could be attractive when she wanted to be, but life had taught her that efficiency and competence often paid better results, and avoided painful complications. At the moment she was concentrating on being everything that a secretary to a headmistress of a famous girls' school should be.

From time to time, as she inserted a fresh sheet in her machine, she looked out of the window and registered interest in the arrivals.

"Goodness!" said Ann to herself, awed, "I didn't know there were so many chauffeurs left in England!"

Then she smiled in spite of herself, as a majestic Rolls moved away and a very small Austin of battered age drove up. A harassed looking father emerged from it with a daughter who looked far calmer than he did.

As he paused uncertainly, Miss Vansittart emerged from the house and took charge.

"Major Hargreaves? And this is Alison? Do come into the house. I'd like you to see Alison's room for yourself. I . . ."

Ann grinned and began to type again.

"Good old Vansittart, the glorified understudy," she said to herself. "She can copy all the Bulstrode's tricks. In fact she's word perfect!"

An enormous and almost incredibly opulent Cadillac, painted in two tones, raspberry red and azure blue, swept

(with difficulty, owing to its length) into the drive and
drew up behind Major the Hon. Alistair Hargreaves'
ancient Austin.

The chauffeur sprang to open the door. An immense,
bearded, dark-skinned man, wearing a flowing aba,
stepped out; a Parisian fashion plate followed; and then a
slim dark girl.

"That's probably Princess Whatshername herself,"
thought Ann. "Can't imagine her in school uniform, but I
suppose the miracle will be apparent tomorrow . . ."

Both Miss Vansittart and Miss Chadwick appeared on
this occasion.

"They'll be taken to the Presence," decided Ann.

Then she thought that, strangely enough, one didn't
quite like making jokes about Miss Bulstrode. Miss Bulstrode was Someone.

"So you'd better mind your P's and Q's, my girl," she
said to herself, "and finish these letters without making
any mistakes."

Not that Ann was in the habit of making mistakes. She
could take her pick of secretarial posts. She had been
personal assistant to the chief executive of an oil company, private secretary to Sir Mervyn Todhunter, renowned
alike for his erudition, his irritability and the illegibility of
his handwriting. She numbered two Cabinet Ministers
and an important Civil Servant among her employers.
But on the whole, her work had always lain among men.
She wondered how she was going to like being, as she put
it to herself, completely submerged in women. Well—it
was all experience! And there was always Denis! Faithful
Denis, returning from Malaya, from Burma, from various
parts of the world, always the same, devoted, asking her
once again to marry him. Dear Denis! But it would be
very dull to be married to Denis.

She would miss the company of men in the near future. All these schoolmistressy characters—not a man
about the place, except a gardener of about eighty.

But here Ann got a surprise. Looking out of the window, she saw there was a man clipping the hedge just
beyond the drive—clearly a gardener but a long way
from eighty. Young, dark, good-looking. Ann wondered

about him—there had been some talk of getting extra labour—but this was no yokel. Oh, well, nowadays people did every kind of job. Some young man trying to get together some money for some project or other, or indeed just to keep body and soul together. But he was cutting the hedge in a very expert manner. Presumably he was a real gardener after all!

"He looks," said Ann to herself, "he looks as though he might be amusing . . ."

Only one more letter to do, she was pleased to note, and then she might stroll round the garden.

iii.

Upstairs, Miss Johnson, the matron, was busy allotting rooms, welcoming newcomers, and greeting old pupils.

She was pleased it was term time again. She never knew quite what to do with herself in the holidays. She had two married sisters with whom she stayed in turn, but they were naturally more interested in their own doings and families than in Meadowbank. Miss Johnson, though dutifully fond of her sisters, was really only interested in Meadowbank.

Yes, it was nice that term had started.

"Miss Johnson?"

"Yes, Pamela."

"I say, Miss Johnson, I think something's broken in my case. It's oozed all over things. I think it's hair oil."

"Chut, chut!" said Miss Johnson, hurrying to help.

iv.

On the grass sweep of lawn beyond the gravelled drive, Mademoiselle Blanche, the new French mistress, was walking. She looked with appreciative eyes at the powerful young man clipping the hedge.

"*Assez bien,*" thought Mademoiselle Blanche.

Mademoiselle Blanche was slender and mouselike and not very noticeable, but she herself noticed everything.

Her eyes went to the procession of cars sweeping up to the front door. She assessed them in terms of money. This

Meadowbank was certainly *formidable!* She summed up mentally the profits that Miss Bulstrode must be making.

Yes, indeed! *Formidable!*

v.

Miss Rich, who taught English and geography, advanced toward the house at a rapid pace, stumbling a little now and then because, as usual, she forgot to look where she was going. Her hair, also as usual, had escaped from its bun. She had an eager ugly face.

She was saying to herself:

"To be back again! To be *here* . . . It seems years . . ." She fell over a rake, and the young gardener put out an arm and said:

"Steady, miss."

Eileen Rich said, "Thank you," without looking at him.

vi.

Miss Rowan and Miss Blake, the two junior mistresses, were strolling toward the Sports Pavilion. Miss Rowan was thin and dark and intense; Miss Blake was plump and fair. They were discussing with animation their recent adventures in Florence; the pictures they had seen, the sculpture, the fruit blossoms, and the attentions (hoped to be dishonourable) of two young Italian gentlemen.

"Of course one knows," said Miss Blake, "how Italians go on."

"Uninhibited," said Miss Rowan who had studied psychology as well as economics. "Thoroughly healthy, one feels. No repressions."

"But Giuseppe was quite impressed when he found I taught at Meadowbank," said Miss Blake. "He became much more respectful at once. He has a cousin who wants to come here, but Miss Bulstrode was not sure she had a vacancy."

"Meadowbank is a school that really counts," said Miss Rowan, happily. "Really, the new Sports Pavilion looks most impressive. I never thought it would be ready in time."

"Miss Bulstrode said it had to be," said Miss Blake in the tone of one who has said the last word.

"Oh," she added in a startled kind of way.

The door of the Sports Pavilion had opened abruptly, and a bony young woman with ginger-coloured hair emerged. She gave them a sharp unfriendly stare and moved rapidly away.

"That must be the new games mistress," said Miss Blake. "How uncouth!"

"Not a very pleasant addition to the staff," said Miss Rowan. "Miss Lorrimer was always so friendly and sociable."

"She absolutely glared at us," said Miss Blake resentfully.

They both felt quite ruffled.

vii.

Miss Bulstrode's sitting room had windows looking out in two directions, one over the drive and lawn beyond, and another toward a bank of rhododendrons behind the house. It was quite an impressive room, and Miss Bulstrode was rather more than quite an impressive woman. She was tall and rather noble looking, with well dressed grey hair, grey eyes with plenty of humour in them and a firm mouth. The success of her school (and Meadowbank was one of the most successful schools in England) was entirely due to the personality of its Headmistress. It was a very expensive school, but that was not really the point. It could be put better by saying that though you paid through the nose, you got what you paid for.

Your daughter was educated in the way you wished, and also in the way Miss Bulstrode wished, and the result of the two together seemed to give satisfaction. Owing to the high fees, Miss Bulstrode was able to employ a full staff. There was nothing mass produced about the school, but if it was individualistic, it also had disicipline. Discipline without regimentation was Miss Bulstrode's motto. Discipline, she held, was reassuring to the young, it gave them a feeling of security; regimentation gave rise to irritation. Her pupils were a varied lot. They included several foreigners of good family, often foreign royalty. There were also English girls of good family or of wealth, who wanted a training in culture and the arts, with a general knowledge of life and social facility, who would be turned out agreeable, well groomed and able to take part in intelligent discussion on any subject. There were girls who wanted to work hard and pass entrance examinations, and eventually take degrees and who, to do so, needed only good teaching and special attention. There were girls who had reacted unfavourably to school life of the conventional type. But Miss Bulstrode had her rules. She did not accept morons, or juvenile delinquents, and she preferred to accept girls whose parents she liked, and girls in whom she herself saw a prospect of development. The ages of her pupils varied within wide limits. There were girls who would have been labelled in the past as being "finished," and there were girls little more than children, some of them with parents abroad, and for whom Miss Bulstrode had a scheme of interesting holidays. The last and final court of appeal was Miss Bulstrode's own approval.

She was standing now by the chimneypiece listening to Mrs. Gerald Hope's slightly whining voice. With great foresight, she had not suggested that Mrs. Hope should sit down.

"Henrietta, you see, is very highly strung. Very highly strung indeed. Our doctor says . . ."

Miss Bulstrode nodded, with gentle reassurance, refraining from the caustic phrase she sometimes was tempted to utter.

"Don't you know, you idiot, that that is what every fool of a woman says about her child?"

She spoke with firm sympathy.

"You need have no anxiety, Mrs. Hope. Miss Rowan, a member of our staff, is a fully trained psychologist. You'll be surprised, I'm sure, at the change you'll find in Henrietta (who's a nice intelligent child, and far too good for you) after a term or two here."

"Oh, I know. You did wonders for the Lambeth child— absolutely wonders! So I'm quite happy. And I—oh, yes, I forgot. We're going to the South of France in six weeks' time. I thought I'd take Henrietta. It would make a little break for her."

"I'm afraid that's quite impossible," said Miss Bulstrode—briskly and with a charming smile, as though she were granting a request instead of refusing one.

"Oh! but—" Mrs. Hope's weak petulant face wavered, showed temper. "Really, I must insist. After all, she's *my* child."

"Exactly. But it's *my* school," said Miss Bulstrode.

"Surely I can take the child away from a school any time I like?"

"Oh, yes," said Miss Bulstrode. "You can. Of course you can. But then, *I* wouldn't have her back."

Mrs. Hope was in a real temper now.

"Considering the size of the fees I pay here . . ."

"Exactly," said Miss Bulstrode. "You wanted my school for your daughter, didn't you? But it's take it as it is, or leave it. Like that very charming Balenciaga model you are wearing. It is Balenciaga, isn't it? It is so delightful to meet a woman with a real clothes sense."

Her hand enveloped Mrs. Hope's, shook it, and imperceptibly guided her toward the door.

"Don't worry at all. Ah, here is Henrietta waiting for you." She looked with approval at Henrietta, a nice well balanced intelligent child if ever there was one, and who deserved a better mother. "Margaret, take Henrietta Hope to Miss Johnson."

Miss Bulstrode retired into her sitting room and a few moments later was talking French.

"But certainly, Excellence, your niece can study modern ballroom dancing. Most important socially. And languages, also, are most necessary."

The next arrivals were prefaced by such a gust of expensive perfume as almost to knock Miss Bulstrode backward.

"Must pour a whole bottle of the stuff over herself every day," Miss Bulstrode noted mentally, as she greeted the exquisitely dressed, dark-skinned woman.

"*Enchantée,* madame."

Madame giggled very prettily.

The big bearded man in Oriental dress took Miss Bulstrode's hand, bowed over it, and said in very good

English, "I have the honour to bring to you the Princess Shaista."

Miss Bulstrode knew all about her new pupil who had just come from a school in Switzerland, but was a little hazy as to who it was escorting her. Not the Emir himself, she decided; probably the Minister, or a chargé d'affaires. As usual when in doubt, she used that useful title *Excellence,* and assured him that Princess Shaista would have the best of care.

Shaista was smiling politely. She also was fashionably dressed and perfumed. Her age, Miss Bulstrode knew, was fifteen, but like many Eastern and Mediterranean girls, she looked older—quite mature. Miss Bulstrode spoke to her about her projected studies and was relieved to find that she answered promptly in excellent English and without giggling. In fact, her manners compared favourably with the awkward ones of many English schoolgirls of fifteen. Miss Bulstrode had often thought that it might be an excellent plan to send English girls abroad to the Near Eastern countries to learn courtesy and manners there. More compliments were uttered on both sides and then the room was empty again though still filled with such heavy perfume that Miss Bulstrode opened both windows to their full extent to let some of it out.

The next comers were Mrs. Upjohn and her daughter Julia.

Mrs. Upjohn was an agreeable young woman in the late thirties, with sandy hair, freckles and an unbecoming hat which was clearly a concession to the seriousness of the occasion, since she was obviously the type of young woman who usually went hatless.

Julia was a plain freckled child, with an intelligent forehead, and an air of good humor.

The preliminaries were quickly gone through and Julia was dispatched via Margaret to Miss Johnson, saying cheerfully as she went, "So long, Mum. Do be careful lighting that gas heater now I'm not there to do it."

Miss Bulstrode turned smilingly to Mrs. Upjohn, but did not ask her to sit. It was possible that, despite Julia's appearance of cheerful common sense, her mother, too, might want to explain that her daughter was highly strung.

"Is there anything special you want to tell me about Julia?" she asked.

Mrs. Upjohn replied cheerfully:

"Oh, no, I don't think so. Julia's a very ordinary sort of child. Quite healthy and all that. I think she's got reasonably good brains, too, but I daresay mothers usually think that about their children, don't they?"

"Mothers," said Miss Bulstrode grimly, "vary!"

"It's wonderful for her to be able to come here," said Mrs. Upjohn. "My aunt's paying for it, really, or helping. I couldn't afford it myself. But I'm awfully pleased about it. And so is Julia." She moved to the window as she said enviously, "How lovely your garden is. And so tidy. You must have lots of real gardeners."

"We had three," said Miss Bulstrode, "but just now we're short-handed except for local labour."

"Of course the trouble nowadays," said Mrs. Upjohn, "is that what one calls a gardener usually isn't a gardener, just a milkman who wants to do something in his spare time, or an old man of eighty. I sometimes think . . . Why!" exclaimed Mrs. Upjohn, still gazing out of the window, "how extraordinary!"

Miss Bulstrode paid less attention to this sudden exclamation than she should have done. For at that moment she herself had glanced casually out of the other window which gave onto the rhododendron shrubbery, and had perceived a highly unwelcome sight, none other than Lady Veronica Carlton-Sandways, weaving her way along the path, her large black velvet hat on one side, muttering to herself and clearly in a state of advanced intoxication.

Lady Veronica was not an unknown hazard. She was a charming woman, deeply attached to her twin daughters, and very delightful when she was, as they put it, herself—but unfortunately at unpredictable intervals, she was not herself. Her husband, Major Carlton-Sandways, coped fairly well. A cousin lived with them, who was usually at hand to keep an eye on Lady Veronica and head her off if necessary. On Sports Day with both Major Carlton-Sandways and the cousin in close attendance Lady

Veronica arrived completely sober and beautifully dressed and was a pattern of what a mother should be. But there were times when Lady Veronica gave her well wishers the slip, tanked herself up and made a beeline for her daughters to assure them of her maternal love. The twins had arrived by train early today, and no one had expected Lady Veronica.

Mrs. Upjohn was still talking. But Miss Bulstrode was not listening. She was reviewing various courses of action, for she recognized that Lady Veronica was fast approaching the truculent stage. But suddenly, an answer to prayer, Miss Chadwick appeared at a brisk trot, slightly out of breath. Faithful Chaddy, thought Miss Bulstrode. Always to be relied upon, whether it was a severed artery or an intoxicated parent.

"Disgraceful," said Lady Veronica to her loudly. "Tried to keep me away—didn't want me to come down here—I fooled Edith all right. Went have my rest—got out car—gave silly old Edith slip . . . regular old maid . . . no man would ever look at her twice . . . Had a row with police on the way . . . said I was unfit to drive car . . . nonshense . . . Going to tell Miss Bulstrode I'm taking the girls home—want 'em home, mother love. Wonderful thing, mother love . . ."

"Splendid, Lady Veronica," said Miss Chadwick. "We're so pleased you've come. I particularly want you to see the new Sports Pavilion. You'll love it."

Adroitly she turned Lady Veronica's unsteady footsteps in the opposite direction, leading her away from the house.

"I expect we'll find your girls there," she said brightly. "Such a nice Sports Pavilion, new lockers, and a drying room for the sports swim suits . . ." Their voices trailed away.

Miss Bulstrode watched. Once Lady Veronica tried to break away and return to the house, but Miss Chadwick was a match for her. They disappeared round the corner of the rhododendrons, headed for the distant loneliness of the new Sports Pavilion.

Miss Bulstrode heaved a sigh of relief. Excellent Chaddy. So reliable! Not modern. Not brainy—apart from mathematics. But always a present help in time of trouble.

She turned with a sigh and a sense of guilt to Mrs. Upjohn who had been talking happily for some time.

". . . though, of course," she was saying, "never real cloak and dagger stuff. Not dropping by parachute, or sabotage, or being a courier. I shouldn't have been brave enough. It was mostly very dull. Office work. And plotting. Plotting things on a map, I mean—not the storytelling kind of plotting. But of course it was exciting sometimes and it was often quite funny, as I just said—all the secret agents following each other round and round Geneva, all knowing each other by sight, and often ending up in the same bar. I wasn't married then, of course. It was all great fun."

She stopped abruptly with an apologetic and friendly smile.

"I'm sorry I've been talking so much. Taking up your time. When you've got such lots of people to see."

She held out a hand, said goodby and departed.

Miss Bulstrode stood frowning for a moment. Without knowing exactly why, she felt uneasy. Some instinct warned her that she had missed something that might be important.

She brushed the feeling aside. This was the opening day of summer term, and she had many more parents to see. Never had her school been more popular, more assured of success. Meadowbank was at its zenith.

There was nothing to tell her that within a few weeks Meadowbank would be plunged into a sea of trouble; that disorder, confusion and murder would reign there, that already certain events had been set in motion . . .

1

Revolution in Ramat

ABOUT TWO MONTHS earlier than the first day of the summer term at Meadowbank, certain events had taken place which were to have unexpected repercussions in that celebrated girls' school.

In the Palace at Ramat, two young men sat smoking and considering the immediate future. One young man was dark, with a smooth olive face and large melancholy eyes. He was Prince Ali Yusuf, Hereditary Sheik of Ramat, which, though small, was one of the richest states in the Middle East. The other young man was sandy-haired and freckled, and more or less penniless except for the handsome salary he drew as private pilot to His Highness Prince Ali Yusuf. In spite of this difference in status, they were on terms of perfect equality. They had been at the same public school and had been friends then and ever since.

"They shot at us, Bob," said Prince Ali almost incredulously.

"They shot at us all right," said Bob Rawlinson.

"And they meant it. They meant to bring us down."

"The bastards meant it all right," said Bob grimly.

Ali considered for a moment.

"It would hardly be worth while trying it again?"

"We mightn't be so lucky this time. The truth is, Ali, we've left things too late. You should have got out two weeks ago. I told you so."

"One doesn't like to run away," said the ruler of Ramat.

"I see your point. But remember what Shakespeare or one of those poetical fellows said about those who run away living to fight another day."

"To think," said the young Prince with feeling, "of the

money that has gone into making this a Welfare State. Hospitals, schools, a health service . . ."

Bob Rawlinson interrupted the catalogue.

"Couldn't the Embassy do something?"

Ali Yusuf flushed angrily.

"Take refuge in your Embassy? That, never. The extremists would probably storm the place—they wouldn't respect diplomatic immunity. Besides, if I did that, it really would be the end! Already the chief accusation against me is of being pro-Western." He sighed. "It is so difficult to understand." He sounded wistful, younger than his twenty-five years. "My grandfather was a cruel man, a real tyrant. He had hundreds of slaves and treated them ruthlessly. In his tribal wars, he killed his enemies unmercifully and executed them horribly. The mere whisper of his name made everyone turn pale. And yet—he is a legend still! Admired! Respected! The great Achmed Abdullah! And I? What have I done? Built hospitals and schools, welfare, housing . . . all the things people are said to want. Don't they want them? Would they prefer a reign of terror like my grandfather's?"

"I expect so," said Bob Rawlinson. "Seems a bit unfair, but there it is."

"But why, Bob? Why?"

Bob Rawlinson sighed, wriggled and endeavoured to explain what he felt. He had to struggle with his own inarticulateness.

"Well," he said. "He put up a show—I suppose that's it really. He was—sort of—dramatic, if you know what I mean."

He looked at his friend who was definitely not dramatic. A nice quiet decent chap, sincere and perplexed, that was what Ali was, and Bob liked him for it. He was neither picturesque nor violent, but while in England people who are picturesque and violent cause embarrassment and are not much liked, in the Middle East, Bob was fairly sure, it was different.

"But democracy—" began Ali.

"Oh, democracy—" Bob waved his pipe. "That's a word that means different things everywhere. One thing's certain, it never means what the Greeks originally meant by it. I bet you anything you like that if they boot you out of here, some spouting hot-air merchant will take over, yelling his own praises, building himself up into God Almighty, and stringing up, or cutting off the heads of anyone who dares to disagree with him in any way. And, mark you, he'll say it's a democratic government, of the people and for the people. I expect the people will like it, too. Exciting for them. Lots of bloodshed."

"But we are not savages! We are civilized nowadays."

"There are different kinds of civilization . . ." said Bob vaguely. "Besides—I rather think we've all got a bit of the savage in us—if we can think up a good excuse for letting it rip."

"Perhaps you are right," said Ali sombrely.

"The thing people don't seem to want anywhere, nowadays," said Bob, "is anyone who's got a bit of ordinary common sense. I've never been a brainy chap— well, you know that well enough, Ali—but I often think that that's the only thing the world really needs—just a bit of common sense." He laid aside his pipe and sat up in his chair. "But never mind all that. The thing is how we're going to get you out of here. Is there anybody in the Army you can really trust?"

Slowly, Prince Ali Yusuf shook his head.

"A fortnight ago I should have said Yes. But now, I do not know . . . cannot be sure . . ."

Bob nodded. "That's the hell of it. As for this Palace of yours, it gives me the creeps."

Ali acquiesced without emotion.

"Yes, there are spies everywhere in palaces . . . They hear everything—they—know everything."

"Even down at the hangars—" Bob broke off. "Old Achmed's all right. He's got a kind of sixth sense. Found one of the mechanics trying to tamper with the plane—one of the men we'd have sworn was absolutely trustworthy. Look here, Ali, if we're going to have a shot at getting you away, it will have to be soon."

"I know—I know. I think—I am quite certain now— that if I stay I shall be killed."

He spoke without emotion, or any kind of panic; with a mild detached interest.

"We'll stand a good chance of being killed anyway," Bob warned him. "We'll have to fly out North, you know.

They can't intercept us that way. But it means going over the mountains—and at this time of year . . ."

He shrugged his shoulders. "You've got to understand. It's damned risky."

Ali Yusuf looked distressed.

"If anything happened to you, Bob—"

"Oh, don't worry about me, Ali. That's not what I meant. I'm not important. And anyway, I'm the sort of chap that's sure to get killed sooner or later. I'm always doing crazy things. No—it's you—I don't want to persuade you one way or the other. If a portion of the Army is loyal . . ."

"I do not like the idea of running away," said Ali simply. "But I do not in the least want to be a martyr, and be cut to pieces by a mob."

He was silent for a moment or two.

"Very well then," he said at last with a sigh. "We will make the attempt. When?"

Bob shrugged his shoulders.

"Sooner the better. We've got to get you to the airstrip in some natural way. How about saying you're going to inspect the new road construction out at Al Jasar? Sudden whim. Go this afternoon. Then, as your car passes the airstrip, stop there—I'll have the bus all ready and tuned up. The idea will be to go up to inspect the road construction from the air, see? We take off and go! We can't take any baggage, of course. It's got to be all quite impromptu."

"There is nothing I wish to take with me—except one thing—"

He smiled, and suddenly the smile altered his face and made a different person of him. He was no longer the modern conscientious Westernized young man—the smile held all the racial guile and craft which had enabled a long line of his ancestors to survive.

"You are my friend, Bob, you shall see."

His hand went inside his shirt and fumbled. Then he held out a little chamois leather bag.

"This?" Bob frowned and looked puzzled.

Ali took it back from him, untied the neck, and poured the contents on the table.

Bob held his breath for a moment, then expelled it in a soft whistle.

"Good Lord. Are they real?"

Ali looked amused.

"Of course they are real. Most of them belonged to my father. He acquired new ones every year. I, too. They have come from many places, bought for our family by men we can trust. From London, from Calcutta, from South Africa. It is a tradition of our family. To have these in case of need." He added in a matter-of-fact voice: "They are worth, at today's prices, about three quarters of a million."

"Three quarters of a million pounds." Bob let out a whistle, picked up the stones, let them run through his fingers. "It's fantastic. Like a fairy tale. It does things to you."

"Yes." The dark young man nodded. Again that age-long weary look was on his face. "Men are not the same when it comes to jewels. There is always a trail of violence to follow such things. Death, bloodshed, murder. And women will be the worst. For with women it will not only be the value. It is something to do with the jewels themselves. Beautiful jewels drive women mad. They want to own them. To wear them round their throats, on their bosoms. I would not trust any woman with these. But I shall trust you."

"Me?" Bob stared.

"Yes. I do not want those stones to fall into the hands of my enemies. I do not know when the rising against me will take place. It may be planned for today. I may not live to reach the airstrip this afternoon. Take the stones and do the best you can."

"But look here—I don't understand. What am I to do with them?"

"Arrange somehow to get them safely out of the country."

Ali stared placidly at his perturbed friend.

"You mean, you want me to carry them instead of you?"

"You can put it that way. But I think, really, you will be able to think of some better plan to get them to Europe."

"But look here, Ali, I haven't the first idea how to set about such a thing."

Ali leaned back in his chair. He was smiling in a quietly amused manner.

"You have common sense. And you are honest. And I remember, from the days when you were my fag, that you could always think up some ingenious idea. I will give you the name and address of a man who deals with such matters for me—that is—in case I should not survive. Do not look so worried, Bob. Do the best you can. That is all I ask. I shall not blame you if you fail. It is as Allah wills. For me, it is simple. I do not want those stones taken from my dead body. For the rest—" he shrugged his shoulders. "It is as I have said. All will go as Allah wills."

"You're nuts!"

"No. I am a fatalist, that is all."

"But look here, Ali. You said just now I was honest. But three quarters of a million. Don't you think that might sap any man's honesty?"

Ali Yusuf looked at his friend with affection.

"Strangely enough," he said, "I have no doubts on that score."

■
2

The Woman on the Balcony

As Bob Rawlinson walked along the echoing marble corridors of the Palace, he had never felt so unhappy in his life. The knowledge that he was carrying three quarters of a million pounds in his trousers pocket caused him acute misery. He felt as though every Palace official he encountered must know the fact. He felt, even, that the knowledge of his precious burden must show in his face. He would have been relieved to learn that his freckled countenance bore exactly its usual expression of cheerful good nature.

The sentries outside presented arms with a clash. Bob walked down the crowded main street of Ramat, his mind still dazed. Where was he going? What was he planning to do? He had no idea. And time was short.

The main street was like most main streets in the Middle East. It was a mixture of squalor and magnificence. Banks reared their vast newly built magnificence. Innumerable small shops presented a collection of cheap plastic goods. Babies' bootees and cheap cigarette lighters were displayed in unlikely juxtaposition. There were sewing machines, and spare parts for cars. Pharmacies displayed flyblown proprietary medicines, and large notices of penicillin in every form and antibiotics galore. In very few of the shops was there anything that you would normally want to buy, except possibly the latest Swiss watches, hundreds of which were displayed crowded into a tiny window. The assortment was so great that even there one would have shrunk from purchase, dazzled by sheer mass.

Bob, still walking in a kind of stupor, jostled by figures in native or European dress, pulled himself together and asked himself again where the hell he was going.

He turned into a native café and ordered lemon tea. As he sipped it, he began, slowly, to come to. The atmosphere of the café was soothing. At a table opposite him an elderly Arab was peacefully clicking through a string of amber beads. Behind him two men played trictrac. It was a good place to sit and think.

And he'd got to think. Jewels worth three quarters of a million had been handed to him, and it was up to him to devise some plan of getting them out of the country. No time to lose, either. At any minute the balloon might go up.

Ali was crazy, of course. Tossing three quarters of a million light-heartedly to a friend that way. And then sitting back quietly himself and leaving everything to Allah. Bob had not got that recourse. Bob's God expected his servants to decide on and perform their own actions to the best of the ability their God had given them.

What the hell was he going to do with those damned stones?

He thought of the Embassy. No, he couldn't involve the Embassy. The Embassy would almost certainly refuse to be involved.

What he needed was some person, some perfectly ordinary person, who was leaving the country in some perfectly ordinary way. A businessman, or a tourist would be best. Someone with no political connections whose baggage would, at most, be subjected to a superficial search or more probably no search at all. There was, of course, the other end to be considered. Sensation at London Air Port. Attempt to smuggle in jewels worth three quarters of a million. And so on and so on. One would have to risk that.

Somebody ordinary—a bona fide traveller. And suddenly Bob kicked himself for a fool. Joan, of course. His sister Joan Sutcliffe. Joan had been out here for two months with her daughter Jennifer, who after a bad bout of pneumonia had been ordered sunshine and a dry climate. They were going by "long sea" in four or five days.

Joan was the ideal person. What was it Ali had said about women and jewels? Bob smiled to himself. Good old Joan! *She* wouldn't lose her head over jewels. Trust her to keep her feet on the earth. Yes—he could trust Joan.

Wait a minute, though . . . could he trust Joan? Her honesty, yes. But her discretion? Regretfully Bob shook his head. Joan would talk, would not be able to help talking. Even worse, she would hint. "I'm taking home something very important. I mustn't say a word to anyone. It's really rather exciting . . ."

Joan had never been able to keep a thing to herself though she was always very incensed if one told her so. Joan, then, mustn't know what she was taking. It would be safer for her that way. He'd make the stones up into a parcel, an innocent-looking parcel. Tell her some story. A present for someone? A commission? He'd think of something . . .

Bob glanced at his watch and rose to his feet. Time was getting on.

He strode along the street oblivious of the midday heat Everything seemed so normal. There was nothing to show on the surface Only in the Palace was one consciou of the banked-down fires, of the spying, the whispers The Army—it all depended on the Army. Who was loyal? Who was disloyal? A *coup d'état* would certainly be attempted Would it succeed or fail?

Bob frowned as he turned into Ramat's leading hotel. It was modestly called the Ritz Savoy and had a grand modernistic facade. It had opened with a flourish three years ago with a Swiss manager, a Viennese chef. and an Italian maître d'hôtel. Everything had been wonderful. The Viennese chef had gone first, then the Swiss manager Now the Italian head waiter had gone too. The food was still ambitious, but bad, the service abominable and a good deal of the expensive plumbing had gone wrong.

The clerk behind the desk knew Bob well and beamed at him.

"Good morning, Squadron Leader. You want your sister? She has gone for a picnic with the little girl."

"A picnic?" Bob was taken aback—of all the silly times to go for a picnic.

"With Mr. and Mrs. Hurst from the oil company," said the clerk informatively. Everyone always knew everything. "They have gone to the Kalat Diwa dam."

Bob swore under his breath. Joan wouldn't be home for hours.

"I'll go up to her room," he said and held out his hand for the key which the clerk gave him.

He unlocked the door and went in. The room, a large double-bedded one, was in its usual confusion. Joan Sutcliffe was not a tidy woman. Golf clubs lay across a chair, tennis racquets had been flung on the bed. Clothing lay about the table was littered with rolls of films, postcards, paperback books and an assortment of native curios from the Souk, mostly made in Birmingham and Japan.

Bob looked round him, at the suitcases and the zip bags. He was faced with a problem. He wouldn't be able to see Joan before flying Ali out. There wouldn't be time to get to the dam and back. He could parcel up the stuff and leave it with a note—but almost immediately he shook his head. He knew quite well that he was nearly always followed. He'd probably been followed from the Palace to the café and from the café here. He hadn't spotted anyone—but he knew that they were good at the job. There was nothing suspicious in his coming to the hotel to see his sister—but if he left a parcel and a note, the note would be read and the parcel opened.

Time . . . time . . . He'd no time . . .

Three quarters of a million in precious stones in his trousers pocket.

He looked round the room.

Then, with a grin, he fished out from his pocket the little tool kit he always carried. His niece Jennifer had some modeling clay, he noted, that would help.

He worked quickly and skilfully. Once he looked up, suspicious, his eyes going to the open window. No, there was no balcony outside this room. It was just his nerves that had made him feel that someone was watching him.

He finished his task and nodded in approval. Nobody would notice what he had done—he felt sure of that. Neither Joan nor anyone else. Certainly not Jennifer, a self-centered child, who never saw or noticed anything outside herself.

He swept up all evidences of his toil and put them into his pocket. Then he hesitated, looking round.

He drew Mrs. Sutcliffe's writing pad toward him and sat frowning. He must leave a note for Joan.

But what could he say? It must be something that Joan would understand—but which would mean nothing to anyone who read the note.

And really that was impossible! In the kind of thriller that Bob liked reading to fill up his spare moments, you left a kind of cryptogram which was always successfully puzzled out by someone. But he couldn't even begin to think of a cryptogram—and in any case Joan was the sort of common-sense person who would need the i's dotted and the t's crossed before she noticed anything at all.

Then his brow cleared. There was another way of doing it. Divert attention away from Joan—leave an ordinary everyday note. Then leave a message with someone else to be given to Joan in England.

He wrote rapidly:

> *Dear Joan,*
>
> *Dropped in to ask if you'd care to play a round of golf this evening but if you've been up to the dam, you'll probably be dead to the world. What about tomorrow? Five o'clock at the Club.*
>
> > *Yours,*
> > *Bob*

A casual sort of message to leave for a sister that he might never see again—but in some ways the more casual the better. Joan mustn't be involved in any funny business, mustn't even know that there was any funny business. Joan could not dissimulate. Her protection would be the fact that she clearly knew nothing.

And the note would accomplish a dual purpose. It would seem that he, Bob, had no plan for departure himself.

He thought for a minute or two, then he crossed to the telephone and gave the number of the British Embassy. Presently he was connected with Edmundson, the third secretary, a friend of his.

"John? Bob Rawlinson here. Can you meet me somewhere when you get off? Make it a bit earlier than that? You've got to, old boy. It's important. Well, actually, it's a girl . . ." He gave an embarrassed cough. "She's wonderful, quite wonderful. Out of this world. Only it's a bit tricky."

Edmundson's voice, sounding slightly stuffed shirt and disapproving, said, "Really, Bob, you and your girls. All right, two o'clock do you?" and rang off. Bob heard the little echoing click as whoever had been listening in replaced the receiver.

Good old Edmundson. Since all telephones in Ramat had been tapped, Bob and John Edmundson had worked out a little code of their own. A wonderful girl who was "out of this world" meant something urgent and important.

Edmundson would pick him up in his car outside the

new Merchants Bank at two o'clock and he'd tell Edmundson of the hiding place. Tell him that Joan didn't know about it but that, if anything happened to him, it was important. Going by the long sea route, Joan and Jennifer wouldn't be back in England for six weeks. By that time the revolution would almost certainly have happened and either been successful or have been put down. Ali Yusuf might be in Europe, or he and Bob might both be dead. He would tell Edmundson enough, but not too much.

Bob took a last look round the room. It looked exactly the same, peaceful, untidy, domestic. The only thing added was his harmless note to Joan. He propped it up on the table and went out. There was no one in the long corridor.

ii.

The woman in the room next to that occupied by Joan Sutcliffe stepped back from the balcony. There was a mirror in her hand.

She had gone out on the balcony originally to examine more closely a single hair that had the audacity to spring up on her chin. She dealt with it with tweezers, then subjected her face to a minute scrutiny in the clear sunlight.

It was then, as she relaxed, that she saw something else. The angle at which she was holding her mirror was such that it reflected the mirror of the hanging wardrobe in the room next to hers, and in that mirror she saw a man doing something very curious.

So curious and unexpected that she stood there motionless, watching. He could not see her from where he sat at the table, and she could only see him by means of the double reflection.

If he had turned his head, he might have caught sight of her mirror in the wardrobe mirror, but he was too absorbed in what he was doing to look behind him.

Once, it was true, he did look up suddenly toward the window, but since there was nothing to see there, he lowered his head again.

The woman watched him while he finished what he

was doing. After a moment's pause he wrote a note which he propped up on the table. Then he moved out of her line of vision but she could just hear enough to realize that he was making a telephone call. She couldn't quite catch what was said, but it sounded light-hearted—casual. Then she heard the door close.

The woman waited a few moments. Then she opened her door. At the far end of the passage an Arab was flicking idly, with a feather duster. He turned the corner, out of sight.

The woman slipped quickly to the door of the next room. It was locked, but she had expected that. The hairpin she had with her and the blade of a small knife did the job quickly and expertly.

She went in, pushing the door to behind her. She picked up the note. The flap had only been stuck down lightly and opened easily. She read the note, frowning. There was no explanation there.

She sealed it up, put it back, and walked across the room.

There, with her hand outstretched, she was disturbed by voices through the window from the terrace below.

One was a voice that she knew to be the occupier of the room in which she was standing. A decided, didactic voice, fully assured of itself.

She darted to the window.

Below on the terrace, Joan Sutcliffe, accompanied by her daughter Jennifer, a pale solid child of fifteen, was telling the world and a tall unhappy-looking Englishman from the British Consulate just what she thought of the arrangements he had come to make.

"But it's absurd! I never heard such nonsense. Everything's perfectly quiet here and everyone quite pleasant. I think it's all a lot of panicky fuss."

"We hope so, Mrs. Sutcliffe, we certainly hope so. But H.E. feels that the responsibility is such . . ."

Mrs. Sutcliffe cut him short. She did not propose to consider the responsibility of Ambassadors.

"We've a lot of baggage, you know. We were going home by long sea—next Wednesday. The sea voyage will be good for Jennifer. The doctor said so. I really must absolutely decline to alter all my arrangements and be flown to England in this silly flurry."

The unhappy-looking man said encouragingly that Mrs. Sutcliffe and her daughter could be flown, not to England, but to Aden and catch their boat there.

"With our baggage?"

"Yes, yes, that can be arranged. I've got a car waiting with a station wagon. We can load everything right away."

"Oh, well." Mrs. Sutcliffe capitulated. "I suppose we'd better pack."

"At once, if you don't mind."

The woman in the bedroom drew back hurriedly. She took a quick glance at the address on a luggage label on one of the suitcases. Then she slipped out of the room and back into her own just as Mrs. Sutcliffe turned the corner of the corridor.

The clerk from the office was running after her.

"Your brother, the Squadron Leader, has been here, Mrs. Sutcliffe. He went up to your room. But I think that he has left again. You must just have missed him."

"How tiresome," said Mrs. Sutcliffe. "Thank you," she said to the clerk and went on to Jennifer, "I suppose Bob's fussing too. I can't see any sign of disturbance myself in the streets. This door's unlocked. How careless these people are."

"Perhaps it was Uncle Bob," said Jennifer.

"I wish I hadn't missed him. Oh, there's a note." She tore it open.

"At any rate Bob isn't fussing," she said triumphantly. "He obviously doesn't know a thing about all this. Diplomatic wind up, that's all it is. How I hate trying to pack in the heat of the day. This room's like an oven. Come on, Jennifer, get your things out of the chest of drawers and the wardrobe. We must just shove everything in anyhow. We can repack later."

"I've never been in a revolution," said Jennifer thoughtfully.

"I don't expect you'll be in one this time," said her mother sharply. "It will be just as I say. Nothing will happen."

Jennifer looked disappointed.

3

Introducing Mr. Robinson

IT WAS SOME six weeks later that a young man tapped
discreetly on the door of a room in Bloomsbury and was
told to come in.

It was a small room. Behind a desk sat a fat middle-
aged man slumped in a chair. He was wearing a
crumpled suit, the front of which was smothered in cigar
ash. The windows were closed and the atmosphere was
almost unbearable.

"Well?" said the fat man testily, and speaking with
half-closed eyes. "What is it now, eh?"

It was said of Colonel Pikeaway that his eyes were
always just closing in sleep, or just opening after sleep. It
was also said that his name was not Pikeaway and that
he was not a Colonel. But some people will say anything!

"Edmundson, from the Foreign Office, is here, sir."

"Oh," said Colonel Pikeaway.

He blinked, appeared to be going to sleep again and
muttered:

"Third secretary at our Embassy in Ramat at the time
of the revolution. Right?"

"That's right, sir."

"I suppose, then, I'd better see him," said Colonel
Pikeaway without any marked relish. He pulled himself
into a more upright position and brushed off a little of the
ash from his paunch.

Mr. Edmundson was a tall fair young man, very correctly dressed with manners to match, and a general air
of quiet disapproval.

"Colonel Pikeaway? I'm John Edmundson. They said
you—er—might want to see me."

"Did they? Well, they should know," said Colonel
Pikeaway. "Siddown," he added.

27

His eyes began to close again, but before they did so, he spoke:

"You were in Ramat at the time of the revolution?"

"Yes, I was. A nasty business."

"I suppose it would be. You were a friend of Bob Rawlinson's, weren't you?"

"I know him fairly well, yes."

"Wrong tense," said Colonel Pikeaway. "He's dead."

"Yes, sir, I know. But I wasn't sure . . ." He paused.

"You don't have to take pains to be discreet here," said Colonel Pikeaway. "We know everything here. Or if we don't, we pretend we do. Rawlinson flew Ali Yusuf out of Ramat on the day of the revolution. Plane wasn't heard of since. Could have landed in some inaccessible place, or could have crashed. Wreckage of a plane has been found in the Arolez mountains. Two bodies. News will be released to the press tomorrow. Right?"

Edmundson admitted that it was quite right.

"We know all about things here," said Colonel Pikeaway. "That's what we're for. Plane flew into the mountain. Could have been weather conditions. Some reason to believe it was sabotage. Delayed action bomb. We haven't got the full reports yet. The plane crashed in a pretty inaccessible place. There was a reward offered for finding it, but these things take a long time to filter through. Then we had to fly out experts to make an examination. All the red tape, of course. Applications to a foreign government, permission from ministers, palm greasing—to say nothing of the local peasantry appropriating anything that might come in useful."

He paused and looked at Edmundson.

"Very sad, the whole thing," said Edmundson. "Prince Ali Yusuf would have made a most enlightened ruler, with firm democratic principles."

"That's what probably did the poor chap in," said Colonel Pikeaway. "But we can't waste time in telling sad stories of the deaths of kings. We've been asked to make certain—inquiries. By interested parties. Parties, that is, to whom Her Majesty's Government is well disposed." He looked hard at the other. "Know what I mean?"

"Well, I have heard something." Edmundson spoke reluctantly.

"You've heard, perhaps, that nothing of value was found on the bodies, or among the wreckage, or as far as is known, had been pinched by the locals. Though as to that, you never can tell with peasants. They can clam up as well as the Foreign Office itself. And what else have you heard?"

"Nothing else."

"You haven't heard that perhaps something of value ought to have been found? What did they send you to me for?"

"They said you might want to ask me certain questions," said Edmundson primly.

"If I ask you questions, I shall expect answers," Colonel Pikeaway pointed out.

"Naturally."

"Doesn't seem natural to you, son. Did Bob Rawlinson say anything to you before he flew out of Ramat? He was in Ali's confidence if anyone was. Come now, let's have it. Did he say anything?"

"As to what, sir?"

Colonel Pikeaway stared hard at him and scratched his ear.

"Oh, all right," he grumbled. "Hush up this and don't say that. Overdo it in my opinion! If you don't know what I'm talking about, you don't know, and there it is."

"I think there was something—" Edmundson spoke cautiously and with reluctance. "Something important that Bob might have wanted to tell me."

"Ah," said Colonel Pikeaway, with the air of a man who has at last pulled a cork out of a bottle. "Interesting. Let's have what you know."

"It's very little, sir. Bob and I had a kind of simple code. We'd cottoned on to the fact that all the telephones in Ramat were being tapped. Bob was in the way of hearing things at the Palace, and I sometimes had a bit of useful information to pass on to him. So if one of us rang the other up and mentioned a girl or girls, in a certain way, using the term 'out of this world' for her, it meant something was up!"

"Important information of some kind or other?"

"Yes. Bob rang me up using those terms the day the whole show started. I was to meet him at our usual rendezvous—outside one of the banks. But rioting broke out in that particular quarter and the police closed the road. I couldn't make contact with Bob or he with me. He flew Ali out that same afternoon."

"I see," said Pikeaway. "No idea where he was telephoning from?"

"No. It might have been anywhere."

"Pity." He paused and then threw out casually:

"Do you know Mrs. Sutcliffe?"

"You mean Bob Rawlinson's sister? I met her out there, of course. She was there with a schoolgirl daughter. I don't know her well."

"Were she and Bob Rawlinson very close?"

Edmundson considered.

"No, I shouldn't say so. She was a good deal older than he was, rather much of the elder sister. And he didn't much like his brother-in-law—always referred to him as a pompous ass."

"So he is! One of our prominent industrialists—and how pompous can they get! So you don't think it likely that Bob Rawlinson would have confided an important secret to his sister?"

"It's difficult to say—but no, I shouldn't think so."

"I shouldn't either," said Colonel Pikeaway.

He sighed. "Well, there we are. Mrs. Sutcliffe and her daughter are on their way home by the long sea route. Dock at Tilbury on the *Eastern Queen* tomorrow."

He was silent for a moment or two, while his eyes made a thoughtful survey of the young man opposite him. Then, as though having come to a decision, he held out his hand and spoke briskly.

"Very good of you to come."

"I'm only sorry I've been of such little use. You're sure that there's nothing I can do?"

"No. No. I'm afraid not."

John Edmundson went out.

The discreet young man came back.

"Thought I might have sent him to Tilbury to break the news to the sister," said Pikeaway. "Friend of her brother's—all that. But I decided against it. Inelastic type. That's the F.O. training. Not an opportunist. I'll send what's his name."

"Derek?"

"That's right," Colonel Pikeaway nodded approval. "Getting to know what I mean quite well, ain't you?"

"I try my best, sir."

"Trying's not enough. You have to succeed. Send me along Ronnie first. I've got an assignment for him."

ii.

Colonel Pikeaway was apparently just going off to sleep again when the young man called Ronnie entered the room. He was tall, dark, muscular, and had a gay and rather impertinent manner.

Colonel Pikeaway looked at him for a moment or two and then grinned.

"How'd you like to penetrate into a girls' school?" he asked.

"A girls' school?" The young man lifted his eyebrows. "That will be something new! What are they up to? Making bombs in the chemistry class?"

"Nothing of that kind. Very superior high-class school. Meadowbank."

"Meadowbank!" the young man whistled. "I can't believe it!"

"Hold your impertinent tongue and listen to me. Princess Shaista, first cousin and only near relative of the late Prince Ali Yusuf of Ramat, goes there this next term. She's been at school in Switzerland up to now."

"What do I do? Abduct her?"

"Certainly not. I think it possible she may become a focus of interest in the near future. I want you to keep an eye on developments. I'll have to leave it vague. I don't know what or who may turn up, but if any of our more unlikable friends seem to be interested, report it. A watching brief, that's what you've got."

The young man nodded.

"And how do I get in to watch? Shall I be the drawing master?"

"The visiting staff is all female." Colonel Pikeaway looked at him in a considering manner. "I think I'll have to make you a gardener."

"A gardener?"

"Yes. I'm right in thinking you know something about gardening?"

"Yes, indeed. I ran a column on 'Your Garden' in the Sunday *Mail* for a year in my younger days."

"Tush!" said Colonel Pikeaway. "That's nothing! I could do a column on gardening myself without knowing a thing about it—just crib from a few luridly illustrated nurserymen's catalogues and a gardening encyclopedia. I know all the patter. *'Why not break away from tradition and sound a really tropical note in your border this year? Lovely Amabellis Gossiporia, and some of the wonderful new Chinese hybrids of Sinensis Maka foolia. Try the rich blushing beauty of a clump of Sinistra Hopaless, not very hardy but they should be all right against a west wall.'*" He broke off and grinned. "Nothing to it! The fools buy the things and early frost sets in and kills them and they wish they'd stuck to wallflowers and forget-me-nots! No, my boy, I mean the real stuff. Spit on your hands and use the spade, be well acquainted with the compost heap, mulch diligently, use the Dutch hoe and every other kind of hoe, trench really deep for your sweet peas—and all the rest of the beastly business. Can you do it?"

"All these things I have done from my youth upward!"

"Of course you have. I know your mother. Well, that's settled."

"Is there a job going as gardener at Meadowbank?"

"Sure to be," said Colonel Pikeaway. "Every garden in England is short staffed. I'll write you some nice testimonials. You'll see, they'll simply jump at you. No time to waste, summer term begins on the twenty-ninth."

"I garden and I keep my eyes open, is that right?"

"That's it, and if any oversexed teenagers make passes at you, Heaven help you if you respond. I don't want you thrown out on your ear too soon."

He drew a sheet of paper toward him. "What do you fancy as a name?"

"Adam would seem appropriate."

"Last name?"

"How about Eden?"

"I'm not sure I like the way your mind is running. Adam Goodman will do very nicely. Go and work out

your past history with Jenson and then get cracking." He
looked at his watch. "I've no more time for you. I don't
want to keep Robinson waiting. He ought to be here by
now."

Adam (to give him his new name) stopped as he was
moving to the door.

"Robinson?" he asked curiously. "Is *he* coming?"

"I said so." A buzzer went on the desk. "There he is
now. Always punctual, Mr. Robinson."

"Tell me," said Adam curiously. "Who is he really?
What's his real name?"

"His name," said Pikeaway, "is Mr. Robinson. That's
all I know, and that's all anybody knows."

iii.

The man who came into the room did not look as
though his name was, or could ever have been, Robinson.
It might have been Demetrius, or Isaacstein, or Perenna—
though not one or the other in particular. He was not
definitely Jewish, nor definitely Greek nor Portuguese nor
Spanish, nor South American. What did seem highly unlikely was that he was an Englishman called Robinson.
He was fat and well dressed, with a yellow face, melancholy dark eyes, a broad forehead, and a generous mouth
that displayed rather overlarge very white teeth. His
hands were well shaped and beautifully kept. His voice
was English with no trace of accent.

He and Colonel Pikeaway greeted each other rather in
the manner of two reigning monarchs. Politenesses were
exchanged.

Then, as Mr. Robinson accepted a cigar, Colonel
Pikeaway said:

"It is very good of you to offer to help us."

Mr. Robinson lit his cigar, savoured it appreciatively,
and finally spoke.

"My dear fellow. I just thought— I hear things, you
know. I know a lot of people, and they tell me things. I
don't know why."

Colonel Pikeaway did not comment on the reason
why.

He said:

"I gather you've heard that Prince Ali Yusuf's plane has been found?"

"Wednesday of last week," said Mr. Robinson. "Young Rawlinson was the pilot. A tricky flight. But the crash wasn't due to any error on Rawlinson's part. The plane had been tampered with—by a certain Achmed—senior mechanic. Completely trustworthy—or so Rawlinson thought. But he wasn't. He's got a very lucrative job with the new regime now."

"So it was sabotage! We didn't know for sure. It's a sad story."

"Yes. That poor young man—Ali Yusuf, I mean—was ill equipped to cope with corruption and treachery. His public school education was unwise—or at least that is my view. But we do not concern ourselves with him now, do we? He is yesterday's news. Nothing is so dead as a dead king. We are concerned, you in your way, I in mine, with what dead kings leave behind them."

"Which is?"

Mr. Robinson shrugged his shoulders.

"A substantial bank balance in Geneva, a modest balance in London, considerable assets in his own country now taken over by the glorious new regime (and a little bad feeling as to how the spoils have been divided, or so I hear!), and finally a small personal item."

"Small?"

"These things are relative. Anyway, small in bulk. Handy to carry upon the person."

"They weren't on Ali Yusuf's person, as far as we know."

"No. Because he had handed them over to young Rawlinson."

"Are you sure of that?" asked Pikeaway sharply.

"Well, one is never sure," said Mr. Robinson apologetically. "In a Palace there is so much gossip. It cannot all be true. But there was a very strong rumour to that effect."

"They weren't on young Rawlinson's person, either."

"In that case," said Mr. Robinson, "it seems as though they must have been got out of the country by some other means."

"What other means? Have you any idea?"

"Rawlinson went to a café in the town after he had received the jewels. He was not seen to speak to anyone or approach anyone while he was there. Then he went to the Ritz Savoy Hotel where his sister was staying. He went up to her room and was there for about twenty minutes. She herself was out. He then left the hotel and went to the Merchants Bank in Victory Square where he cashed a check. When he came out of the bank a disturbance was beginning. Students rioting about something. It was some time before the Square was cleared. Rawlinson then went straight to the airstrip where, in company with Sergeant Achmed, he went over the plane.

"Ali Yusuf drove out to see the new road construction, stopped his car at the airstrip, joined Rawlinson and expressed a desire to take a short flight and see the dam and the new highway construction from the air. They took off and did not return."

"And your deductions from that?"

"My dear fellow, the same as yours. Why did Bob Rawlinson spend twenty minutes in his sister's room when she was out and he had been told that she was not likely to return until evening? He left her a note which would have taken him at most three minutes to scribble. What did he do for the rest of the time?"

"You are suggesting that he concealed the jewels in some appropriate place among his sister's belongings?"

"It seems indicated, does it not? Mrs. Sutcliffe was evacuated that same day with other British subjects. She was flown to Aden with her daughter. She arrives at Tilbury, I believe, tomorrow."

Pikeaway nodded.

"Look after her," said Mr. Robinson.

"We're going to look after her," said Pikeaway. "That's all arranged."

"If she has the jewels, she will be in danger." He closed his eyes. "I so much dislike violence."

"You think there is likely to be violence?"

"There are people interested. Various undesirable people—if you understand me."

"I understand you," said Pikeaway grimly.

"And they will, of course, all double-cross each other." Mr. Robinson shook his head. "So confusing."

Colonel Pikeaway asked delicately: "Have you yourself any—er—special interest in the matter?"

"I represent a certain group of interests," said Mr. Robinson. His voice was faintly reproachful. "Some of the stones in question were supplied by my syndicate to his late Highness—at a very fair and reasonable price. The group of people I represent who are interested in the recovery of the stones would, I may venture to say, have had the approval of the late owner. I shouldn't like to say more. These matters are so delicate."

"But you are definitely on the side of the angels," Colonel Pikeaway smiled.

"Ah, angels! Angels—yes." He paused. "Do you happen to know who occupied the rooms in the Ritz Savoy Hotel on either side of the room occupied by Mrs. Sutcliffe and her daughter?"

Colonel Pikeaway looked vague.

"Let me see now—I believe I do. On the left-hand side was Señora Angelica da Toredo—a Spanish—er—dancer appearing at the local cabaret. Perhaps not strictly Spanish and perhaps not a very good dancer. But popular with the clientele. On the other side was one of a group of school teachers, I understand."

Mr. Robinson beamed approvingly.

"You are always the same. I come to tell you things, but nearly always you know them already."

"No, no." Colonel Pikeaway made a polite disclaimer.

"Between us," said Mr. Robinson, "we know a good deal."

Their eyes met.

"I hope," Mr. Robinson said, rising, "that we know enough."

4

Return of a Traveller

"REALLY!" SAID MRS. SUTCLIFFE, in an annoyed voice, as she looked out of her hotel window, "I don't see why it always has to rain when one comes back to England. It makes it all seem so depressing."

"I think it's lovely to be back," said Jennifer. "Hearing everyone talk English in the streets! And we'll be able to have a really good tea presently. Bread and butter and jam and proper cakes."

"I wish you weren't so insular, darling," said Mrs. Sutcliffe. "What's the good of my taking you abroad all the way to the Persian Gulf if you're going to say you'd rather have stayed at home?"

"I don't mind going abroad just for a month or two," said Jennifer. "All I said was I'm glad to be back."

"Now do get out of the way, dear, and let me make sure that they've brought up all the luggage. Really, I do feel—I've felt ever since the war that people have got very dishonest nowadays. I'm sure if I hadn't kept an eye on things that man would have gone off with my green zip bag at Tilbury. And there was another man hanging about near the luggage. I saw him afterward on the train. I believe, you know, that these sneak-thieves meet the boats and if the people are flustered or seasick they go off with some of the suitcases."

"Oh, you're always thinking things like that, Mother," said Jennifer. "You think everybody you meet's dishonest."

"Most of them are," said Mrs. Sutcliffe grimly.

"Not English people," said the loyal Jennifer.

"That's worse," said her mother. "One doesn't expect anything else from Arabs and foreigners, but in England one's off one's guard and that makes it easier for dishon-

37

est people. Now do let me count. That's the big green suitcase and the black one, and the two small brown and the zip bag and the golf clubs and the racquets and the hold-all and the canvas suitcase—and where's the green bag? Oh, there it is. And that local tin trunk we bought to put the extra things in—yes, one, two, three, four, five, six—yes, that's right. All fourteen things are here."

"Can't we have some tea now?" said Jennifer.

"Tea? It's only three o'clock."

"I'm awfully hungry."

"All right, all right. Can you go down by yourself and order it? I really feel I must have rest, and then I'll just unpack the things we'll need for tonight. It's too bad your father couldn't have met us. Why he had to have an important directors' meeting in Newcastle-on-Tyne today I simply cannot imagine. You'd think his wife and daughter would come first. Especially as he hadn't seen us for three months. Are you sure you can manage by yourself?"

"Good gracious, Mummy," said Jennifer, "what age do you think I am? Can I have some money, please? I haven't got any English money."

She accepted the ten-shilling note her mother handed to her, and went out scornfully.

The telephone rang by the bed. Mrs. Sutcliffe went to it and picked up the receiver.

"Hullo . . . yes . . . yes, Mrs. Sutcliffe speaking . . ."

There was a knock on the door. Mrs. Sutcliffe said, "Just one moment" to the receiver, laid it down and went over to the door. A young man in dark blue overalls was standing there with a small kit of tools.

"Electrician," he said briskly. "The lights in this suite aren't satisfactory. I've been sent up to see to them."

"Oh—all right . . ."

She drew back. The electrician entered.

"Bathroom?"

"Through there—beyond the other bedroom."

She went back to the telephone.

"I'm sorry . . . What were you saying?"

"My name is Derek O'Connor. Perhaps I might come up to your suite, Mrs. Sutcliffe. It's about your brother."

"Bob? Is there—news of him?"

"I'm afraid so—yes."

"Oh . . . Oh, I see . . . Yes, come up. It's on the third floor, 310."

She sat down on the bed. She already knew what the news must be.

Presently there was a knock on the door and she opened it to admit a young man who shook hands in a suitably subdued manner.

"Are you from the Foreign Office?"

"My name's Derek O'Connor. My chief sent me round as there didn't seem to be anybody else who could break it to you."

"Please tell me," said Mrs. Sutcliffe. "He's killed. Is that it?"

"Yes, that's it, Mrs. Sutcliffe. He was flying Prince Ali Yusuf out from Ramat and they crashed in the mountains."

"Why haven't I heard—why didn't someone wireless it to the boat?"

"There was no definite news until a few days ago. It was known that the plane was missing, that was all. But under the circumstances there might still have been hope. But now the wreck of the plane has been found. I am sure you will be glad to know that death was instantaneous."

"The Prince was killed as well?"

"Yes."

"I'm not at all surprised," said Mrs. Sutcliffe. Her voice shook a little but she had full command of herself. "I knew Bob would die young. He was always reckless, you know—always flying new planes, trying new stunts. I've hardly seen anything of him for the last four years. Oh, well, one can't change people, can one?"

"No," said her visitor, "I'm afraid not."

"Henry always said he'd smash himself up sooner or later," said Mrs. Sutcliffe. She seemed to derive a kind of melancholy satisfaction from the accuracy of her husband's prophecy. A tear rolled down her cheek and she looked for her handkerchief. "It's been a shock," she said.

"I know—I'm awfully sorry."

"Bob couldn't run away, of course," said Mrs. Sutcliffe. "I mean, he'd taken on the job of being the Prince's pilot. I wouldn't have wanted him to throw in his hand. And he was a good flyer too. I'm sure if he ran into a mountain it wasn't his fault."

"No," said O'Connor, "it certainly wasn't his fault. The only hope of getting the Prince out was to fly in no matter what conditions. It was a dangerous flight to undertake and it went wrong."

Mrs. Sutcliffe nodded.

"I quite understand," she said. "Thank you for coming to tell me."

"There's something more," said O'Connor, "something I've got to ask you. Did your brother entrust anything to you to take back to England?"

"Entrust something to me?" said Mrs. Sutcliffe. "What do you mean?"

"Did he give you any—package—any small parcel to bring back and deliver to anyone in England?"

She shook her head wonderingly. "No. Why should you think he did?"

"There was a rather important package which we think your brother may have given to someone to bring home. He called on you at your hotel that day—the day of the revolution, I mean."

"I know. He left a note. But there was nothing in that—just some silly thing about playing tennis or golf the next day. I suppose when he wrote that note, he couldn't have known that he'd have to fly the Prince out that very afternoon."

"That was all it said?"

"The note? Yes."

"Have you kept it, Mrs. Sutcliffe?"

"Kept the note he left? No, of course I haven't. It was quite trivial. I tore it up and threw it away. Why should I keep it?"

"No reason," said O'Connor. "I just wondered."

"Wondered what?" said Mrs. Sutcliffe crossly.

"Whether there might have been some—other message concealed in it. After all—" he smiled, "there is such a thing as invisible ink, you know."

"Invisible ink!" said Mrs. Sutcliffe, with a great deal of

distaste. "Do you mean the sort of thing they use in spy stories?"

"Well, I'm afraid I do mean just that," said O'Connor, rather apologetically.

"How idiotic," said Mrs. Sutcliffe. "I'm sure Bob would never use anything like invisible ink. Why should he? He was a dear, matter-of-fact sensible person." A tear dripped down her cheek again. "Oh, dear, where is my bag? I must have a handkerchief. Perhaps I left it in the other room."

"I'll get it for you," said O'Connor.

He went through the communicating door and stopped as a young man in overalls who was bending over a suitcase straightened up to face him, looking rather startled.

"Electrician," said the young man hurriedly. "Something wrong with the lights here."

O'Connor flicked a switch.

"They seem all right to me," he said pleasantly.

"Must have given me the wrong room number," said the electrician.

He gathered up his tool bag and slipped out quickly through the door to the corridor.

O'Connor frowned, picked up Mrs. Sutcliffe's bag from the dressing table and took it back to her.

"Excuse me," he said, and picked up the telephone receiver.

"Room 310 here. Have you just sent up an electrician to see to the lights in this suite? Yes . . . yes, I'll hang on."

He waited.

"No? No, I thought you hadn't. No, there's nothing wrong."

He replaced the receiver and turned to Mrs. Sutcliffe.

"There's nothing wrong with any of the lights here," he said. "And the office didn't send up an electrician."

"Then what was that man doing? Was he a thief?"

"He may have been."

Mrs. Sutcliffe looked hurriedly in her bag. "He hasn't taken anything out of my bag. The money is all right."

"Are you sure, Mrs. Sutcliffe, absolutely sure that your

brother didn't give you anything to take home, to pack among your belongings?"

"I'm absolutely sure," said Mrs. Sutcliffe.

"Or your daughter—you have a daughter, haven't you?"

"Yes. She's downstairs having tea. Oh, I dread having to tell her about Bob. Maybe it would be better to wait until we get home . . ."

"Could your brother have given anything to her?"

"No, I'm sure he couldn't."

"There's another possibility," said O'Connor, "he might have hidden something in your baggage among your belongings that day when he was waiting for you in your room."

"But why should Bob do such a thing? It sounds absolutely absurd."

"It's not quite so absurd as it sounds. It seems possible that Prince Ali Yusuf gave your brother something to keep for him and that your brother thought it would be safer among your possessions than if he kept it himself."

"Sounds very unlikely to me," said Mrs. Sutcliffe.

"I wonder now, would you mind if we searched?"

"Searched through my luggage, do you mean? Unpack?" Mrs. Sutcliffe's voice rose with a wail on that word.

"I know," said O'Connor, "it's a terrible thing to ask you. But it might be very important. I could help you, you know," he said persuasively. "I often used to pack for my mother. She said I was quite a good packer."

He exerted all the charm which was one of his assets to Colonel Pikeaway.

"Oh, well," said Mrs. Sutcliffe yielding, "I suppose—if you say so—if, I mean, it's really important—"

"It might be very important," said Derek O'Connor. "Well, now," he smiled at her. "Suppose we begin."

ii.

Three quarters of an hour later Jennifer returned from her tea. She looked round the room and gave a gasp of surprise.

"Mummy, what *have* you been doing?"

"We've been unpacking," said Mrs. Sutcliffe crossly. "Now we're packing things up again. This is Mr. O'Connor. My daughter Jennifer."

"But why are you packing and unpacking?"

"Don't ask me why," snapped her mother. "There seems to be some idea that your Uncle Bob put something in my luggage to bring home. He didn't give you anything, I suppose, Jennifer?"

"Uncle Bob give me anything to bring back? No. Have you been unpacking my things too?"

"We've unpacked everything," said Derek O'Connor cheerfully, "and we haven't found a thing and now we're packing them up again. I think you ought to have a drink of tea or something, Mrs. Sutcliffe. Can I order you something? A brandy and soda perhaps?" He went to the telephone.

"I wouldn't mind a good cup of tea," said Mrs. Sutcliffe.

"I had a smashing tea," said Jennifer. "Bread and butter and sandwiches and cake and then the waiter brought me more sandwiches because I asked him if he'd mind and he said he didn't. It was lovely."

O'Connor ordered the tea, then he finished packing up Mrs. Sutcliffe's belongings again with a neatness and a dexterity which forced her unwilling admiration.

"Your mother seems to have trained you to pack very well," she said.

"Oh, I've all sorts of handy accomplishments," said O'Connor smiling.

His mother was long since dead, and his skill in packing and unpacking had been acquired solely in the service of Colonel Pikeaway.

"There's just one thing more, Mrs. Sutcliffe. I'd like you to be very careful of yourself."

"Careful of myself? In what way?"

"Well," O'Connor left it vague. "Revolutions are tricky things. There are a lot of ramifications. Are you staying in London long?"

"We're going down to the country tomorrow. My husband will be driving us down."

"That's all right then. But—don't take any chances. If

anything in the least out of the ordinary happens, ring
999 straightaway."

"Ooh!" said Jennifer, in high delight. "Dial 999. I've
always wanted to."

"Don't be silly, Jennifer," said her mother.

iii.

Extract from account in a local paper:

> *A man appeared before the Magistrate's Court
> yesterday charged with breaking into the residence of
> Mr. Henry Sutcliffe with intent to steal. Mrs. Sut-
> cliffe's bedroom was ransacked and left in wild con-
> fusion while the members of the family were at
> Church on Sunday morning. The kitchen staff, who
> were preparing the midday meal, heard nothing.
> Police arrested the man as he was making his es-
> cape from the house. Something had evidently
> alarmed him and he had fled without taking anything.*
>
> *Giving his name as Andrew Ball of no fixed
> abode, he pleaded guilty. He said he had been out
> of work and was looking for money. Mrs. Sutcliffe's
> jewellery, apart from a few pieces which she was
> wearing, is kept at her bank.*

"I told you to have the lock of that drawing-room
French window seen to," was the comment of Mr. Sutcliffe in the family circle.

"My dear Henry," said Mrs. Sutcliffe, "you don't seem
to realize that I have been abroad for the last three
months. And anyway, I'm sure I've read somewhere that
if burglars *want* to get in they always can."

She added wistfully, as she glanced again at the local
paper:

"How beautifully grand 'kitchen staff' sounds. So different from what it really is, old Mrs. Ellis who is quite
deaf and can hardly stand up and that half-witted daughter of the Bardwells who comes in to help on Sunday
mornings."

"What I don't see," said Jennifer, "is how the police

found out the house was being burgled and got here in time to catch him."

"It seems extraordinary that he didn't take anything," commented her mother.

"Are you quite sure about that, Joan?" demanded her husband. "You were a little doubtful at first."

Mrs. Sutcliffe gave an exasperated sigh.

"It's impossible to tell about a thing like that straight-away. The mess in my bedroom—things thrown about everywhere, drawers pulled out and overturned. I had to look through everything before I could be sure—though now I come to think of it, I don't remember seeing my best Jacqmar scarf."

"I'm sorry, Mummy. That was me. It blew overboard in the Mediterranean. I'd borrowed it. I meant to tell you but I forgot."

"Really, Jennifer, how often have I asked you not to borrow things without telling me first?"

"Can I have some more pudding?" said Jennifer, creating a diversion.

"I suppose so. Really, Mrs. Ellis has a wonderfully light hand. It makes it worth while having to shout at her so much. I do hope, though, that they won't think you too greedy at school. Meadowbank isn't quite an ordinary school, remember."

"I don't know that I really want to go to Meadow-bank," said Jennifer. "I knew a girl whose cousin had been there, and she said it was awful. They spent all their time telling you how to get in and out of Rolls-Royces, and how to behave if you went to lunch with the Queen."

"That will do, Jennifer," said Mrs. Sutcliffe. "You don't appreciate how extremely fortunate you are in being admitted to Meadowbank. Miss Bulstrode doesn't take every girl, I can tell you. It's entirely owing to your father's important position and the influence of your Aunt Rosamond. You are exceedingly lucky. And if," added Mrs. Sutcliffe, "you are ever asked to lunch with the Queen, it will be a good thing for you to know how to behave."

"Oh, well," said Jennifer. "I expect the Queen often has to have people to lunch who don't know how to behave—African chiefs and jockeys and sheiks."

"African chiefs have the most polished manners," said her father, who had recently returned from a short business trip to Ghana.

"So do Arab sheiks," said Mrs. Sutcliffe. "Really courtly."

"D'you remember that sheik's feast we went to?" said Jennifer. "And how he picked out the sheep's eye and gave it to you, and Uncle Bob nudged you not to make a fuss and to eat it? I mean, if a sheik did that with roast lamb at Buckingham Palace, it would give the Queen a bit of a jolt, wouldn't it?"

"That will do, Jennifer," said her mother and closed the subject.

iv.

When Andrew Ball of no fixed abode had been sentenced to three months for breaking and entering, Derek O'Connor, who had been occupying a modest position at the back of the Magistrate's Court, put through a call to a Museum number.

"Not a thing on the fellow when we picked him up," he said. "We gave him plenty of time too."

"Who was he? Anyone we know?"

"One of the Gecko lot, I think. Small time. They hire him out for this sort of thing. Not much brain but he's said to be thorough."

"And he took his sentence like a lamb?" At the other end of the line Colonel Pikeaway grinned as he spoke.

"Yes. Perfect picture of a stupid fellow lapsed from the straight and narrow path. You'd never connect him with any big-time stuff. That's his value, of course."

"And he didn't find anything," mused Colonel Pikeaway. "And you didn't find anything. It rather looks, doesn't it, as though there isn't anything to find? Our idea that Rawlinson planted these things on his sister seems to have been wrong."

"Other people appear to have the same idea."

"It's a bit obvious really. Maybe we were meant to take the bait."

"Could be. Any other possibilities?"

"Plenty of them. The stuff may still be in Ramat.

Hidden somewhere in the Ritz Savoy Hotel, maybe. Or Rawlinson passed it to someone on his way to the airstrip. Or there may be something in that hint of Mr. Robinson's. A woman may have got hold of it. Or it could be that Mrs. Sutcliffe had it all the time unbeknown to herself, and flung it overboard in the Red Sea with something she had no further use for.

"And that," he added thoughtfully, "might be all for the best."

"Oh, come now, it's worth a lot of money, sir."

"Human life is worth a lot, too," said Colonel Pikeaway.

■

5

Letters from Meadowbank School

LETTER FROM Julia Upjohn to her mother:

Dear Mummy,

I've settled in now and am liking it very much. There's a girl who is new this term too called Jennifer and she and I rather do things together. We're both awfully keen on tennis. She's rather good. She has a really smashing serve when it comes off, but it doesn't usually. She says her racquet's got warped from being out in the Persian Gulf. It's very hot out there. She was in all that revolution that happened. I said wasn't it very exciting, but she said no, they didn't see anything at all. They were taken away to the Embassy or something and missed it.

Miss Bulstrode is rather a lamb, but she's pretty frightening too—or can be. She goes easy on you when you're new. Behind her back everyone calls

her The Bull, or Bully. We're taught English literature by Miss Rich, who's terrific. When she gets in a
real state her hair comes down. She's got a queer
but rather exciting face and when she reads bits of
Shakespeare it seems all different and real. She went
on at us the other day about Iago, and what he
felt—and a lot about jealousy and how it ate into
you and you suffered until you went quite mad
wanting to hurt the person you loved. It gave us all
the shivers—except Jennifer, because nothing upsets
her. Miss Rich teaches us geography, too. I always
thought it was such a dull subject, but it isn't with
Miss Rich. This morning she told us all about the
spice trade and why they had to have spices because
of things going bad so easily.

I'm starting art with Miss Laurie. She comes twice
a week and takes us up to London to see picture
galleries as well. We do French with Mademoiselle
Blanche. She doesn't keep order very well. Jennifer
says French people can't. She doesn't get cross,
though, only bored. She says "Enfin, vous m'en-
nuiez, mes enfants!" Miss Springer is awful. She
does gym and P.T. She's got ginger hair and smells
when she's hot. Then there's Miss Chadwick (Chaddy)—she's been here since the school started. She
teaches mathematics and is rather fussy, but quite
nice. And there's Miss Vansittart who teaches history and German. She's a sort of second Miss Bulstrode with the pep left out.

There are a lot of foreign girls here, two Italians
and some Germans, and a rather jolly Swede (she's
a Princess or something) and a girl who's half Turkish and half Persian and who says she would have
been married to Prince Ali Yusuf who got killed in
that aeroplane crash, but Jennifer says that isn't
true, that Shaista only says so because she was a
kind of cousin, and you're supposed to marry a
cousin. But Jennifer says he wasn't going to. He
liked someone else. Jennifer knows a lot of things
but she won't usually tell them.

I suppose you'll be starting off on your trip soon.
Don't leave your passport behind like you did last

time!!! And take your first-aid kit in case you have an accident.

Love from Julia

Letter from Jennifer Sutcliffe to her mother:

Dear Mummy,

It really isn't bad here. I'm enjoying it more than I expected to do. The weather has been very fine. We had to write a composition yesterday on "Can a good quality be carried to excess?" I couldn't think of anything to say. Next week it will be "Contrast the characters of Juliet and Desdemona." That seems silly too. Do you think I could have a new tennis racquet? I know you had mine restrung last autumn—but it feels all wrong. Perhaps it's got warped. I'd rather like to learn Greek. Can I? I love languages. Some of us are going to London to see the ballet next week. It's "Swan Lake." The food here is jolly good. Yesterday we had chicken for lunch, and we have lovely homemade cakes for tea.

I can't think of any more news—have you had any more burglaries?

Your loving daughter,
Jennifer

Letter from Margaret Gore-West, Senior Prefect, to her mother:

Dear Mummy,

There is very little news. I am doing German with Miss Vansittart this term. There is a rumour that Miss Bulstrode is going to retire and that Miss Vansittart will succeed her, but they've been saying that for over a year now, and I'm sure it isn't true. I asked Miss Chadwick (of course I wouldn't dare ask Miss Bulstrode!) and she was quite sharp about it. Said certainly not and don't listen to gossip. We went to the ballet on Tuesday. "Swan Lake." Too dreamy for words!

Princess Ingrid is rather fun. Very blue eyes, but she wears braces on her teeth. There are two new German girls. They speak English quite well.

Miss Rich is back and looking quite well. We did miss her last term. The new games mistress is called Miss Springer. She's terribly bossy and nobody likes her much. She coaches you at tennis very well, though. One of the new girls, Jennifer Sutcliffe, is going to be really good, I think. Her backhand's a bit weak. Her great friend is a girl called Julia. We call them the Jays!

You won't forget about taking me out on the 20th, will you? Sports Day is June 19th.

Your loving
Margaret

Letter from Ann Shapland to Denis Rathbone:

Dear Denis,

I shan't get any time off until the third week of term. I should like to dine with you then very much. It would have to be Saturday or Sunday. I'll let you know.

I find it rather fun working in a school. But thank God I'm not a schoolmistress! I'd go raving mad.

Yours ever,
Ann

Letter from Miss Johnson to her sister:

Dear Denis,

Everything much the same as usual here. The summer term is always nice. The garden is looking beautiful and we've got a new gardener to help old Briggs—young and strong! Rather good-looking, too, which is a pity. Girls are so silly.

Miss Bulstrode hasn't said anything more about retiring, so I hope she's got over the idea. Miss Vansittart wouldn't be at all the same thing. I really don't believe I would stay on.

Give my love to Dick and to the children, and

remember me to Oliver and Kate when you see them.

Yours affectionately,
Elspeth

Letter from Mademoiselle Angele Blanche to René Dupont, Poste Restante, Bordeaux:

Dear René,
All is well here, though I cannot say that I amuse myself. The girls are neither respectful nor well behaved. I think it better, however, not to complain to Miss Bulstrode. One has to be on one's guard when dealing with that one!
There is nothing interesting at present to tell you.
Mouche

Letter from Miss Vansittart to a friend:

Dear Gloria,
The summer term has started smoothly. A very satisfactory set of new girls. The foreigners are settling down well. Our little Princess (the Middle East one, not the Scandinavian) is inclined to lack application, but I suppose one has to expect that. She has very charming manners.
The new games mistress, Miss Springer, is not a success. The girls dislike her and she is far too high-handed with them. After all, this is not an ordinary school. We don't stand or fall by P.T.! She is also very inquisitive, and asks far too many personal questions. That sort of thing can be very trying, and is so ill bred. Mademoiselle Blanche, the new French mistress, is quite amiable but not up to the standard of Mademoiselle Depuy.
We had a near escape on the first day of term. Lady Veronica Carlton-Sandways turned up completely intoxicated!! But for Miss Chadwick spotting it and heading her off, we might have had a most unpleasant incident. The twins are such nice girls, too.

Miss Bulstrode has not said anything definite yet about the future—but from her manner, I think her mind is definitely made up. Meadowbank is a really fine achievement, and I shall be proud to carry on its traditions.

Give my love to Marjorie when you see her.

Yours ever,
Eleanor

Letter to Colonel Pikeaway, sent through the usual channels:

Talk of sending a man into danger! I'm the only able-bodied male in an establishment of, roughly, some hundred and fifty females.

Her Highness arrived in style. Cadillac of squashed strawberry and pastel blue, with Wog Notable in native dress, fashion-plate-from-Paris wife, and junior edition of same (H.R.H.).

Hardly recognized her the next day in her school uniform. There will be no difficulty in establishing friendly relations with her. She has already seen to that. Was asking me the names of various flowers in a sweet innocent way, when a female Gorgon with freckles, red hair, and a voice like a corncrake bore down upon her and removed her from my vicinity. She didn't want to go. I'd always understood these Oriental girls were brought up modestly behind the veil. This one must have had a little worldly experience during her schooldays in Switzerland, I think.

The Gorgon, alias Miss Springer, the games mistress, came back to give me a raspberry. Garden staff were not to talk to the pupils, etc. My turn to express innocent surprise. "Sorry, miss. The young lady was asking what these here delphiniums was. Suppose they don't have them in the parts she comes from." The Gorgon was easily pacified, in the end she almost simpered. Less success with Miss Bulstrode's secretary. One of these coat and skirt county girls. French mistress is more cooperative. Demure and mousy to look at, but not such a mouse really.

Have also made friends with three pleasant gigglers,
Christian names, Pamela, Lois, and Mary, surnames
unknown, but of aristocratic lineage. A sharp old
war-horse, called Miss Chadwick, keeps a wary eye
on me, so I'm careful not to blot my copybook.

My boss, old Briggs, is a crusty kind of character
whose chief subject of conversation is what things
used to be in the good old days, when he was, I
suspect, the fourth of a staff of five. He grumbles
about most things and people, but has a wholesome
respect for Miss Bulstrode herself. So have I. She
had a few words (very pleasant) with me, but I had
a horrid feeling she was seeing right through me
and knowing all about me.

No sign, so far, of anything sinister—but I live in
hope.

■

6

Early Days

IN THE MISTRESSES' Common Room news was being
exchanged. Foreign travel, plays seen, art exhibitions visited. Snapshots were handed round. The menace of
coloured transparencies was in the offing. All the enthusi-
asts wanted to show their own pictures, but to get out of
being forced to see other people's.

Presently conversation became less personal. The new
Sports Pavilion was both criticized and admired. It was
admitted to be a fine building, but naturally everybody
would have liked to improve its design in one way or
another.

The new girls were then briefly passed in review, and,
on the whole, the verdict was favourable.

A little pleasant conversation was made to the two new

members of the staff. Had Mademoiselle Blanche been in England before? What part of France did she come from?

Mademoiselle Blanche replied politely but with reserve.

Miss Springer was more forthcoming.

She spoke with emphasis and decision. It might almost have been said that she was giving a lecture. Subject: the excellence of Miss Springer. How much she had been appreciated as a colleague. How headmistresses had accepted her advice with gratitude and had reorganized their schedules accordingly.

Miss Springer was not sensitive. A restlessness in her audience was not noticed by her. It remained for Miss Johnson to ask in her mild tones:

"All the same, I expect your ideas haven't always been accepted in the way they—er—should have been."

"One must be prepared for ingratitude," said Miss Springer. Her voice, already loud, became louder. "The trouble is, people are so cowardly—won't face the facts. They often prefer not to see what's under their noses all the time. I'm not like that. I go straight to the point. More than once I've unearthed a nasty scandal—brought it into the open. I've got a good nose—once I'm on the trail, I don't leave it—not till I've pinned down my quarry." She gave a loud jolly laugh. "In my opinion, no one should teach in a school whose life isn't an open book. If anyone's got anything to hide, one can soon tell. Oh! you'd be surprised if I told you some of the things I've found out about people. Things that nobody else had dreamt of."

"You enjoyed that experience, yes?" said Mademoiselle Blanche.

"Of course not. Just doing my duty. But I wasn't backed up. Shameful laxness. So I resigned—as a protest."

She looked round and gave her jolly sporting laugh again.

"Hope nobody here has anything to hide," she said gaily.

Nobody was amused. But Miss Springer was not the kind of woman to notice that.

ii.

"Can I speak to you, Miss Bulstrode?"

Miss Bulstrode laid her pen aside and looked up into the flushed face of the matron, Miss Johnson.

"Yes, Miss Johnson."

"It's that girl Shaista—the Egyptian girl or whatever she is."

"Yes?"

"It's her—er—underclothing."

Miss Bulstrode's eyebrows rose in patient surprise.

"Her—well—her bust bodice."

"What is wrong with her brassière?"

"Well—it isn't an ordinary kind—I mean it doesn't hold her in, exactly. It—er—well it pushes her up—really quite unnecessarily."

Miss Bulstrode bit her lip to keep back a smile, as so often when in colloquy with Miss Johnson.

"Perhaps I'd better come and look at it," she said gravely.

A kind of inquest was then held with the offending contraption held up to display by Miss Johnson, while Shaista looked on with lively interest.

"It's this sort of wire and—er—boning arrangement," said Miss Johnson with disapprobation.

Shaista burst into animated explanation.

"But you see my breasts they are not very big—not nearly big enough. I do not look enough like a woman. And it is very important for a girl—to show she is a woman and not a boy."

"Plenty of time for that. You're only fifteen," said Miss Johnson.

"Fifteen—that *is* a woman! And I look like a woman, do I not?"

She appealed to Miss Bulstrode who nodded gravely.

"Only my breasts, they are poor. So I want to make them look not so poor. You understand?"

"I understand perfectly," said Miss Bulstrode. "And I quite see your point of view. But in this school, you see, you are among girls who are, for the most part, English, and English girls are not very often women at the age of fifteen. I like my girls to use make-up discreetly and to wear clothes suitable to their stage of growth. I suggest that you wear your brassière when you are dressed for a party or for going to London, but not every day here. We do a good deal of sports and games here and for that your body needs to be free to move easily."

"It is too much—all this running and jumping," said Shaista sulkily, *"and* the P.T. I do not like Miss Springer— she always says, 'Faster, faster, do not slack.' I get tired."

"That will do, Shaista," said Miss Bulstrode, her voice becoming authoritative. "Your family has sent you here to learn English ways. All this exercise will be very good for your complexion, *and* for developing your bust."

Dismissing Shaista, she smiled at the agitated Miss Johnson.

"It's quite true," she said. "The girl is fully mature. She might easily be over twenty by the look of her. And that is what she feels like. You can't expect her to feel the same age as Julia Upjohn, for instance. Intellectually Julia is far ahead of Shaista. Physically, she could quite well wear a liberty bodice still."

"I wish they were all like Julia Upjohn," said Miss Johnson.

"I don't," said Miss Bulstrode briskly. "A school full of girls all alike would be very dull."

Dull, she thought, as she went back to her marking of Scripture essays. That word had been repeating itself in her brain for some time now. Dull. . . .

If there was one thing her school was not, it was dull. During her career as its headmistress, she herself had never felt dull. There had been difficulties to combat, unforeseen crises, irritations with parents, with children; domestic upheavals. She had met and dealt with incipient disasters and turned them into triumphs. It had all been stimulating, exciting, supremely worth while. And even now, though she had made up her mind to it, she did not want to go.

She was physically in excellent health, almost as tough as when she and Chaddy (faithful Chaddy!) had started the great enterprise with a mere handful of children, and backing from a banker of unusual foresight. Chaddy's academic distinctions had been better than hers, but it was she who had had the vision to plan and make of the school a place of such distinction that it was known all over Europe. She had never been afraid to experiment, whereas Chaddy had been content to teach soundly but unexcitingly what she knew. Chaddy's supreme achievement had always been to be there, at hand, the faithful buffer, quick to render assistance when assistance was needed. As on the opening day of term with Lady Veronica. It was on her stolidity, Miss Bulstrode reflected, that an exciting edifice had been built.

Well, from the material point of view, both women had done very well out of it. If they retired now, they would both have a good assured income for the rest of their lives. Miss Bulstrode wondered if Chaddy would want to retire when she herself did. Probably not. Probably, to her, the school was home. She would continue, faithful and reliable, to buttress up Miss Bulstrode's successor.

Because Miss Bulstrode had made up her mind—a successor there must be. Firstly associated with herself in joint rule and then to rule alone. To know when to go—that was one of the great necessities of life. To go before one's powers began to fail, one's sure grip to loosen, before one felt the faint staleness, the unwillingness to envisage continuing effort.

Miss Bulstrode finished marking the essays and noted that the Upjohn child had an original mind. Jennifer Sutcliffe had a complete lack of imagination, but showed an unusually sound grasp of facts. Mary Vyse, of course, was scholarship class—a wonderfully retentive memory. But what a dull girl! Dull—that word again. Miss Bulstrode dismissed it from her mind and rang for her secretary.

She began to dictate letters.

Dear Lady Valence. Jane has had some trouble with her ears. I enclose the doctor's report . . .

Dear Baron Von Eisenger. We can certainly arrange for Hedwig to go to the Opera on the occasion of Hellstern's taking the role of Isolde . . .

An hour passed swiftly. Miss Bulstrode seldom paused for a word. Ann Shapland's pencil raced over the pad.

A very good secretary, Miss Bulstrode thought to herself. Better than Vera Lorrimer. Tiresome girl, Vera.

Throwing up her post so suddenly. A nervous break-down, she had said. Something to do with a man, Miss Bulstrode thought resignedly. It was usually a man.

"That's the lot," said Miss Bulstrode, as she dictated the last word. She heaved a sigh of relief.

"So many dull things to be done," she remarked. "Writing letters to parents is like feeding dogs. Pop some soothing platitude into every waiting mouth."

Ann laughed. Miss Bulstrode looked at her appraisingly.

"What made you take up secretarial work?"

"I don't quite know. I had no special bent for anything in particular, and it's the sort of thing almost everybody drifts into."

"You don't find it monotonous?"

"I suppose I've been lucky. I've had a lot of different jobs. I was with Sir Mervyn Todhunter, the archaeologist, for a year, then I was with Sir Andrew Peters in Shell. I was secretary to Monica Lord, the actress, for a while— that really was hectic!" She smiled in remembrance.

"There's a lot of that nowadays among you girls," said Miss Bulstrode. "All this chopping and changing." She sounded disapproving.

"Actually, I can't do anything for very long. I've got an invalid mother. She's rather—well—difficult from time to time. And then I have to go back home and take charge."

"I see."

"But all the same, I'm afraid I should chop and change anyway. I haven't got the gift for continuity. I find chopping and changing far less dull."

"Dull . . ." murmured Miss Bulstrode, struck again by the fatal word.

Ann looked at her in surprise.

"Don't mind me," said Miss Bulstrode. "It's just that sometimes one particular word seems to crop up all the time. How would you have liked to be a schoolmistress?" she asked, with some curiosity.

"I'm afraid I should hate it," said Ann frankly.

"Why?"

"I'd find it terribly dull. Oh, I am sorry."

She stopped in dismay.

"Teaching isn't in the least dull," said Miss Bulstrode with spirit. "It can be the most exciting thing in the world. I shall miss it terribly when I retire."

"But surely—" Ann stared at her. "Are you thinking of retiring?"

"It's decided—yes. Oh, I shan't go for another year—or even two years."

"But—why?"

"Because I've given my best to the school—and had the best from it. I don't want the second best."

"The school will carry on?"

"Oh yes. I have a good successor."

"Miss Vansittart, I suppose?"

"So you fix on her automatically?" Miss Bulstrode looked at her sharply. "That's interesting—"

"I'm afraid I hadn't really thought about it. I've just overheard the staff talking. I should think she'll carry on very well—exactly in your tradition. And she's very striking looking, handsome and with quite a presence. I imagine that's important, isn't it?"

"Yes, it is. Yes, I'm sure Eleanor Vansittart is the right person."

"She'll carry on where you leave off," said Ann gathering up her things.

"But do I want that?" thought Miss Bulstrode to herself as Ann went out. "Carry on where I leave off? That's just what Eleanor will do! No new experiments, nothing revolutionary. That wasn't the way I made Meadowbank what it is. I took chances. I upset lots of people. I bullied and cajoled, and refused to follow the pattern of other schools. Isn't that what I want to follow on here now? Someone to pour new life into the school. Some dynamic personality . . . like—yes—Eileen Rich."

But Eileen wasn't old enough, hadn't enough experience. She was stimulating though, she could teach. She had ideas. She would never be dull. Nonsense, she must get that word out of her mind. Eleanor Vansittart was not dull . . .

She looked up as Miss Chadwick came in.

"Oh, Chaddy," she said. "I *am* pleased to see you!"

Miss Chadwick looked a little surprised.

"Why? Is anything the matter?"

"I'm the matter. I don't know my own mind."

"That's very unlike you, Honoria."

"Yes, isn't it? How's the term going, Chaddy?"

"Quite all right, I think." Miss Chadwick sounded a little unsure.

Miss Bulstrode pounced.

"Now then. Don't hedge. What's wrong?"

"Nothing. Really, Honoria, nothing at all. It's just . . ." Miss Chadwick wrinkled up her forehead and looked rather like a perplexed Boxer dog. "Oh, a feeling. But really it's nothing that I can put my finger on. The new girls seem a pleasant lot. I don't care for Mademoiselle Blanche very much. But then I didn't like Genevieve Depuy, either. Sly."

Miss Bulstrode did not pay very much attention to this criticism. Chaddy always accused the French mistresses of being sly.

"She's not a good teacher," said Miss Bulstrode. "Surprising really. Her testimonials were so good."

"The French never can teach. No discipline," said Miss Chadwick. "And really Miss Springer is a little too much of a good thing! Leaps about so. Springer by nature as well as by name . . ."

"She's good at her job."

"Oh, yes, first class."

"New staff is always upsetting," said Miss Bulstrode.

"Yes," agreed Miss Chadwick eagerly. "I'm sure it's nothing more than that. By the way, that new gardener is quite young. So unusual nowadays. No gardeners seem to be young. A pity he's so good looking. We shall have to keep a sharp eye open."

The two ladies nodded their heads in agreement. They knew, none better, the havoc caused by a good-looking young man to the hearts of adolescent girls.

7

Straws in the Wind

"Not too bad, boy," said old Briggs grudgingly, "not too bad."

He was expressing approval of his new assistant's performance in digging a strip of ground. It wouldn't do, thought Briggs, to let the young fellow get above himself.

"Mind you," he went on, "you don't want to rush at things. Take it steady, that's what I say. Steady is what does it."

The young man understood that his performance had compared rather too favourably with Briggs' own tempo of work.

"Now, along this here," continued Briggs, "we'll put some nice asters out. She don't like asters—but I pay no attention. Females has their whims, but if you don't pay no attention, ten to one they never notice. Though I will say she is the noticing kind on the whole. You'd think she 'ad enough to bother her head about, running a place like this."

Adam understood that the "she" who figured so largely in Briggs' conversation referred to Miss Bulstrode.

"And who was it I saw you talking to just now?" went on Briggs suspiciously, "when you went along to the potting shed for them bamboos?"

"Oh, that was just one of the young ladies," said Adam.

"Ah. One of them two Eye-ties, wasn't it? Now you be very careful, my boy. Don't you get mixed up with no Eye-ties. I know what I'm talkin' about. I knew Eye-ties, I did, in the first war and if I'd known then what I know now I'd have been more careful. See?"

"Wasn't no harm in it," said Adam, putting on a sulky

manner. "Just passed the time of day with me, she did, and asked the names of one or two things."

"Ah," said Briggs, "but you be careful. It's not your place to talk to any of the young ladies. She wouldn't like it."

"I wasn't doing no harm and I didn't say anything I shouldn't."

"I don't say you did, boy. But I say a lot o' young females penned up together here with not so much as a drawing master to take their minds off things—well, you'd better be careful. That's all. Ah, here comes the Old Bitch now. Wanting something difficult, I'll be bound."

Miss Bulstrode was approaching with a rapid step. "Good morning, Briggs," she said. "Good morning—er—"

"Adam, miss."

"Ah, yes, Adam. Well, you seem to have got that piece dug very satisfactorily. The wire netting's coming down by the far tennis court, Briggs. You'd better attend to that."

"All right, ma'am, all right. It'll be seen to."

"What are you putting in front here?"

"Well, ma'am, I had thought—"

"Not asters," said Miss Bulstrode, without giving him time to finish. "Pompon dahlias," she departed briskly.

"Coming along—giving orders," said Briggs. "Not that she isn't a sharp one. She soon notices if you haven't done work properly. And remember what I've said and be careful, boy. About Eye-ties and the others."

"If she's any fault to find with me, I'll soon know what I can do," said Adam sulkily. "Plenty o' jobs going."

"Ah. That's like you young men all over nowadays. Won't take a word from anybody. All I say is, mind your step."

Adam continued to look sulky, but bent to his work once more.

Miss Bulstrode walked back along the path toward the school. She was frowning a little.

Miss Vansittart was coming in the opposite direction.

"What a hot afternoon," said Miss Vansittart.

"Yes, it's very sultry and oppressive." Again Miss Bulstrode frowned. "Have you noticed that young man—the young gardener?"

"No, not particularly."

"He seems to me—well—an odd type," said Miss Bulstrode thoughtfully. "Not the usual kind around here."

"Perhaps he's just come down from Oxford and wants to make a little money."

"He's good looking. The girls notice him."

"The usual problem."

Miss Bulstrode smiled. "To combine freedom for the girls and strict supervision—is that what you mean, Eleanor?"

"Yes."

"We manage," said Miss Bulstrode.

"Yes, indeed. You've never had a scandal at Meadowbank, have you?"

"We've come near it once or twice," said Miss Bulstrode. She laughed. "Never a dull moment in running a school." She went on, "Do you ever find life dull here, Eleanor?"

"No, indeed," said Miss Vansittart. "I find the work here most stimulating and satisfying. You must feel very proud and happy, Honoria, at the great success you have achieved."

"I think I've made a good job of things," said Miss Bulstrode thoughtfully. "Nothing, of course, is ever quite as one first imagined it . . .

"Tell me, Eleanor," she said suddenly, "if you were running this place instead of me, what changes would you make? Don't mind saying, I shall be interested to hear."

"I don't think I should want to make any changes," said Eleanor Vansittart. "It seems to me the spirit of the place and the whole organization is well-nigh perfect."

"You'd carry on on the same lines, you mean?"

"Yes, indeed. I don't think they could be bettered."

Miss Bulstrode was silent for a moment. She was thinking to herself: "I wonder if she said that in order to please me. One never knows with people. However close to them you may have been for years. Surely, she can't really mean that. Anybody with any creative feeling at all must want to make changes. It's true, though, that it mightn't have seemed tactful to say so . . . And tact is very important. It's important with parents, it's important with the girls, it's important with the staff. Eleanor certainly has tact."

Aloud, she said, "There must always be adjustments, though, mustn't there? I mean with changing ideas and conditions of life generally."

"Oh, that, yes," said Miss Vansittart. "One has, as they say, to go with the times. But it's your school, Honoria, you've made it what it is and your traditions are the essence of it. I think tradition is very important, don't you?"

Miss Bulstrode did not answer. She was hovering on the brink of irrevocable words. The offer of a partnership hung in the air. Miss Vansittart, though seeming unaware in her well-bred way, must be conscious of the fact that it was there. Miss Bulstrode did not know really what was holding her back. Why did she so dislike to commit herself? Probably, she admitted ruefully, because she hated the idea of giving up control. Secretly, of course, she wanted to stay, she wanted to go on running her school. But surely nobody could be a worthier successor than Eleanor? So dependable, so reliable. Of course, as far as that went, so was dear Chaddy—reliable as they came. And yet you could never envisage Chaddy as headmistress of an outstanding school.

"What do I want?" said Miss Bulstrode to herself. "How tiresome I am being! Really, indecision has never been one of my faults up to now."

A bell sounded in the distance.

"My German class," said Miss Vansittart. "I must go in." She moved at a rapid but dignified step toward the school buildings. Following her more slowly, Miss Bulstrode almost collided with Eileen Rich, hurrying from a side path.

"Oh, I'm so sorry, Miss Bulstrode. I didn't see you." Her hair, as usual, was escaping from its untidy bun. Miss Bulstrode noted anew the ugly but interesting bones of her face, a strange, eager, compelling young woman.

"You've got a class?" she asked.

"Yes. English."

"You enjoy teaching, don't you?" said Miss Bulstrode.

"I love it. It's the most fascinating thing in the world."

"Why?"

Eileen Rich stopped dead. She ran a hand through her hair. She frowned with the effort of thought.

"How interesting. I don't know that I've ever really thought about it. Why does one like teaching? Is it because it makes one feel grand and important? No, no . . . it's not as bad as that. No, it's more like fishing, I think. You don't know what catch you're going to get, what you're going to drag up from the sea. It's the quality of the response. It's so exciting when it comes. It doesn't very often, of course."

Miss Bulstrode nodded in agreement. She had been right! This girl had something!

"I expect you'll run a school of your own some day," she said.

"Oh, I hope so," said Eileen Rich. "I do hope so. That's what I'd like above anything."

"You've got ideas already, haven't you, as to how a school should be run?"

"Everyone has ideas, I suppose," said Eileen Rich. "I daresay a great many of them are fantastic and they'd go utterly wrong. That would be a risk, of course. But one would have to try them out. I would have to learn by experience. The awful thing is that one can't go by other people's experience, can one?"

"Not really," said Miss Bulstrode. "In life one has to make one's own mistakes."

"That's all right in life," said Eileen Rich, "in life you can pick yourself up and start again." Her hands, hanging at her sides, clenched themselves into fists. Her expression was grim. Then suddenly it relaxed into humour. "But if a school's gone to pieces, you can't very well pick that up and start again, can you?"

"If you ran a school like Meadowbank," said Miss Bulstrode, "would you make changes—experiment?"

Eileen Rich looked embarrassed. "That's—that's an awfully hard thing to say," she said.

"You mean you would," said Miss Bulstrode. "Don't mind speaking your mind, child."

"One would always want, I suppose, to use one's own ideas," said Eileen Rich. "I don't say they'd work. They mightn't."

"But it would be worth taking a risk?"

"It's always worth taking a risk, isn't it?" said Eileen Rich. "I mean if you feel strongly enough about anything."

"You don't object to leading a dangerous life. I see . . ." said Miss Bulstrode.

"I think I've always led a dangerous life." A shadow passed over the girl's face. "I must go. They'll be waiting." She hurried off.

Miss Bulstrode stood looking after her. She was still standing there lost in thought when Miss Chadwick came hurrying to find her.

"Oh! there you are. We've been looking everywhere for you. Professor Anderson has just rung up. He wants to know if he can take out Meroe this next week end. He knows it's against the rules so soon, but he's going off quite suddenly to—somewhere that sounds like Azure Basin."

"Azerbaijan," said Miss Bulstrode automatically, her mind still on her own thoughts.

"Not enough experience," she murmured to herself. "That's the risk. What did you say, Chaddy?"

Miss Chadwick repeated her message.

"I told Miss Shapland to say that we'd ring him back, and sent her to find you."

"Say it will be quite all right," said Miss Bulstrode. "I recognize that this is an exceptional occasion."

Miss Chadwick looked at her keenly.

"You're worrying, Honoria."

"Yes, I am. I don't really know my own mind. That's unusual for me—and it upsets me. I know what I'd like to do—but I feel that to hand over to someone without the necessary experience wouldn't be fair to the school."

"I wish you'd give up this idea of retirement. You belong here. Meadowbank needs you."

"Meadowbank means a lot to you, Chaddy, doesn't it?"

"There's no other school like it anywhere in England," said Miss Chadwick. "We can be proud of ourselves, you and I, for having started it."

Miss Bulstrode put an affectionate arm round her shoulders. "We can indeed, Chaddy. As for you, you're the comfort of my life. There's nothing about Meadow-bank you don't know. You care for it as much as I do. And that's saying a lot, my dear."

Miss Chadwick flushed with pleasure. It was so seldom that Honoria Bulstrode broke through her reserve.

ii.

"I simply can't play with the beastly thing. It's no good." Jennifer flung her racquet down in despair.

"Oh, Jennifer, what a fuss you make."

"It's the balance." Jennifer picked it up again and waggled it experimentally. "It doesn't balance right."

"It's much better than my old thing," Julia compared her racquet. "Mine's like a sponge. Listen to the sound of it." She twanged. "We meant to have it restrung, but Mummy forgot."

"I'd rather have it than mine, all the same," Jennifer took it and tried a swish or two with it.

"Well, I'd rather have yours. I could really hit something then. I'll swop, if you will."

"All right then, swop."

The two girls peeled off the small pieces of adhesive tape on which their names were written, and reaffixed them, each to the other's racquet.

"I'm not going to swop back again," said Julia warningly. "So it's no use your saying you don't like the old sponge."

iii.

Adam whistled cheerfully as he tacked up the wire netting round the tennis court. The door of the Sports Pavilion opened and Mademoiselle Blanche, the little mousy French mistress, looked out. She seemed startled at the sight of Adam. She hesitated for a moment and then went back inside.

"Wonder what she's been up to," said Adam to himself. It would not have occurred to him that Mademoiselle Blanche had been up to anything, if it had not been for her manner. She had a guilty look which immediately roused surmise in his mind. Presently she came out again, closing the door behind her, and paused to speak as she passed him.

"Ah, you repair the netting, I see?"

"Yes, miss."

"They are very fine courts here, and the swimming pool and the pavilion too. Oh, *le sport!* You think a lot in England of *le sport*, do you not?"

"Well, I suppose we do, miss."

"Do you play tennis yourself?" Her eyes appraised him in a definitely feminine way and with a faint invitation in her glance. Adam wondered once more about her. It struck him that Mademoiselle Blanche was a somewhat unsuitable French mistress for Meadowbank.

"No," he said untruthfully, "I don't play tennis. Haven't got the time."

"You play the cricket, then?"

"Oh, well, I played cricket as a boy. Most chaps do."

"I have not had much time to look round," said Angele Blanche. "Not until today and it was so fine I thought I would like to examine the Sports Pavilion. I wish to write home to my friends in France who keep a school."

Again Adam wondered a little. It seemed a lot of unnecessary explanation. It was almost as though Mademoiselle Blanche wished to excuse her presence out here at the Sports Pavilion. But why should she? She had a perfect right to go anywhere in the school grounds that she pleased. There was certainly no need to apologize for it to a gardener's assistant. It raised queries again in his mind. What had this young woman been doing in the Sports Pavilion?

He looked thoughtfully at Mademoiselle Blanche. It would be a good thing perhaps to know a little more about her. Subtly, deliberately, his manner changed. It was still respectful but not quite so respectful. He permitted his eyes to tell her that she was an attractive-looking young woman.

"You must find it a bit dull sometimes working in a girls' school, miss," he said.

"It does not amuse me very much, no."

"Still," said Adam, "I suppose you get your times off, don't you?"

There was a slight pause. It was as though she were debating with herself. Then, he felt it was with slight regret, the distance between them was deliberately widened.

"Oh, yes," she said, "I have very adequate time off. The conditions of employment here are excellent." She gave him a little nod of the head. "Good morning." She walked off toward the house.

"You've been up to something," said Adam to himself, "in the Sports Pavilion."

He waited till she was out of sight, then he left his work, went across to the Sports Pavilion and looked inside. But nothing that he could see was out of place. "All the same," he said to himself, "she was up to something."

As he came out again, he was confronted unexpectedly by Ann Shapland.

"Do you know where Miss Bulstrode is?" she asked.

"I think she's gone back to the house, miss. She was talking to Briggs just now."

Ann was frowning.

"What are you doing in the Sports Pavilion?"

Adam was slightly taken aback. "Nasty suspicious mind she's got," he thought. He said, with a faint inso-lence in his voice:

"Thought I'd like to take a look at it. No harm in looking, is there?"

"Oughtn't you to be getting on with your work?"

"I've just about finished nailing the wire round the tennis court." He turned, looking up at the building be-hind him. "This is new, isn't it? Must have cost a packet. The best of everything the young ladies here get, don't they?"

"They pay for it," said Ann drily.

"Pay through the nose, so I've heard," agreed Adam.

He felt a desire he hardly understood himself, to wound or annoy this girl. She was so cool always, so self-sufficient. He would really enjoy seeing her angry.

But Ann did not give him that satisfaction. She merely said:

"You'd better finish tacking up the netting," and went

back toward the house. Halfway there, she slackened
speed and looked back. Adam was busy at the tennis
wire. She looked from him to the Sports Pavilion in a
puzzled manner.

8

Murder

ON NIGHT DUTY in Hurst St. Cyprian Police Station,
Sergeant Green yawned. The telephone rang and he
picked up the receiver. A moment later his manner had
changed completely. He began scribbling rapidly on a
pad.

"Yes? Meadowbank? Yes—and the name? Spell it,
please. S—P—R—I—N—G—for greengage?—E—R.
Springer. Yes. Yes, please see that nothing is disturbed.
Someone'll be with you very shortly."

Rapidly and methodically he then proceeded to put
into motion the various procedures indicated.

"Meadowbank?" said Detective Inspector Kelsey when
his turn came. "That's the girls' school, isn't it? Who is it
who's been murdered?"

"Seems to be Miss Springer, the games mistress."

"Death of a games mistress," said Kelsey, thoughtfully.
"Sounds like the title of a thriller on a railway bookstall."

"Who's likely to have done her in, d'you think?" said
the Sergeant. "Seems unnatural."

"Even games mistresses may have their love lives,"
said Detective Inspector Kelsey. "Where did they say the
body was found?"

"In the Sports Pavilion. I suppose that's a fancy name
for the gymnasium."

"Could be," said Kelsey. "Death of a Games Mistress
in the Gymnasium. Sounds a highly athletic crime,
doesn't it? Did you say she was shot?"

"Yes."

"They find the pistol?"

"No."

"Interesting," said Detective Inspector Kelsey, and having assembled his retinue, he departed to carry out his duties.

ii.

The front door at Meadowbank was open, with light streaming from it, and here Inspector Kelsey was received by Miss Bulstrode herself. He knew her by sight, as indeed most people in the neighbourhood did. Even in this moment of confusion and uncertainty, Miss Bulstrode remained eminently herself, in command of the situation and in command of her subordinates.

"Detective Inspector Kelsey, madam," said the Inspector.

"What would you like to do first, Inspector Kelsey? Do you wish to go out to the Sports Pavilion or do you want to hear full details?"

"The doctor is with me," said Kelsey. "If you will show him and two of my men to where the body is, I should like a few words with you."

"Certainly. Come into my sitting room. Miss Rowan, will you show the doctor and the others the way?" She added, "One of my staff is out there seeing that nothing is disturbed."

"Thank you, madam."

Kelsey followed Miss Bulstrode into her sitting room. "Who found the body?"

"The matron, Miss Johnson. One of the girls had an earache and Miss Johnson was up attending to her. As she did so, she noticed the curtains were not pulled properly and going to pull them she observed that there was a light on in the Sports Pavilion which there should not have been at one A.M.," finished Miss Bulstrode drily.

"Quite so," said Kelsey. "Where is Miss Johnson now?"

"She is here if you want to see her."

"Presently. Will you go on, madam?"

"Miss Johnson went and woke up another member of

my staff, Miss Chadwick. They decided to go out and investigate. As they were leaving by the side door they heard the sound of a shot, whereupon they ran as quickly as they could toward the Sports Pavilion. On arrival there—"

The Inspector broke in. "Thank you, Miss Bulstrode. If, as you say, Miss Johnson is available, I will hear the next part from her. But first, perhaps you will tell me something about the murdered woman."

"Her name is Grace Springer."

"She has been with you long?"

"No. She came to me this term. My former games mistress left to take up a post in Australia."

"And what did you know about this Miss Springer?"

"Her testimonials were excellent," said Miss Bulstrode.

"You didn't know her personally before that?"

"No."

"Have you any idea at all, even the vaguest, of what might have precipitated this tragedy? Was she unhappy? Any unfortunate entanglements?"

Miss Bulstrode shook her head. "Nothing that I know of. I may say," she went on, "that it seems to me most unlikely. She was not that kind of a woman."

"You'd be surprised," said Inspector Kelsey darkly.

"Would you like me to fetch Miss Johnson now?"

"If you please. When I've heard her story I'll go out to the gym—or the—what d'you call it?—Sports Pavilion."

"It is a newly built addition to the school this year," said Miss Bulstrode. "It is built adjacent to the swimming pool and it comprises a squash court and other features. The racquets, lacrosse and hockey sticks are kept there, and there is a drying room for swim suits."

"Was there any reason why Miss Springer should be in the Sports Pavilion at night?"

"None whatever," said Miss Bulstrode unequivocally.

"Very well, Miss Bulstrode. I'll talk to Miss Johnson now."

Miss Bulstrode left the room and returned bringing the matron with her. Miss Johnson had had a sizable dollop of brandy administered to her to pull her together after her discovery of the body. The result was a slightly added loquacity.

"This is Detective Inspector Kelsey," said Miss Bulstrode. "Pull yourself together, Elspeth, and tell him exactly what happened."

"It's dreadful," said Miss Johnson, "it's really dreadful. Such a thing has never happened before in all my experience. Never! I couldn't have believed it, I really couldn't've believed it. Miss Springer too!"

Inspector Kelsey was a perceptive man. He was always willing to deviate from the course of routine if a remark struck him as unusual or worth following up.

"It seems to you, does it," he said, "very strange that it was Miss Springer who was murdered?"

"Well, yes, it does, Inspector. She was so—well, so tough, you know. So hearty. Like the sort of woman one could imagine taking on a burglar singlehanded—or two burglars."

"Burglars? Hm," said Inspector Kelsey. "Was there anything to steal in the Sports Pavilion?"

"Well, no, really I can't see what there can have been. Swim suits of course, sports paraphernalia."

"The sort of thing a sneak-thief might have taken," agreed Kelsey. "Hardly worth breaking in for, I should have thought. Was it broken into, by the way?"

"Well, really, I never thought to look," said Miss Johnson. "I mean, the door was open when we got there and . . ."

"It had not been broken into," said Miss Bulstrode.

"I see," said Kelsey. "A key was used." He looked at Miss Johnson. "Was Miss Springer well liked?" he asked.

"Well, really, I couldn't say. I mean, after all, she's dead."

"So you didn't like her," said Kelsey perceptively, ignoring Miss Johnson's finer feelings.

"I don't think anyone could have liked her very much," said Miss Johnson. "She had a very positive manner, you know. Never minded contradicting people flatly. She was very efficient and took her work very seriously I should say, wouldn't you, Miss Bulstrode?"

"Certainly," said Miss Bulstrode.

Kelsey returned from the by-path he had been pursuing. "Now, Miss Johnson, let's hear just what happened."

"Jean, one of our pupils, had earache. She woke up

with a rather bad attack of it and came to me. I got some remedies and when I'd got her back to bed, I saw the window curtains were ajar and thought perhaps it would be better for once if her window was not opened at night as it was blowing rather in that direction. Of course the girls always sleep with their windows open. We have difficulties sometimes with the foreigners, but I always insist that—"

"That really doesn't matter now," said Miss Bulstrode. "Our general rules of hygiene would not interest Inspector Kelsey."

"No, no, of course not," said Miss Johnson. "Well, as I say I went to shut the window and what was my surprise to see a light in the Sports Pavilion. It was quite distinct, I couldn't mistake it. It seemed to be moving about."

"You mean it was not the electric light turned on but the light of a flashlight?"

"Yes, yes, that's what it must have been. I thought at once, 'Dear me, what's anyone doing out there at this time of night?' Of course I didn't think of burglars. That would have been a very fanciful idea, as you said just now."

"What did you think of?" asked Kelsey.

Miss Johnson shot a glance at Miss Bulstrode and back again.

"Well, really,, I don't know that I had any ideas in particular. I mean, well—well really, I mean I couldn't think—"

Miss Bulstrode broke in. "I should imagine that Miss Johnson had the idea that one of our pupils might have gone out there to keep an assignation with someone," she said. "Is that right, Elspeth?"

Miss Johnson gasped. "Well, yes, the idea did come into my head just for the moment. One of our Italian girls, perhaps. Foreigners are so much more precocious than English girls."

"Don't be so insular," said Miss Bulstrode. "We've had plenty of English girls trying to make unsuitable assignations. It was a very natural thought to have occurred to you and probably the one that would have occurred to me."

"Go on," said Inspector Kelsey.

"So I thought the best thing," went on Miss Johnson, "was to go to Miss Chadwick and ask her to come out with me and see what was going on."

"Why Miss Chadwick?" asked Kelsey. "Any particular reason for selecting that particular mistress?"

"Well, I didn't want to disturb Miss Bulstrode," said Miss Johnson, "and I'm afraid it's rather a habit of ours always to go to Miss Chadwick if we don't want to disturb Miss Bulstrode. You see, Miss Chadwick's been here a very long time and has had so much experience."

"Anyway," said Kelsey, "you went to Miss Chadwick and woke her up. Is that right?"

"Yes. She agreed with me that we must go out there immediately. We didn't wait to dress or anything, just put on pullovers and coats and went out by the side door. And it was then, just as we were standing in the path, that we heard a shot from the Sports Pavilion. So we ran along the path as fast as we could. Rather stupidly we hadn't taken a flashlight with us and it was hard to see where we were going. We stumbled once or twice but we got there quite quickly. The door was open. We switched on the light and—"

Kelsey interrupted. "There was no light then when you got there? Not a flashlight or any other light?"

"No. The place was in darkness. We switched on the light and there she was. She—"

"That's all right," said Inspector Kelsey kindly, "you needn't describe anything. I shall be going out there now and I shall see for myself. You didn't meet anyone on your way there?"

"No."

"Or hear anybody running away?"

"No. We didn't hear anything."

"Did anybody else hear the shot in the school building?" asked Kelsey looking at Miss Bulstrode.

She shook her head. "No. Not that I know of. Nobody has said that they heard it. The Sports Pavilion is some distance away and I rather doubt if the shot would be noticeable."

"Perhaps from one of the rooms on the side of the house giving on the Sports Pavilion?"

"Hardly, I think, unless one were listening for such a

thing. I'm sure it wouldn't be loud enough to wake anybody up."

"Well, thank you," said Inspector Kelsey. "I'll be going out to the Sports Pavilion now."

"I will come with you," said Miss Bulstrode.

"Do you want me to come too?" asked Miss Johnson. "I will if you like. I mean it's no good shirking things, is it? I always feel that one must face whatever comes and . . ."

"Thank you," said Inspector Kelsey, "there's no need, Miss Johnson. I wouldn't think of putting you to any further strain."

"So awful," said Miss Johnson, "it makes it worse to feel I didn't like her very much. In fact, we had a disagreement only last night in the Common Room. I stuck to it that too much P.T. was bad for some girls—the more delicate girls. Miss Springer said nonsense, that they were just the ones who needed it. Toned them up and made new women of them, she said. I said to her that really she didn't know everything though she might think she did. After all I have been professionally trained and I know a great deal more about delicacy and illness than Miss Springer does—did, though I've no doubt that Miss Springer knows everything about parallel bars and vaulting horses and coaching tennis. But, oh, dear, now I think of what's happened, I wish I hadn't said quite what I did. I suppose one always feels like that afterward when something dreadful has occurred. I really do blame myself."

"Now sit down there, dear," said Miss Bulstrode settling her on the sofa. "You just sit down and rest and pay no attention to any little disputes you may have had. Life would be very dull if we agreed with each other on every subject."

Miss Johnson sat down shaking her head, then yawned. Miss Bulstrode followed Kelsey into the hall.

"I gave her rather a lot of brandy," she said, apologetically. "It's made her a little voluble. But not confused, do you think?"

"No," said Kelsey. "She gave quite a clear account of what happened."

Miss Bulstrode led the way to the side door.

"Is this the way Miss Johnson and Miss Chadwick went out?"

"Yes. You see it leads straight on to the path through the rhododendrons there which comes out at the Sports Pavilion."

The Inspector had a powerful flashlight and he and Miss Bulstrode soon reached the building where the lights were now glaring.

"Fine bit of building," said Kelsey, looking at it.

"It cost us a pretty penny," said Miss Bulstrode, "but we can afford it," she added serenely.

The open door led into a fair-sized room. There were lockers with the names of the various girls on them. At the end of the room there was a stand for tennis racquets and one for lacrosse sticks. The door at the side led off to showers and changing cubicles. Kelsey paused before going in. Two of his men had been busy. A photographer had just finished his job and another man who was busy testing for fingerprints looked up and said:

"You can walk straight across the floor, sir. You'll be all right. We haven't finished down this end yet."

Kelsey walked forward to where the police surgeon was kneeling by the body. The latter looked up as Kelsey approached.

"She was shot from about four feet away," he said. "Bullet penetrated the heart. Death must have been pretty well instantaneous."

"Shot from the front?"

"Yes."

"How long ago?"

"Say an hour or thereabouts."

Kelsey nodded. He strolled round to look at the tall figure of Miss Chadwick where she stood grimly, like a watchdog against one wall. About fifty-five, he judged, good forehead, obstinate mouth, untidy grey hair, no trace of hysteria. The kind of woman, he thought, who could be depended upon in a crisis though she might be overlooked in ordinary everyday life.

"Miss Chadwick?" he said.

"Yes."

"You came out with Miss Johnson and discovered the body?"

"Yes. She was just as she is now. She was dead."

"And the time?"

"I looked at my watch when Miss Johnson roused me. It was ten minutes to one."

Kelsey nodded. That agreed with the time that Miss Johnson had given him. He looked down thoughtfully at the dead woman. Her bright red hair was cut short. She had a freckled face, with a chin which jutted out strongly, and a spare, athletic figure. She was wearing a tweed skirt and a heavy, dark pullover. She had brogues on her feet with no stockings.

"Any sign of the weapon?" asked Kelsey.

One of his men shook his head. "No sign at all, sir."

"What about the light?"

"There's a flashlight there in the corner."

"Any prints on it?"

"Yes. The dead woman's."

"So she's the one who had the light," said Kelsey thoughtfully. "She came out here with a flashlight—why?" He asked it partly of himself, partly of his men, partly of Miss Bulstrode and Miss Chadwick. Finally he seemed to concentrate on the latter. "Any ideas?"

Miss Chadwick shook her head. "No idea at all. I suppose she might have left something here—forgotten it this afternoon or evening—and come out to fetch it. But it seems rather unlikely in the middle of the night."

"It must have been something very important if she did," said Kelsey.

He looked round him. Nothing seemed disturbed except the stand of racquets at the end. That seemed to have been pulled violently forward. Several of the racquets were lying about on the floor.

"Of course," said Miss Chadwick, "she could have seen a light here, like Miss Johnson did later, and have come out to investigate. That seems the most likely thing to me."

"I think you're right," said Kelsey. "There's just one small matter. Would she have come out alone?"

"Yes." Miss Chadwick answered without hesitation.

"Miss Johnson," Kelsey reminded her, "came and woke you up."

"I know," said Miss Chadwick, "and that's what I

should have done if I'd seen the light. I would have woken up Miss Bulstrode or Miss Vansittart or somebody. But Miss Springer wouldn't. She would have been quite confident—indeed would have preferred to tackle an intruder on her own."

"Another point," said the Inspector. "You came out through the side door with Miss Johnson. Was the side door unlocked?"

"Yes, it was."

"Presumably left unlocked by Miss Springer?"

"That seems the natural conclusion," said Miss Chadwick.

"So we assume," said Kelsey, "that Miss Springer saw a light out here in the gymnasium—Sports Pavilion—whatever you call it—that she came out to investigate and that whoever was here shot her." He wheeled round on Miss Bulstrode as she stood motionless in the doorway. "Does that seem right to you?" he asked.

"It doesn't seem right at all," said Miss Bulstrode. "I grant you the first part. We'll say Miss Springer saw a light out here and that she went out to investigate by herself. That's perfectly probable. But that the person she disturbed here should shoot her—that seems to me all wrong. If anyone was here who had no business to be here they would be more likely to run away, or to try to run away. Why should someone come to this place at this hour of night with a pistol? It's ridiculous, that's what it is. Ridiculous! There's nothing here worth stealing, certainly nothing for which it would be worth while doing murder."

"You think it more likely that Miss Springer disturbed a rendezvous of some kind?"

"That's the natural and most probable explanation," said Miss Bulstrode. "But it doesn't explain the fact of murder, does it? Girls in my school don't carry pistols about with them and any young man they might be meeting seems very unlikely to have a pistol either."

Kelsey agreed. "He'd have had a flick knife at most," he said. "There's an alternative," he went on. "Say Miss Springer came out here to meet a man—"

Miss Chadwick giggled suddenly. "Oh, no," she said, "not Miss Springer."

"I do not mean necessarily an amorous assignment," said the Inspector drily. "I'm suggesting that the murder was deliberate, that someone intended to murder Miss Springer, that they arranged to meet her here and shot her."

■

9

Cat Among the Pigeons

LETTER FROM Jennifer Sutcliffe to her mother:

Dear Mummy,
We had a murder last night. Miss Springer, the gym mistress. It happened in the middle of the night and the police came and this morning they're asking everybody questions.

Miss Chadwick told us not to talk to anybody about it but I thought you'd like to know.

With love,
Jennifer

ii.

Meadowbank was an establishment of sufficient importance to merit the personal attention of the Chief Constable. While routine investigation was going on Miss Bulstrode had not been inactive. She rang up a press magnate and the Home Secretary, both personal friends of hers. As a result of these maneuvers, very little had appeared about the event in the papers. A games mistress had been found dead in the School gymnasium. She had been shot, whether by accident or not was as yet not determined. Most of the notices of the event had an almost apologetic note in them, as though it were thoroughly tactless of any games mistress to get herself shot in such circumstances.

Ann Shapland had a busy day taking down letters to parents. Miss Bulstrode did not waste time in telling her pupils to keep quiet about the event. She knew that it would be a waste of time. More or less lurid reports would be sure to be penned to anxious parents and guardians. She intended her own balanced and reasonable account of the tragedy to reach them at the same time.

Later that afternoon she sat in conclave with Mr. Stone, the Chief Constable, and Inspector Kelsey. The police were perfectly amenable to having the press play the thing down as much as possible. It enabled them to pursue their inquiries quietly and without interference.

"I'm very sorry about this, Miss Bulstrode, very sorry indeed," said the Chief Constable. "I suppose it's—well—a bad thing for you."

"Murder's a bad thing for any school, yes," said Miss Bulstrode. "It's no good dwelling on that now, though. We shall weather it, no doubt, as we have weathered other storms. All I do hope is that the matter will be cleared up quickly."

"Don't see why it shouldn't, eh?" said Stone. He looked at Kelsey.

Kelsey said, "It may help when we get her background."

"D'you really think so?" asked Miss Bulstrode drily.

"Somebody may have had it in for her," Kelsey suggested.

Miss Bulstrode did not reply.

"You think it's tied up with this place?" asked the Chief Constable.

"Inspector Kelsey does really," said Miss Bulstrode. "He's only trying to save my feelings, I think."

"I think it does tie up with Meadowbank," said the Inspector slowly. "After all, Miss Springer had her times off like all the other members of the staff. She could have arranged a meeting with anyone if she had wanted to do so at any spot she chose. Why choose the gymnasium here in the middle of the night?"

"You have no objection to a search being made of the

school premises, Miss Bulstrode?" asked the Chief Constable.

"None at all. You're looking for the pistol or revolver or whatever it is, I suppose?"

"Yes. It was a small pistol of foreign make."

"Foreign," said Miss Bulstrode thoughtfully.

"To your knowledge, do any of your staff or any of the pupils have such a thing as a pistol in their possession?"

"Certainly not to my knowledge," said Miss Bulstrode. "I am fairly certain that none of the pupils have. Their possessions are unpacked for them when they arrive and such a thing would have been seen and noted, and would, I may say, have aroused considerable comment. But please, Inspector Kelsey, do exactly as you like in that respect. I see your men have been searching the grounds today."

The Inspector nodded. "Yes."

He went on: "I should also like interviews with the other members of your staff. One or other of them may have heard some remark made by Miss Springer that will give us a clue. Or may have observed some oddity of behaviour on her part." He paused, then went on, "The same thing might apply to the pupils."

Miss Bulstrode said: "I had formed the plan of making a short address to the girls this evening after prayers. I would ask that if any of them has any knowledge that might possibly bear upon Miss Springer's death that they should come and tell me of it."

"Very sound idea," said the Chief Constable.

"But you must remember this," said Miss Bulstrode, "one or other of the girls may wish to make herself important by exaggerating some incident or even by inventing one. Girls do very odd things; but I expect you are used to dealing with that form of exhibitionism."

"I've come across it," said Inspector Kelsey. "Now," he added, "please give me a list of your staff, also the servants."

iii.

"I've looked through all the lockers out in the Pavilion, sir."

"And you didn't find anything?" said Kelsey.

"No, sir, nothing of importance. Funny things in some of them, but nothing in our line."

"None of them were locked, were they?"

"No, sir, they can lock. There were keys in them, but none of them were locked."

Kelsey looked round the bare floor thoughtfully. The tennis racquets and lacrosse sticks had been replaced on their stands.

"Oh, well," he said, "I'm going up to the house now to have a talk with the staff."

"You don't think it was an inside job, sir?"

"It could have been," said Kelsey. "Nobody's got an alibi except those two mistresses, Chadwick and Johnson, and the child Jean that had the earache. Theoretically, everyone else was in bed and asleep, but there's no one to vouch for that. The girls all have separate rooms and naturally the staff do. Any one of them, including Miss Bulstrode herself, could have come out and met Springer here, or could have followed her here. Then, after she'd been shot, whoever it was could dodge back quietly into the house through the bushes to the side door, and be nicely back in bed again when the alarm was given. It's motive that's difficult. Yes," said Kelsey, "it's motive. Unless there's something going on here that we don't know anything about, there doesn't seem to *be* any motive."

He stepped out of the Pavilion and made his way slowly back to the house. Although it was past working hours, old Briggs, the gardener, was putting in a little work on a flower bed and he straightened up as the Inspector passed.

"You work late hours," said Kelsey, smiling.

"Ah," said Briggs. "Young 'uns don't know what gardening is. Come on at eight and knock off at five—that's what they think it is. You've got to study your weather, some days you might as well not be out in the garden at all, and there's other days as you can work from seven in the morning until eight at night. That is if you love the place and have pride in the look of it."

"You ought to be proud of this one," said Kelsey. "I've never seen any place better kept these days."

"These days is right," said Briggs. "But I'm lucky I am. I've got a strong young fellow to work for me. A couple of boys, too, but they're not much good. Most of these boys and young men won't come and do this sort of work. All for going into factories, they are, or white collars and working in an office. Don't like to get their hands soiled with a bit of honest earth. But I'm lucky, as I say. I've got a good man working for me as came and offered himself."

"Recently?" said Inspector Kelsey.

"Beginning of the term," said Briggs. "Adam, his name is. Adam Goodman."

"I don't think I've seen him about," said Kelsey.

"Asked for the day off today, he did," said Briggs. "I give it him. Didn't seem to be much doing today with you people tramping all over the place."

"Somebody should have told me about him," said Kelsey sharply.

"What do you mean, told you about him?"

"He's not on my list," said the Inspector. "Of people employed here, I mean."

"Oh, well, you can see him tomorrow, mister," said Briggs. "Not that he can tell you anything, I don't suppose."

"You never know," said the Inspector.

A strong young man who had offered himself at the beginning of the term? It seemed to Kelsey that here was the first thing that he had come across which might be a little out of the ordinary.

iv.

The girls filed into the hall for prayers that evening as usual, and afterward Miss Bulstrode arrested their departure by raising her hand.

"I have something to say to you all. Miss Springer, as you know, was shot last night in the Sports Pavilion. If any of you has heard or seen anything in the past week——anything that has puzzled you relating to Miss Springer, anything Miss Springer may have said or someone else may have said of her that strikes you as at all significant,

I should like to know it. You can come to me in my sitting room any time this evening."

"Oh," Julia Upjohn sighed, as the girls filed out, "how I wish we did know something! But we don't, do we, Jennifer?"

"No," said Jennifer, "of course we don't."

"Miss Springer always seemed so very ordinary," said Julia, sadly, "much too ordinary to get killed in a mysterious way."

"I don't suppose it was so mysterious," said Jennifer. "Just a burglar."

"Stealing our tennis racquets, I suppose," said Julia with sarcasm.

"Perhaps someone was blackmailing her," suggested one of the other girls hopefully.

"What about?" said Jennifer.

But nobody could think of any reason for blackmailing Miss Springer.

v.

Inspector Kelsey started his interviewing of the staff with Miss Vansittart. A handsome woman, he thought, summing her up. Possibly forty or a little over; tall, well built, grey hair tastefully arranged. She had dignity and composure, with a certain sense, he thought, of her own importance. She reminded him a little of Miss Bulstrode herself; she was the schoolmistress type all right. All the same, he reflected, Miss Bulstrode had something that Miss Vansittart had not. Miss Bulstrode had a quality of unexpectedness. He did not feel that Miss Vansittart would ever be unexpected.

Question and answer followed routine. In effect, Miss Vansittart had seen nothing, had noticed nothing, had heard nothing. Miss Springer had been excellent at her job. Yes, her manner had perhaps been a trifle brusque, but not, she thought, unduly so. She had not perhaps had a very attractive personality but that was really not a necessity in a games mistress. It was better, in fact, *not* to have mistresses who had attractive personalities. It did not do to let the girls get emotional about the mistresses.

Miss Vansittart, having contributed nothing of value, made her exit.

"See no evil, hear no evil, think no evil. Same like the monkeys," observed Sergeant Percy Bond, who was assisting Inspector Kelsey in his task.

Kelsey grinned. "That's about right, Percy," he said.

"There's something about schoolmistresses that gives me the hump," said Sergeant Bond. "Had a terror of them ever since I was a kid. Knew one that was a holy terror. So upstage and la-di-da you never knew what she was trying to teach you."

The next mistress to appear was Eileen Rich. Ugly as sin was Inspector Kelsey's first reaction. Then he qualified it, she had a certain attraction. He started his routine questions, but the answers were not quite so routine as he had expected. After saying No, she had not heard or noticed anything special that anyone else had said about Miss Springer or that Miss Springer herself had said, Eileen Rich's next answer was not what he anticipated. He had asked:

"There was no one as far as you know who had a personal grudge against her?"

"Oh, no," said Eileen Rich quickly. "One couldn't have. I think that was her tragedy, you know. That she wasn't a person one could ever hate."

"Now just what do you mean by that, Miss Rich?"

"I mean she wasn't a person one could ever have wanted to destroy. Everything she did and was, was on the surface. She annoyed people. They often had sharp words with her, but it didn't mean anything. Not anything deep. I'm sure she wasn't killed for herself, if you know what I mean."

"I'm not quite sure that I do, Miss Rich."

"I mean if you had something like a bank robbery, she might quite easily be the cashier that gets shot, but it would be as a cashier not as Grace Springer. Nobody would love her or hate her enough to want to do away with her. I think she probably felt that without thinking about it, and that's what made her so officious. About finding fault, you know, and enforcing rules and finding out what people were doing that they shouldn't be doing, and showing them up."

"Snooping?" asked Kelsey.

"No, not exactly snooping." Eileen Rich considered. "She wouldn't tiptoe round on sneakers or anything of that kind. But if she found something going on that she didn't understand she'd be quite determined to get to the bottom of it. And she *would* get to the bottom of it."

"I see." He paused a moment. "You didn't like her yourself much, did you, Miss Rich?"

"I don't think I ever thought about her. She was just the games mistress. Oh! what a horrible thing that is to say about anybody! Just this—just that! But that's how *she* felt about her job. It was a job that she took pride in doing well. She didn't find it fun. She wasn't keen when she found a girl who might be really good at tennis, or really fine at some form of athletics. She didn't rejoice in it or triumph."

Kelsey looked at her curiously. An odd young woman, this, he thought.

"You seem to have your ideas on most things, Miss Rich," he said.

"Yes. Yes, I suppose I do."

"How long have you been at Meadowbank?"

"Just over a year and a half."

"There's never been any trouble before?"

"At Meadowbank?" She sounded startled.

"Yes."

"Oh, no. Everything's been quite all right until this term."

Kelsey pounced.

"What's been wrong this term? You don't mean the murder, do you? You mean something else—"

"I don't—" she stopped. "Yes, perhaps I do—but it's all very nebulous."

"Go on."

"Miss Bulstrode's not been happy lately," said Eileen slowly. "That's one thing. You wouldn't know it. I don't think anybody else has even noticed it. But I have. And she's not the only one who's unhappy. But that isn't what you mean, is it? That's just people's feelings. The kind of things you get when you're cooped up together and think about one thing too much. You meant, was there anything that didn't seem right just this term. That's it, isn't it?"

"Yes," said Kelsey, looking at her curiously, "yes, that's it. Well, what about it?"

"I think there is something wrong here," said Eileen Rich slowly. "It's as though there were someone among us who didn't belong." She looked at him, smiled, almost laughed and said, "Cat among the pigeons, that's the sort of feeling. We're the pigeons, all of us, and the cat's among us. But we can't *see* the cat."

"That's very vague, Miss Rich."

"Yes, isn't it? It sounds quite idiotic. I can hear that myself. What I really mean, I suppose, is that there has been something, some little thing that I've noticed but I don't know what I've noticed."

"About anyone in particular?"

"No, I told you, that's just it. I don't know who it is. The only way I can sum it up is to say that there's someone here, who's—somehow—wrong! There's someone here—I don't know who—who makes me uncomfortable. Not when I'm looking at her but when she's looking at me because it's when she's looking at me that it shows, whatever it is. Oh, I'm getting more incoherent than ever. And anyway, it's only a feeling. It's not what you want. It isn't evidence."

"No," said Kelsey, "it isn't evidence. Not yet. But it's interesting, and if your feeling gets any more definite, Miss Rich, I'd be glad to hear about it."

She nodded. "Yes," she said, "because it's serious, isn't it? I mean, someone's been killed—we don't know why—and the killer may be miles away, or, on the other hand, the killer may be here in the school. And if so that pistol or revolver or whatever it is, must be here too. That's not a very nice thought, is it?"

She went out with a slight nod. Sergeant Bond said:

"Crackers—or don't you think so?"

"No," said Kelsey, "I don't think she's crackers. I think she's what's called a sensitive. You know, like the people who know when there's a cat in the room long before they see it. If she'd been born in an African tribe she might have been a witch doctor."

"They go round smelling out evil, don't they?" said Sergeant Bond.

"That's right, Percy," said Kelsey. "And that's exactly what I'm trying to do myself. Nobody's come across with any concrete facts so I've got to go about smelling out things. We'll have the Frenchwoman next."

■
10

Fantastic Story

MADEMOISELLE ANGELE BLANCHE was thirty-five at a guess. No make-up, dark brown hair arranged neatly but unbecomingly. A severe coat and skirt.

It was Mademoiselle Blanche's first term at Meadowbank, she explained. She was not sure that she wished to remain for a further term.

"It is not nice to be in a school where murders take place," she said disapprovingly.

Also, there did not seem to be burglar alarms anywhere in the house—that was very dangerous.

"There's nothing of any great value, Mademoiselle Blanche, to attract burglars."

Mademoiselle Blanche shrugged her shoulders.

"How does one know? These girls who come here, some of them have very rich fathers. They may have something with them of great value. A burglar knows about that, perhaps, and he comes here because he thinks this is an easy place to steal it."

"If a girl had something of value with her it wouldn't be in the gymnasium."

"How do you know?" said Mademoiselle. "They have lockers there, do they not, the girls?"

"Only to keep their sports kit in, and things of that kind."

"Ah, yes, that is what is supposed. But a girl could

hide anything in the toe of a gym shoe, or wrapped up in an old pullover or in a scarf."

"What sort of thing, Mademoiselle Blanche?"

But Mademoiselle Blanche had no idea what sort of thing.

"Even the most indulgent fathers don't give their daughters diamond necklaces to take to school," the Inspector said.

Again Mademoiselle Blanche shrugged her shoulders.

"Perhaps it is something of a different kind of value—a scarab, say, or something that a collector would give a lot of money for. One of the girls has a father who is an archaeologist."

Kelsey smiled. "I don't really think that's likely, you know, Mademoiselle Blanche."

She shrugged her shoulders. "Oh, well, I only make the suggestion."

"Have you taught in any other English schools, Mademoiselle Blanche?"

"One in the north of England some time ago. Mostly I have taught in Switzerland and in France. Also in Germany. I think I will come to England to improve my English. I have a friend here. She went sick and she told me I could take her position here as Miss Bulstrode would be glad to find somebody quickly. So I came. But I do not like it very much. As I tell you, I do not think I shall stay."

"Why don't you like it?" Kelsey persisted.

"I do not like places where there are shootings," said Mademoiselle Blanche. "And the children, they are not respectful."

"They are not quite children, are they?"

"Some of them behave like babies, some of them might be twenty-five. There are all kinds here. They have much freedom. I prefer an establishment with more routine."

"Did you know Miss Springer well?"

"I knew her practically not at all. She had bad manners and I conversed with her as little as possible. She was all bones and freckles and a loud ugly voice. She was like caricatures of Englishwomen. She was rude to me often and I did not like it."

"What was she rude to you about?"

"She did not like me coming to her Sports Pavilion. That seems to be how she feels about it—or felt about it I mean—that it was her Sports Pavilion! I go there one day because I am interested. I have not been in it before and it is a new building. It is very well arranged and planned and I am just looking round. Then Miss Springer she comes and says, 'What are you doing here? This is no business of yours to be in here.' She says that to me—me, a mistress in the school! What does she think I am, a pupil?"

"Yes, yes, very irritating I'm sure," said Kelsey, soothingly.

"The manners of a pig, that is what she had. And then she calls out, 'Do not go away with the key in your hand.' She upset me. When I pull the door open the key fell out and I pick it up. I forget to put it back, because she has offended me. And then she shouts after me as though she thinks I was meaning to steal it. Her key, I suppose, as well as her Sports Pavilion."

"That seems a little odd, doesn't it?" said Kelsey, "that she should feel like that about the gymnasium, I mean. As though it were her private property, as though she were afraid of people finding something she had hidden there." He made the faint feeler tentatively, but Angele Blanche merely laughed.

"Hide something there—what could you hide in a place like that? Do you think she hides her love letters there? I am sure she has never had a love letter written to her! The other mistresses, they are at least polite. Miss Chadwick, she is old-fashioned and she fusses. Miss Vansittart, she is very nice, *grande dame,* sympathetic. Miss Rich, she is a little crazy I think, but friendly. And the younger mistresses are quite pleasant."

Angele Blanche was dismissed after a few more unimportant questions.

"Touchy," said Bond. "All the French are touchy."

"All the same, it's interesting," said Kelsey. "Miss Springer didn't like people prowling about her gymnasium—Sports Pavilion—I don't know what to call the thing. Now why?"

"Perhaps she thought the Frenchwoman was spying on her," suggested Bond.

"Well, but why should she think so? I mean, ought it to
have mattered to her that Angele Blanche should spy on
her unless there was something she was afraid of Angele
Blanche finding out?

"Who have we got left?" he added.

"The two junior mistresses, Miss Blake and Miss
Rowan, and Miss Bulstrode's secretary."

Miss Blake was young and earnest with a round good-
natured face. She taught botany and physics. She had
nothing much to say that could help. She had seen very
little of Miss Springer and had no idea of what could
have led to her death.

Miss Rowan, as befitted one who held a degree in
psychology, had views to express. It was highly probable,
she said, that Miss Springer had committed suicide.

Inspector Kelsey raised his eyebrows.

"Why should she? Was she unhappy in any way?"

"She was aggressive," said Miss Rowan, leaning forward and peering eagerly through her thick lenses. "Very
aggressive. I consider that significant. It was a defense
mechanism, to conceal a feeling of inferiority."

"Everything I've heard so far," said Inspector Kelsey,
"points to her being very sure of herself."

"Too sure of herself," said Miss Rowan darkly. "And
several of the things she said bear out my assumption."

"Such as?"

"She hinted at people being 'not what they seemed.'
She mentioned that at the last school where she was
employed, she had 'unmasked' someone. The Headmistress, however, had been prejudiced, had refused to listen
to what she had found out. Several of the other mistresses, too, had been what she called 'against her.'

"You see what that means, Inspector?" Miss Rowan
nearly fell off her chair as she leaned forward excitedly.
Strands of lank dark hair fell forward across her face.
"The beginning of a persecution complex."

Inspector Kelsey said politely that Miss Rowan might
be correct in her assumptions, but that he couldn't accept
the theory of suicide, unless Miss Rowan could explain
how Miss Springer had managed to shoot herself from a
distance of at least four feet away, and had also been
able to make the pistol disappear into thin air afterward.

Miss Rowan retorted acidly that the police were well known to be prejudiced against psychology.

She then gave place to Ann Shapland.

"Well, Miss Shapland," said Inspector Kelsey, eying her neat and businesslike appearance with favour, "what light can you throw upon this matter?"

"Absolutely none, I'm afraid. I've got my own sitting room, and I don't see much of the staff. The whole thing's unbelievable."

"In what way unbelievable?"

"Well, first that Miss Springer should get shot at all. Say somebody broke into the gymnasium and she went out to see who it was. That's all right, I suppose, but who'd want to break into the gymnasium?"

"Boys, perhaps, or some young locals who wanted to help themselves to equipment of some kind or another, or who did it for a lark."

"If that's so, I can't help feeling that what Miss Springer would have said was: 'Now then, what are you doing here? Be off with you,' and they'd have gone off."

"Did it ever seem to you that Miss Springer adopted any particular attitude about the Sports Pavilion?"

Ann Shapland looked puzzled. "Attitude?"

"I mean did she regard it as her special province and dislike other people going there?"

"Not that I know of. Why should she? It was just part of the school buildings."

"You didn't notice anything yourself? You didn't find that if you went there she resented your presence—anything of that kind?"

Ann Shapland shook her head. "I haven't been out there myself more than a couple of times. I haven't the time. I've gone out there once or twice with a message for one of the girls from Miss Bulstrode. That's all."

"You didn't know that Miss Springer had objected to Mademoiselle Blanche being out there?"

"No, I didn't hear anything about that. Oh, yes, I believe I did. Mademoiselle Blanche was rather cross about something one day, but then she is a little bit touchy, you know. There was something about her going into the drawing class one day and resenting something the drawing mistress said to her. Of course she hasn't really very much to do—Mademoiselle Blanche, I mean. She only teaches one subject—French, and she has a lot of time on her hands. I think"—she hesitated—"I think she is perhaps rather an inquisitive person."

"Do you think it likely that when she went into the Sports Pavilion she was poking about in any of the lockers?"

"The girls' lockers? Well, I wouldn't put it past her. She might amuse herself that way."

"Does Miss Springer herself have a locker out there?"

"Yes, of course."

"If Mademoiselle Blanche was caught poking about in Miss Springer's locker, then I can imagine that Miss Springer *would* be annoyed?"

"She certainly would!"

"You don't know anything about Miss Springer's private life?"

"I don't think anyone did," said Ann. "Did she have one, I wonder?"

"And there's nothing else—nothing connected with the Sports Pavilion, for instance, that you haven't told me?"

"Well—" Ann hesitated.

"Yes, Miss Shapland, let's have it."

"It's nothing really," said Ann slowly. "But one of the gardeners—not Briggs, the young one—I saw him come out of the Sports Pavilion one day, and he had no business to be in there at all. Of course it was probably just curiosity on his part—or perhaps an excuse to slack off for a bit from work—he was supposed to be nailing down the wire on the tennis court. I don't suppose really there's anything in it."

"Still, you remembered it," Kelsey pointed out. "Now why?"

"I think—" She frowned. "Yes, because his manner was a little odd. Defiant. And—he sneered at all the money that was spent here on the girls."

"That sort of attitude . . . I see."

"I don't suppose there's really anything in it."

"Probably not—but I'll make a note of it, all the same."

"Round and round the mulberry bush," said Bond when Ann Shapland had gone. "Same thing over and over again! For goodness' sake let's hope we get something out of the servants."

But they got very little out of the servants.

"It's no use asking me anything, young man," said Mrs. Gibbons, the cook. "For one thing I can't hear what you say, and for another I don't know a thing. I went to sleep last night and I slept unusual heavy. Never heard anything of all the excitement there was. Nobody woke me up and told me anything about it." She sounded injured. "It wasn't until this morning I heard."

Kelsey shouted a few questions and got a few answers that told him nothing.

Miss Springer had come new this term, and she wasn't as much liked as Miss Lorrimer who'd held the post before her. Miss Shapland was new, too, but she was a nice young lady, Mademoiselle Blanche was like all the Frenchies—thought the other mistresses were against her and let the young ladies treat her something shocking in class. "Not a one for crying, though," Mrs. Gibbons admitted. "Some schools I've been in the French mistresses used to cry something awful!"

Most of the domestic staff were dailies.

There was only one other maid who slept in the house, and she proved equally uninformative, though able to hear what was said to her. She couldn't say, she was sure. She didn't know nothing. Miss Springer was a bit sharp in her manner. She didn't know nothing about the Sports Pavilion nor what was kept there, and she'd never seen nothing like a pistol nowhere.

This negative spate of information was interrupted by Miss Bulstrode.

"One of the girls would like to speak to you, Inspector Kelsey," she said.

Kelsey looked up sharply. "Indeed? She knows something?"

"As to that I'm rather doubtful," said Miss Bulstrode, "but you had better talk to her yourself. She is one of our foreign girls, Princess Shaista—niece of the Emir Ibrahim. She is inclined to think, perhaps, that she is of rather more importance than she is. You understand?"

Kelsey nodded comprehendingly. Then Miss Bulstrode went out and a slight dark girl of middle height came in.

She looked at them, almond eyed and demure.

"You are the police?"

"Yes," said Kelsey smiling, "we are the police. Will you sit down and tell me what you know about Miss Springer?"

"Yes, I will tell you."

She sat down, leaned forward, and lowered her voice dramatically.

"There have been people watching this place. Oh, they do not show themselves clearly, but they are there!"

She nodded her head significantly.

Inspector Kelsey thought that he understood what Miss Bulstrode had meant. This girl was dramatizing herself—. and enjoying it.

"And why should they be watching the school?"

"Because of me! They want to kidnap me."

Whatever Kelsey had expected, it was not this. His eyebrows rose.

"Why should they want to kidnap you?"

"To hold me to ransom, of course. Then they would make my relations pay much money."

"Er—well—perhaps," said Kelsey dubiously. "But—er—supposing this is so, what has it got to do with the death of Miss Springer?"

"She must have found out about them," said Shaista. "Perhaps she told them she had found out something. Perhaps she threatened them. Then perhaps they promised to pay her money if she would say nothing. And she believed them. So she goes out to the Sports Pavilion where they say they will pay her the money, and then they shoot her."

"But surely Miss Springer would never have accepted blackmail money?"

"Do you think it is such fun to be a school teacher—to be a teacher of gymnastics?" Shaista was scornful. "Do you not think it would be nice instead to have money, to travel, to do what you want? Especially someone like Miss Springer who is not beautiful, at whom men do not even look! Do you not think that money would attract her more than it would attract other people?"

"Well—er—" said Inspector Kelsey, "I don't know

quite what to say." He had not had this point of view presented to him before.

"This is just—er—your own idea?" he said. "Miss Springer never said anything to you?"

"Miss Springer never said anything except 'Stretch and Bend,' and 'Faster,' and 'Don't slack,' " said Shaista with resentment.

"Yes—quite so. Well, don't you think you may have imagined all this about kidnaping?"

Shaista was immediately much annoyed.

"You do not understand at all! My cousin was Prince Ali Yusuf of Ramat. He was killed in a revolution, or at least in fleeing from a revolution. It was understood that when I grew up I should marry him. So you see I am an important person. It may be perhaps the Communists who come here. Perhaps it is not to kidnap. Perhaps they intend to assassinate me."

Inspector Kelsey looked still more incredulous.

"That's rather farfetched, isn't it?"

"You think such things could not happen? I say they can. They are very, very wicked, the Communists! Everybody knows that."

As he still looked dubious, she went on:

"Perhaps they think I know where the jewels are!"

"What jewels?"

"My cousin had jewels. So had his father. My family always has a hoard of jewels. For emergencies, you comprehend."

She made it sound very matter of fact.

Kelsey stared at her.

"But what has all this got to do with you—or with Miss Springer?"

"But I already tell you! They think, perhaps, I know where the jewels are. So they will take me prisoner and force me to speak."

"Do you know where the jewels are?"

"No, of course I do not know. They disappeared in the revolution. Perhaps the wicked Communists take them. But again, perhaps not."

"Who do they belong to?"

"Now my cousin is dead, they belong to me. No men in his family any more. His aunt, my mother, is dead. He would want them to belong to me. If he were not dead, I marry him."

"That was the arrangement?"

"I have to marry him. He is my cousin, you see."

"And you would have got the jewels when you married him?"

"No, I would have had new jewels. From Cartier in Paris. These others would still be kept for emergencies."

Inspector Kelsey blinked, letting this Oriental insurance scheme for emergencies sink into his consciousness.

Shaista was racing on with great animation.

"I think that is what happens. Somebody gets the jewels out of Ramat. Perhaps good person, perhaps bad. Good person would bring them to me, would say: 'These are yours,' and I should reward him."

She nodded her head regally, playing the part.

"Quite a little actress," thought the Inspector.

"But if it was a bad person, he would keep the jewels and sell them. Or he would come to me and say: 'What will you give me as a reward if I bring them to you?' And if it is worth while, he brings—but if not, then not!"

"But in actual fact, nobody has said anything at all to you?"

"No," admitted Shaista.

Inspector Kelsey made up his mind.

"I think, you know," he said pleasantly, "that you're really talking a lot of nonsense."

Shaista flashed a furious glance at him.

"I tell you what I know, that is all," she said sulkily.

"Yes—well, it's very kind of you, and I'll bear it in mind."

He got up and opened the door for her to go out.

"The Arabian Nights aren't in it," he said, as he returned to the table. "Kidnaping and fabulous jewels! What next?"

11

Conference

WHEN INSPECTOR KELSEY returned to the station, the sergeant on duty said:

"We've got Adam Goodman here, waiting, sir."

"Adam Goodman? Oh, yes. The gardener."

A young man had risen respectfully to his feet. He was tall, dark and good-looking. He wore stained corduroy trousers loosely held up by an aged belt, and an open-necked shirt of very bright blue.

"You wanted to see me, I hear."

His voice was rough, and as that of so many young men of today, slightly truculent.

Kelsey said merely:

"Yes, come into my room."

"I don't know anything about the murder," said Adam Goodman sulkily. "It's nothing to do with me. I was at home and in bed last night."

Kelsey merely nodded noncommittally.

He sat down at his desk, and motioned to the young man to take the chair opposite. A young policeman in plain clothes had followed the two men in unobtrusively and sat down a little distance away.

"Now then," said Kelsey. "You're Goodman—" he looked at a note on his desk, "Adam Goodman."

"That's right, sir. But first, I'd like to show you this."

Adam's manner had changed. There was no truculence or sulkiness in it now. It was quiet and deferential. He took something from his pocket and passed it across the desk. Inspector Kelsey's eyebrows rose very slightly as he studied it. Then he raised his head.

"I shan't need you, Barber," he said.

The discreet young policeman got up and went out. He managed not to look surprised, but he was.

99

"Ah," said Kelsey. He looked across at Adam with speculative interest. "So that's who you are? And what the hell, I'd like to know, are you——"

"Doing in a girls' school?" the young man finished for him. His voice was still deferential, but he grinned in spite of himself. "It's certainly the first time I've had an assignment of that kind. Don't I look like a gardener?"

"Not around these parts. Gardeners are usually rather ancient. Do you know anything about gardening?"

"Quite a lot. I've got one of these gardening mothers. England's specialty. She's seen to it that I'm a worthy assistant to her."

"And what exactly is going on at Meadowbank—to bring you on the scene?"

"We don't know, actually, that there's anything going on at Meadowbank. My assignment is in the nature of a watching brief. Or was—until last night. Murder of a games mistress. Not quite in the school's curriculum."

"It could happen," said Inspector Kelsey. He sighed. "Anything could happen—anywhere. I've learnt that. But I'll admit that it's a little off the beaten track. What's behind all this?"

Adam told him. Kelsey listened with interest.

"I did that girl an injustice," he remarked. "But you'll admit it sounds too fantastic to be true. Jewels worth between half a million and a million pounds? Who do you say they belong to?"

"That's a very pretty question. To answer it, you'd have to have a gaggle of international lawyers on the job, and they'd probably disagree. You could argue the case a lot of ways. They belonged, three months ago, to His Highness Prince Ali Yusuf of Ramat. But now? If they'd turned up in Ramat they'd have been the property of the present government, they'd have made sure of that. Ali Yusuf may have willed them to someone. A lot would then depend on where the will was executed and could be proved. They may belong to his family. But the real essence of the matter is that if you or I happened to pick them up in the street and put them in our pockets, they would for all practical purposes belong to us. That is, I doubt if any legal machinery exists that could get them away from us. They could try, of course, but the intricacies of international law are quite incredible . . ."

"You mean that, practically speaking, it's findings are keepings?" asked Inspector Kelsey. He shook his head disapprovingly. "That's not very nice," he said primly.

"No," said Adam grimly. "It's not very nice. There's more than one lot after them, too. None of them scrupulous. Word's got around, you see. It may be a rumour, it may be true, but the story is that they were got out of Ramat just before the bust up. There are a dozen different tales of how."

"But why Meadowbank? Because of little Princess Butter-won't-melt-in-my-mouth?"

"Princess Shaista, first cousin of Ali Yusuf. Yes. Someone may try and deliver the goods to her or communicate with her. There are some questionable characters from our point of view hanging about the neighbourhood. A Mrs. Kolinsky, for instance, staying at the Grand Hotel. Quite a prominent member of what one might describe as International Riff-Raff, Ltd. Nothing in *your* line, always strictly within the law, all perfectly respectable, but a grand picker-up of useful information. Then there's a woman who was out in Ramat dancing in a cabaret there. She's reported to have been working for a certain foreign government. Where she is now we don't know, we don't even know what she looks like, but there's a rumour that she *might* be in this part of the world. Looks, doesn't it, as though it were all centering round Meadowbank? And last night, Miss Springer gets herself killed."

Kelsey nodded thoughtfully.

"Proper mix-up," he observed. He struggled a moment with his feelings. "You see this sort of thing on the Telly . . . farfetched—that's what you think . . . can't really happen. And it doesn't—not in the normal course of events."

"Secret agents, robbery, violence, murder, double-crossing," agreed Adam. "All preposterous—but that side of life exists."

"But not at Meadowbank!"

The words were wrung from Inspector Kelsey.

"I perceive your point," said Adam. *"Lèse-majesté."*

There was a silence, and then Inspector Kelsey asked:

"What do *you* think happened last night?"

Adam took his time, then he said slowly:

"Springer was in the Sports Pavilion—in the middle of the night. Why? We've got to start there. It's no good asking ourselves who killed her until we've made up our minds why she was there, in the Sports Pavilion at that time of night. We can say that in spite of her blameless and athletic life she wasn't sleeping well, and got up and looked out of her window and saw a light in the Sports Pavilion—her window does look out that way?"

Kelsey nodded.

"Being a tough and fearless woman, she went out to investigate. She disturbed someone there who was—doing what? We don't know. But it was someone desperate enough to shoot her dead."

Again Kelsey nodded.

"That's the way we've been looking at it," he said. "But your last point had me worried all along. You don't shoot to kill—and come prepared to do so, unless—"

"Unless you're after something big? Agreed! Well, that's the case of what we might call Innocent Springer—shot down in the performance of duty. But there's another possibility. Springer, as a result of private information, gets a job at Meadowbank or is detailed for it by her bosses—because of her qualifications. She waits until a suitable night, then slips out to the Sports Pavilion—again our stumbling block of a question—*why?* Somebody is following her—or waiting for her—someone who carries a pistol and is prepared to use it. But again—why? What for? In fact, what the devil is there about the Sports Pavilion? It's not the sort of place that one can imagine hiding anything."

"There wasn't anything hidden there, I can tell you that. We went through it with a fine tooth comb—the girls' lockers, Miss Springer's ditto. Sports equipment of various kinds, all normal and accounted for. *And* a brand new building! There wasn't anything there in the nature of jewellery."

"Whatever it was it could have been removed, of course. By the murderer," said Adam. "The other possibility is that the Sports Pavilion was simply used as a rendezvous—by Miss Springer or by someone else. It's quite a handy place for that. A reasonable distance from the house. Not too far. And if anyone was noticed going out there, a simple answer would be that whoever it was thought they had seen a light, etc., etc. Let's say that Miss Springer went out to meet someone—there was a disagreement and she got shot. Or, a variation, Miss Springer noticed someone leaving the house, followed that someone, intruded upon something she wasn't meant to see or hear."

"I never met her alive," said Kelsey, "but from the way everyone speaks of her, I get the impression that she might have been a nosy woman."

"I think that's really the most probable explanation," agreed Adam. "Curiosity killed the cat. Yes, I think that's the way the Sports Pavilion comes into it."

"But if it was a rendezvous, then—" Kelsey paused.

Adam nodded vigorously.

"Yes. It looks as though there is someone in the school who merits our very close attention. Cat among the pigeons, in fact."

"Cat among the pigeons," said Kelsey, struck by the phrase. "Miss Rich, one of the mistresses, said something like that today."

He reflected a moment or two.

"There were three newcomers to the staff this term," he said. "Shapland, the secretary; Blanche, the French mistress; and, of course, Miss Springer herself. She's dead and out of it. If there is a cat among the pigeons, it would seem that one of the other two would be the most likely bet." He looked toward Adam. "Any ideas, as between the two of them?"

Adam considered.

"I caught Mademoiselle Blanche coming out of the Sports Pavilion one day. She had a guilty look. As though she'd been doing something she ought not to have done. All the same, on the whole—I think I'd plump for the other. For Shapland. She's a cool customer and she's got brains. I'd go into her antecedents rather carefully if I were you. What the devil are you laughing for?"

Kelsey was grinning.

"*She* was suspicious of *you*," he said. "Caught *you*

coming out of the Sports Pavilion—and thought there was
something odd about your manner!"

"Well, I'm damned!" Adam was indignant. "The cheek
of her!"

Inspector Kelsey resumed his authoritative manner.

"The point is," he said, "that we think a lot of Meadowbank round these parts. It's a fine school. And Miss
Bulstrode's a fine woman. The sooner we can get to the
bottom of all this, the better for the school. We want to
clear things up and give Meadowbank a clean bill of
health."

He paused, looking thoughtfully at Adam.

"I think," he said, "we'll have to tell Miss Bulstrode
who you are. She'll keep her mouth shut—don't fear for
that."

Adam considered for a moment. Then he nodded his
head.

"Yes," he said. "Under the circumstances, I think it's
more or less inevitable."

■

12

New Lamps for Old

MISS BULSTRODE HAD another faculty which demon-
strated her superiority over most other women. She
could listen.

She listened in silence to both Inspector Kelsey and
Adam. She did not so much as raise an eyebrow. Then
she uttered one word:

"Remarkable."

"It's you who are remarkable," thought Adam, but he
did not say so aloud.

"Well," said Miss Bulstrode, coming, as was habitual to
her, straight to the point. "What do you want me to do?"

Inspector Kelsey cleared his throat.

"It's like this," he said. "We felt that you ought to be fully informed—for the sake of the school."

Miss Bulstrode nodded.

"Naturally," she said, "the school is my first concern. It has to be. I am responsible for the care and safety of my pupils—and in a lesser degree for that of my staff. And I would like to add now that if there can be as little publicity as possible about Miss Springer's death—the better it will be for me. This is a purely selfish point of view—though I think my school is important in itself— not only to me. And I quite realize that if full publicity is necessary for you, then you will have to go ahead. But is it?"

"No," said Inspector Kelsey. "In this case I should say the less publicity the better. The inquest will be adjourned and we'll let it get about that we think it was a local affair. Young thugs—or juvenile delinquents, as we have to call them nowadays—out with guns among them, trigger happy. It's usually flick knives, but some of these boys do get hold of guns. Miss Springer surprised them. They shot her. That's what I should like to let it go at—then we can get to work quietlike. Not more than can be helped in the press. But of course, Meadowbank's famous. It's news. And murder at Meadowbank will be hot news."

"I think I can help you there," said Miss Bulstrode crisply, "I am not without influence in high places." She smiled and reeled off a few names. These included the Home Secretary, two press barons, a bishop and the Minister of Education. "I'll do what I can." She looked at Adam. "You agree?"

Adam spoke quickly.

"Yes, indeed. We always like things nice and quiet."

"Are you continuing to be my gardener?" inquired Miss Bulstrode.

"If you don't object. It puts me right where I want to be. And I can keep an eye on things."

This time Miss Bulstrode's eyebrows did rise.

"I hope you're not expecting any more murders?"

"No, no."

"I'm glad of that. I doubt if any school could survive two murders in one term."

She turned to Kelsey.

"Have you people finished with the Sports Pavilion? It's awkward if we can't use it."

"We've finished with it. Clean as a whistle—from our point of view, I mean. For whatever reason the murder was committed—there's nothing there now to help us. It's just a Sports Pavilion with the usual equipment."

"Nothing in the girls' lockers?"

Inspector Kelsey smiled.

"Well—this and that—copy of a book—French —called *Candide*—with—er—illustrations. Expensive book."

"Ah," said Miss Bulstrode. "So that's where she keeps it! Giselle d'Aubray, I suppose?"

Kelsey's respect for Miss Bulstrode rose.

"You don't miss much, ma'am," he said.

"She won't come to harm with *Candide,*" said Miss Bulstrode. "It's a classic. Some forms of pornography I do confiscate. Now I come back to my first question. You have relieved my mind about the publicity connected with the school. Can the school help you in any way? Can *I* help you?"

"I don't think so, at the moment. The only thing I can ask is, has anything caused you uneasiness this term? Any incident? Or any person?"

Miss Bulstrode was silent for a moment or two. Then she said slowly:

"The answer, literally, is: I don't know."

Adam said quickly:

"You've got a feeling that something's wrong?"

"Yes—just that. It's not definite. I can't put my finger on any person, or any incident—unless—"

She was silent for a moment, then she said:

"I feel—I felt at the time—that I'd missed something that I ought not to have missed. Let me explain."

She recited briefly the little incident of Mrs. Upjohn and the distressing and unexpected arrival of Lady Veronica.

Adam was interested.

"Let me get this clear, Miss Bulstrode. Mrs. Upjohn, looking out of the window, this front window that gives on the drive, recognized someone. There's nothing in that. You have over a hundred pupils and nothing is more likely than for Mrs. Upjohn to see some parent or relation that she knew. But you are definitely of the opinion that she was *astonished* to recognize that person— in fact, that it was someone she would *not* have expected to see at Meadowbank?"

"Yes, that was exactly the impression I got."

"And then through the window looking in the opposite direction you saw one of the pupils' mother, in a state of intoxication, and that completely distracted your mind from what Mrs. Upjohn was saying?"

Miss Bulstrode nodded.

"She was talking for some minutes?"

"Yes."

"And when your attention did return to her, she was speaking of espionage, of Intelligence work she had done in the war before she married?"

"Yes."

"It might tie up," said Adam thoughtfully. "Someone she had known in her war days. A parent or relation of one of your pupils, or it could have been a member of your teaching staff."

"Hardly a member of my staff," objected Miss Bulstrode.

"It's possible."

"We'd better get in touch with Mrs. Upjohn," said Kelsey. "As soon as possible. You have her address, Miss Bulstrode?"

"Of course. But I believe she is abroad at the moment. Wait—I will find out."

She pressed her desk buzzer twice, then went impatiently to the door and called to a girl who was passing.

"Find Julia Upjohn for me, will you, Paula?"

"Yes, Miss Bulstrode."

"I'd better go before the girl comes," Adam said. "It wouldn't be natural for me to assist at the inquiries the Inspector is making. Ostensibly he's called me in here to get the low-down on me. Having satisfied himself that he's got nothing on me for the moment, he now tells me to take myself off."

"Take yourself off and remember I've got my eye on you!" growled Kelsey with a grin.

"By the way," said Adam, addressing Miss Bulstrode as he paused by the door. "Will it be all right with you if I slightly abuse my position here? If I get, shall we say, a little too friendly with some members of your staff?"

"With which members of my staff?"

"Well—Mademoiselle Blanche, for instance."

"Mademoiselle Blanche? You think that she—"

"I think she's rather bored here."

"Ah!" Miss Bulstrode looked rather grim. "Perhaps you're right. Anyone else?"

"I shall have a good try all round," said Adam cheerfully. "If you should find that some of your girls are being rather silly, and slipping off to assignations in the garden, please believe that my intentions are strictly sleuthial—if there is such a word."

"You think the girls are likely to know something?"

"Everybody always knows something," said Adam, "even if it's something they don't know they know."

"You may be right."

There was a knock on the door, and Miss Bulstrode called "Come in."

Julia Upjohn appeared, very much out of breath.

"Come in, Julia."

Inspector Kelsey growled.

"You can go now, Goodman. Take yourself off and get on with your work."

"I've told you I don't know a thing about anything," said Adam sulkily. He went out, muttering, "Blooming Gestapo."

"I'm sorry I'm so out of breath, Miss Bulstrode," apologized Julia. "I've run all the way from the tennis courts."

"That's quite all right. I just wanted to ask you your mother's address—that is, where I can get in touch with her?"

"Oh! You'll have to write to Aunt Isabel. Mother's abroad."

"I have your aunt's address. But I need to get in touch with your mother personally."

"I don't see how you can," said Julia, frowning. "Mother's gone to Anatolia on a bus."

"On a *bus?*" said Miss Bulstrode, taken aback.

Julia nodded vigorously.

"She likes that sort of thing," she explained. "And of course it's frightfully cheap. A bit uncomfortable, but Mummy doesn't mind that. Roughly, I should think she'd fetch up in Van in about three weeks or so."

"I see—yes. Tell me, Julia, did your mother ever mention to you seeing someone here whom she'd known in her war service days?"

"No, Miss Bulstrode, I don't think so. No, I'm sure she didn't."

"Your mother did Intelligence work, didn't she?"

"Oh, yes. Mummy seems to have loved it. Not that it sounds really exciting to me. She never blew up anything. Or got caught by the Gestapo. Or had her toenails pulled out. Or anything like that. She worked in Switzerland, I think—or was it Portugal?"

Julia added apologetically: "One gets rather bored with all that old war stuff; and I'm afraid I don't always listen properly."

"Well, thank you, Julia. That's all."

"Really!" said Miss Bulstrode, when Julia had departed. "Gone to Anatolia on a bus! The child said it exactly as though she were saying her mother had taken a 73 bus to Marshall and Snelgrove's."

ii.

Jennifer walked away from the tennis courts rather moodily, swishing her racquet. The amount of double faults she had served this morning depressed her. Not, of course, that you could get a hard serve with this racquet, anyway. But she seemed to have lost control of her service lately. Her backhand, however, had definitely improved. Springer's coaching had been helpful. In many ways it was a pity that Springer was dead.

Jennifer took tennis very seriously. It was one of the things she thought about.

"Excuse me—"

Jennifer looked up, startled. A well dressed woman with golden hair, carrying a long flat parcel, was standing a few feet away from her on the path. Jennifer wondered why on earth she hadn't seen the woman coming along toward her before. It did not occur to her that the woman might have been hidden behind a tree or in the rhododendron bushes and just stepped out of them. Such an idea would not have occurred to Jennifer, since why should a woman hide behind rhododendron bushes and suddenly step out of them?

Speaking with a slightly American accent the woman said, "I wonder if you could tell me where I could find a girl called"—she consulted a piece of paper—"Jennifer Sutcliffe."

Jennifer was surprised.

"I'm Jennifer Sutcliffe."

"Why! How ridiculous! That *is* a coincidence. That in a big school like this I should be looking for one girl and I should happen upon the girl herself to ask. And they say things like that don't happen."

"I suppose they do happen sometimes," said Jennifer, uninterested.

"I was coming down to lunch today with some friends down here," went on the woman, "and at a cocktail party yesterday I happened to mention I was coming, and your aunt—or was it your godmother?—I've got such a terrible memory. She told me her name and I've forgotten that too. But anyway, she said could I possibly call here and leave a new tennis racquet for you. She said you had been asking for one."

Jennifer's face lit up. It seemed like a miracle, nothing less.

"It must have been my godmother, Mrs. Campbell. I call her Aunt Gina. It wouldn't have been Aunt Rosamond. She never gives me anything but a mingy ten shillings at Christmas."

"Yes, I remember now. That *was* the name. Campbell."

The parcel was held out. Jennifer took it eagerly. It was quite loosely wrapped. Jennifer uttered an exclamation of pleasure as the racquet emerged from its coverings.

"Oh, it's smashing!" she exclaimed. "A really *good* one. I've been longing for a new racquet. You can't play decently if you haven't got a decent racquet."

"Why I guess that's so."

"Thank you very much for bringing it," said Jennifer gratefully.

"It was really no trouble. Only I confess I felt a little shy. Schools always make me feel shy. So many girls. Oh, by the way, I was asked to bring back your old racquet with me."

She picked up the racquet Jennifer had dropped.

"Your aunt—no—godmother—said she would have it restrung. It needs it badly, doesn't it?"

"I don't think that it's really worth while," said Jennifer, but without paying much attention.

She was still experimenting with the swing and balance of her new treasure.

"But an extra racquet is always useful," said her new friend. "Oh, dear," she glanced at her watch. "It is much later than I thought. I must run."

"Have you—do you want a taxi? I could telephone—"

"No, thank you, dear. My car is right by the gate. I left it there so that I shouldn't have to turn in a narrow space. Goodby. So pleased to have met you. I hope you enjoy the racquet."

She literally ran along the path toward the gate. Jennifer called after her once more. "Thank you *very* much."

Then, gloating, she went in search of Julia.

"Look." She flourished the racquet dramatically.

"I say! Where did you get that?"

"My godmother sent it to me. Aunt Gina. She's not my aunt, but I call her that. She's frightfully rich. I expect Mummy told her about my grumbling about my racquet. It *is* smashing, isn't it? I *must* remember to write and thank her."

"I should hope so!" said Julia virtuously.

"Well, you know how one does forget things sometimes. Even things you really mean to do. Look, Shaista," she added as the latter girl came toward them. "I've got a new racquet. Isn't it a beauty?"

"It must have been very expensive," said Shaista scanning it respectfully. "I wish I could play tennis well."

"You always run into the ball."

"I never seem to know where the ball is going to come," said Shaista vaguely. "Before I go home, I must

have some really good shorts made in London. Or a
tennis dress like the American champion Ruth Allen
wears. I think that is very smart. Perhaps I will have
both," she smiled in pleasurable anticipation.

"Shaista never thinks of anything except things to
wear," said Julia scornfully as the two friends passed on.
"Do you think *we* shall ever be like that?"

"I suppose so," said Jennifer gloomily. "It will be an
awful bore."

They entered the Sports Pavilion, now officially va-
cated by the police, and Jennifer put her racquet carefully into her press.

"Isn't it lovely?" she said, stroking it affectionately.

"What have you done with the old one?"

"Oh, she took it."

"Who?"

"The woman who brought this. She'd met Aunt Gina
at a cocktail party, and Aunt Gina asked her to bring me
this as she was coming down here today, and Aunt Gina
said to bring up my old one and she'd have it restrung."

"Oh, I see . . ." But Julia was frowning.

"What did Bully want with you?" asked Jennifer.

"Bully? Oh, nothing really. Just Mummy's address. But
she hasn't got one because she's on a bus. In Turkey
somewhere. Jennifer—look here. Your racquet didn't
need restringing."

"Oh, it did, Julia. It was like a sponge."

"I know. But it's *my* racquet really. I mean, we exchanged. It was *my* racquet that needed restringing.
Yours, the one I've got now, *was* restrung. You said
yourself your mother had had it restrung before you went
abroad."

"Yes, that's true." Jennifer looked a little startled.
"Oh, well, I suppose this woman—whoever she was—I
ought to have asked her name, but I was so entranced—
just saw that it needed restringing."

"But you said that *she* said that it was your *Aunt Gina*
who had said it needed restringing. And your Aunt Gina
couldn't have thought it needed restringing if it didn't."

"Oh, well—" Jennifer looked impatient. "I suppose—I
suppose—"

"You suppose what?"

"Perhaps Aunt Gina just thought that *if* I wanted a new racquet, it was because the old one wanted restringing. Anyway what does it matter?"

"I suppose it doesn't matter," said Julia slowly. "But I do think it's odd, Jennifer. It's like—like new lamps for old. Aladdin, you know."

Jennifer giggled.

"Fancy rubbing my old racquet—your old racquet, I mean, and having a genie appear! If you rubbed a lamp and a genie did appear, what would you ask him for, Julia?"

"Lots of things," breathed Julia ecstatically. "A tape recorder, and an Alsatian—or perhaps a Great Dane, and a hundred thousand pounds, and a black satin party frock, and oh! lots of other things. What would you?"

"I don't really know," said Jennifer. "Now I've got this smashing new racquet, I don't really want anything else."

■
13

Catastrophe

THE THIRD WEEK END after the opening of term followed the usual plan. It was the first week end on which parents were allowed to take pupils out. As a result Meadowbank was left almost deserted.

On this particular Sunday there would only be twenty girls left at the school itself for the midday meal. Some of the staff had week-end leave, returning late Sunday night or early Monday morning. On this particular occasion Miss Bulstrode herself was proposing to be absent for the week end. This was unusual since it was not her habit to leave the school during term time. But she had her reasons. She was going to stay with the Duchess of Welsham at Welsington Abbey. The Duchess had made a special point of it and had added that Henry Banks would be there. Henry Banks was the Chairman of the Governors. He was an important industrialist and he had been one of the original backers of the school. The invitation was therefore almost in the nature of a command. Not that Miss Bulstrode would have allowed herself to be commanded if she had not wished to do so. But as it happened, she welcomed the invitation gladly. She was by no means indifferent to duchesses and the Duchess of Welsham was an influential duchess, whose own daughters had been sent to Meadowbank. She was also particularly glad to have the opportunity of talking to Henry Banks on the subject of the school's future and also to put forward her own account of the recent tragic occurrence.

Owing to the influential connections at Meadowbank the murder of Miss Springer had been played down very tactfully in the press. It had become a sad fatality rather than a mysterious murder. The impression was given, though not said, that possibly some young thugs had broken into the Sports Pavilion and that Miss Springer's death had been more accident than design. It was reported vaguely that several young men had been asked to come to the police station and "assist the police." Miss Bulstrode herself was anxious to mitigate any unpleasant impression that might have been given to these two influential patrons of the school. She knew that they wanted to discuss the veiled hint that she had thrown out, of her coming retirement. Both the Duchess and Henry Banks were anxious to persuade her to remain on. Now was the time, Miss Bulstrode felt, to push the claims of Eleanor Vansittart, to point out what a splendid person she was, and how well fitted to carry on the traditions of Meadowbank.

On Saturday morning Miss Bulstrode was just finishing off her correspondence with Ann Shapland when the telephone rang. Ann answered it.

"It's the Emir Ibrahim, Miss Bulstrode. He's arrived at Claridge's and would like to take Shaista out tomorrow."

Miss Bulstrode took the receiver from her and had a brief conversation with the Emir's equerry. Shaista would be ready any time from eleven-thirty onward on Sunday morning, she said. The girl must be back at the school by 8 P.M.

She rang off and said:

"I wish Orientals sometimes gave you a little more warning. It has been arranged for Shaista to go out with Giselle d'Aubray tomorrow. Now that will have to be cancelled. Have we finished all the letters?"

"Yes, Miss Bulstrode."

"Good, then I can go off with a clear conscience. Type them and send them off, and then you, too, are free for the week end. I shan't want you until lunchtime on Monday."

"Thank you, Miss Bulstrode."

"Enjoy yourself, my dear."

"I'm going to," said Ann.

"Young man?"

"Well—yes." Ann coloured a little. "Nothing serious, though."

"Then there ought to be. If you're going to marry, don't leave it too late."

"Oh, this is only an old friend. Nothing exciting."

"Excitement," said Miss Bulstrode warningly, "isn't always a good foundation for married life. Send Miss Chadwick to me, will you?"

Miss Chadwick bustled in.

"The Emir Ibrahim, Shaista's uncle, is taking her out tomorrow, Chaddy. If he comes himself, tell him she is making good progress."

"She's not very bright," said Miss Chadwick.

"She's immature intellectually," agreed Miss Bulstrode. "But she has a remarkably mature mind in other ways. Sometimes, when you talk to her, she might be a woman of twenty-five. I suppose it's because of the sophisticated life she's led. Paris, Teheran, Cairo, Istanbul and all the rest of it. In this country we're inclined to keep our children too young. We account it a merit when we say: 'She's still quite a child.' It isn't a merit. It's a grave handicap in life."

"I don't know that I quite agree with you there, dear," said Miss Chadwick. "I'll go now and tell Shaista about her uncle. You go away for your week end and don't worry about anything."

"Oh! I shan't," said Miss Bulstrode. "It's a good opportunity, really, for leaving Eleanor Vansittart in charge and seeing how she shapes. With you and her in charge nothing's likely to go wrong."

"I hope not, indeed. I'll go and find Shaista."

Shaista looked surprised and not at all pleased to hear that her uncle had arrived in London.

"He wants to take me out tomorrow?" she grumbled. "But, Miss Chadwick, it is all arranged that I go out with Giselle d'Aubray and her mother."

"I'm afraid you'll have to do that another time."

"But I would much rather go out with Giselle," said Shaista crossly. "My uncle is not at all amusing. He eats and then he grunts and it is all very dull."

"You mustn't talk like that. It is impolite," said Miss Chadwick. "Your uncle is only in England for a week, I understand, and naturally he wants to see you."

"Perhaps he has arranged a new marriage for me," said Shaista, her face brightening. "If so, that would be fun."

"If that is so, he will no doubt tell you so. But you are too young to get married yet awhile. You must finish your education."

"Education is very boring," said Shaista.

ii.

Sunday morning dawned bright and serene—Miss Shapland had departed soon after Miss Bulstrode on Saturday. Miss Johnson, Miss Rich and Miss Blake left on Sunday morning.

Miss Vansittart, Miss Chadwick, Miss Rowan and Mademoiselle Blanche were left in charge.

"I hope all the girls won't talk too much," said Miss Chadwick dubiously. "About poor Miss Springer I mean."

"Let us hope," said Eleanor Vansittart, "that the whole affair will soon be forgotten." She added: "If any parents talk to *me* about it, I shall discourage them. It will be best, I think, to take quite a firm line."

The girls went to church at ten o'clock accompanied by Miss Vansittart and Miss Chadwick. Four girls who were Roman Catholics were escorted by Angele Blanche to a rival religious establishment. Then, about half past eleven, the cars began to roll into the drive. Miss Vansittart, graceful, poised and dignified, stood in the hall. She greeted mothers smilingly, produced their offspring and adroitly turned aside any unwanted references to the recent tragedy.

"Terrible," she said, "yes, quite terrible, but, you do understand, *we don't talk about it here.* All these young minds—such a pity for them to dwell on it."

Chaddy was also on the spot greeting old friends among the parents, discussing plans for the holidays and speaking affectionately of the various daughters.

"I do think Aunt Isabel might have come and taken *me* out," said Julia, who with Jennifer was standing with her nose pressed against the window of one of the classrooms, watching the comings and goings on the drive outside.

"Mummy's going to take me out next week end," said Jennifer. "Daddy's got some important people coming down this week end so she couldn't come today."

"There goes Shaista," said Julia, "all togged up for London. Oo-ee! Just look at the heels on her shoes. I bet old Johnson doesn't like those shoes."

A liveried chauffeur was opening the door of a large Cadillac. Shaista climbed in and was driven away.

"You can come out with me next week end, if you like," said Jennifer. "I told Mummy I'd got a friend I wanted to bring."

"I'd love to," said Julia. "Look at Vansittart doing her stuff."

"Terribly gracious, isn't she?" said Jennifer.

"I don't know why," said Julia, "but somehow it makes me want to laugh. It's a sort of copy of Miss Bulstrode, isn't it? Quite a good copy, but it's rather like Joyce Grenfell or someone doing an imitation."

"There's Pam's mother," said Jennifer. "She's brought the little boys. How they can all get into that tiny Morris Minor I don't know."

"They're going to have a picnic," said Julia. "Look at all the baskets."

"What are you going to do this afternoon?" asked Jennifer. "I don't think I need write to Mummy this week, do you, if I'm going to see her next week?"

"You are slack about writing letters, Jennifer."

"I never can think of anything to say," said Jennifer.

"I can," said Julia, "I can think of lots to say." She added mournfully, "But there isn't really anyone much to write to at present."

"What about your mother?"

"I told you she's gone to Anatolia in a bus. You can't write letters to people who go to Anatolia in buses. At least you can't write to them all the time."

"Where do you write to when you do write?"

"Oh, consulates here and there. She left me a list. Stamboul is the first and then Ankara and then some funny name." She added, "I wonder why Bully wanted to get in touch with Mummy so badly? She seemed quite upset when I said where she'd gone."

"It can't be about you," said Jennifer. "You haven't done anything awful, have you?"

"Not that I know of," said Julia. "Perhaps she wanted to tell her about Springer."

"Why should she?" said Jennifer. "I should think she'd be jolly glad that there's at least one mother who *doesn't* know about Springer."

"You mean mothers might think that their daughters were going to get murdered too?"

"I don't think my mother's quite as bad as that," said Jennifer. "But she did get in quite a flap about it."

"If you ask me," said Julia, in a meditative manner, "I think there's a lot that they haven't told us about Springer."

"What sort of things?"

"Well, funny things seem to be happening. Like your new tennis racquet."

"Oh, I meant to tell you," said Jennifer, "I wrote and thanked Aunt Gina and this morning I got a letter from her saying she was very glad I'd got a new racquet but that she never sent it to me."

"I told you that racquet business was peculiar," said Julia triumphantly, "and you had a burglary, too, at your home, didn't you?"

"Yes, but they didn't take anything."

"That makes it even more interesting," said Julia. "I

think," she added thoughtfully, "that we shall probably have a second murder soon."

"Oh, really, Julia, why should we have a second murder?"

"Well, there's usually a second murder in books," said Julia. "What I think is, Jennifer, that you'll have to be frightfully careful that it isn't *you* who gets murdered."

"Me?" said Jennifer, surprised. "Why should anyone murder me?"

"Because somehow you're mixed up in it all," said Julia. She added thoughtfully, "We must try and get a bit more out of your mother next week, Jennifer. Perhaps somebody gave her some secret papers out in Ramat."

"What sort of secret papers?"

"Oh, how should I know," said Julia. "Plans or formulas for a new atomic bomb. That sort of thing."

Jennifer looked unconvinced.

iii.

Miss Vansittart and Miss Chadwick were in the Common Room when Miss Rowan entered and said:

"Where is Shaista? I can't find her anywhere. The Emir's car has just arrived to call for her."

"What?" Chaddy looked up surprised. "There must be some mistake. The Emir's car came for her about three quarters of an hour ago. I saw her get into it and drive off myself. She was one of the first to go."

Eleanor Vansittart shrugged her shoulders. "I suppose a car must have been ordered twice over, or something," she said.

She went out herself and spoke to the chauffeur. "There must be some mistake," she said. "The young lady has already left for London three quarters of an hour ago."

The chauffeur seemed surprised. "I suppose there must be some mistake, if you say so, madam," he said. "I was definitely given instructions to call at Meadowbank for the young lady."

"I suppose there's bound to be a muddle sometimes," said Miss Vansittart.

The chauffeur seemed unperturbed and unsurprised.

"Happens all the time," he said. "Telephone messages taken, written down, forgotten. All that sort of thing. But we pride ourselves in our firm that we *don't* make mistakes. Of course, if I may say so, you never know with these Oriental gentlemen. They've sometimes got quite a big entourage with them, and orders get given twice and even three times over. I expect that's what must have happened in this instance." He turned his large car with some adroitness and drove away.

Miss Vansittart looked a little doubtful for a moment or two, but she decided there was nothing to worry about and began to look forward with satisfaction to a peaceful afternoon.

After luncheon the few girls who remained wrote letters or wandered about the grounds. A certain amount of tennis was played and the swimming pool was well patronized. Miss Vansittart took her fountain pen and her writing pad to the shade of the cedar tree. When the telephone rang at half past four it was Miss Chadwick who answered it.

"Meadowbank School?" The voice of a well-bred young Englishman spoke. "Oh, is Miss Bulstrode there?"

"Miss Bulstrode's not here today. This is Miss Chadwick speaking."

"Oh, it's about one of your pupils. I am speaking from Claridge's, the Emir Ibrahim's suite."

"Oh, yes? You mean about Shaista?"

"Yes. The Emir is rather annoyed at not having got a message of any kind."

"A message? Why should he get a message?"

"Well, to say that Shaista couldn't come, or wasn't coming."

"Wasn't coming! Do you mean to say she hasn't arrived?"

"No, no, she's certainly not arrived. Did she leave Meadowbank then?"

"Yes. A car came for her this morning—oh, about half past eleven I should think, and she drove off."

"That's extraordinary because there's no sign of her here . . . I'd better ring up the firm that supplies the Emir's cars."

"Oh, dear," said Miss Chadwick, "I do hope there hasn't been an accident."

"Oh, don't let's assume the worst," said the young man cheerfully. "I think you'd have heard, you know, if there'd been an accident. Or we would. I shouldn't worry if I were you."

But Miss Chadwick did worry.

"It seems to me very odd," she said.

"I suppose—" The young man hesitated.

"Yes?" said Miss Chadwick.

"Well, it's not quite the sort of thing I want to suggest to the Emir, but just between you and me there's no—er— well, no boy friend hanging about, is there?"

"Certainly not," said Miss Chadwick with dignity.

"No, no, well I didn't think there would be, but, well, one never knows with girls, does one? You'd be surprised at some of the things I've run into."

"I can assure you," said Miss Chadwick with dignity, "that anything of that kind is quite impossible."

But was it impossible? Did one ever know with girls?

She replaced the receiver and rather unwillingly went in search of Miss Vansittart. There was no reason to believe that Miss Vansittart would be any better able to deal with the situation than she herself but she felt the need of consulting with someone. Miss Vansittart said at once:

"The second car?"

They looked at each other.

"Do you think," said Chaddy slowly, "that we ought to report this to the police?"

"Not to the *police*," said Eleanor Vansittart in a shocked voice.

"She did say, you know," said Chaddy, "that somebody might try to kidnap her."

"Kidnap her? Nonsense!" said Miss Vansittart sharply.

"You don't think—" Miss Chadwick was persistent.

"Miss Bulstrode left me in charge here," said Eleanor Vansittart, "and I shall certainly not sanction anything of the kind. We don't want any more trouble here with the police."

Miss Chadwick looked at her without affection. She

thought Miss Vansittart was being short-sighted and foolish. She went back into the house and put through a call to the Duchess of Welsham's house. Unfortunately everyone was out.

■
14

Miss Chadwick Lies Awake

MISS CHADWICK was restless. She turned to and fro in her bed, counting sheep, and employing other time-honoured methods of invoking sleep. In vain.

At eight o'clock, when Shaista had not returned, and there had been no news of her, Miss Chadwick had taken matters into her own hands and rung up Inspector Kelsey. She was relieved to find that he did not take the matter too seriously. She could leave it all to him, he assured her. It would be an easy matter to check up on a possible accident. After that, he would get in touch with London. Everything would be done that was necessary. Perhaps the girl herself was playing truant. He advised Miss Chadwick to say as little as possible at the school. Let it be thought that Shaista was staying the night with her uncle at Claridge's.

"The last thing you want, or that Miss Bulstrode would want, is any more publicity," said Kelsey. "It's most unlikely that the girl has been kidnaped. So don't worry, Miss Chadwick. Leave it all to us."

But Miss Chadwick did worry.

Lying in bed, sleepless, her mind went from possible kidnaping back to murder.

Murder at Meadowbank. It was terrible! Unbelievable! *Meadowbank*. Miss Chadwick loved Meadowbank. She loved it, perhaps, even more than Miss Bulstrode did, though in a somewhat different way. It had been such a risky gallant enterprise. Following Miss Bulstrode faithfully into the hazardous undertaking, she had endured panic more than once. Supposing the whole thing should fail. They hadn't really had much capital. If they did not succeed—if their backing was withdrawn—Miss Chadwick had an anxious mind and could always tabulate innumerable ifs. Miss Bulstrode had enjoyed the adventure, the hazard of it all, but Chaddy had not. Sometimes, in an agony of apprehension, she had pleaded for Meadowbank to be run on more conventional lines. It would be *safer,* she urged. But Miss Bulstrode had been uninterested in safety. She had her vision of what a school should be and she had pursued it unafraid. And she had been justified in her audacity. But oh, the relief to Chaddy when success was a *fait accompli.* When Meadowbank was established, safely established, as a great English institution. It was then that her love for Meadowbank had flowed most fully. Doubts, fears, anxieties, all slipped from her. Peace and prosperity had come. She basked in the prosperity of Meadowbank like a purring tabby cat.

She had been quite upset when Miss Bulstrode had first begun to talk of retirement. Retire *now*—when everything was set fair? What madness! Miss Bulstrode talked of travel, of all the things in the world to see. Chaddy was unimpressed. Nothing, anywhere, could be half as good as Meadowbank! It had seemed to her that nothing could affect the well-being of Meadowbank. But now—murder!

Such an ugly violent word—coming in from the outside world like an ill-mannered storm wind. Murder—a word associated by Miss Chadwick only with delinquent boys with flick knives, or evil-minded doctors poisoning their wives. But murder here—at a school—and not any school—at Meadowbank. Incredible.

Really, Miss Springer—poor Miss Springer, naturally it wasn't her fault—but, illogically, Chaddy felt that it must have been her fault in some way. She didn't know the traditions of Meadowbank. A tactless woman. She must in some way have invited murder. Miss Chadwick rolled over, turned her pillow, said, "I mustn't go on thinking of it all. Perhaps I had better get up and take some aspirin. I'll just try counting to fifty . . ."

Before she had got to fifty, her mind was off again on the same track. Worrying. Would all this—and perhaps kidnaping too—get into the papers? Would parents, reading, hasten to take their daughters away . . .

Oh, dear, she *must* calm down and go to sleep. What time was it? She switched on her light and looked at her watch. Just after a quarter to one. Just about the time that poor Miss Springer . . . No, she would *not* think of it any more. And, how stupid of Miss Springer to have gone off by herself like that without waking up somebody else.

"Oh, dear," said Miss Chadwick. "I'll have to take some aspirin."

She got out of bed and went over to the washstand. She took two aspirins with a drink of water. On her way back, she pulled aside the curtain of the window and peered out. She did so to reassure herself more than for any other reason. She wanted to feel that of course there would never again be a light in the Sports Pavilion in the middle of the night . . .

But there was.

In a minute Chaddy had leapt to action. She thrust her feet into stout shoes, pulled on a thick coat, picked up her own flashlight and rushed out of her room and down the stairs. She had blamed Miss Springer for not obtaining support before going out to investigate, but it never occurred to her to do so. She was only eager to get out to the Pavilion and find out who the intruder was. She did pause to pick up a weapon—not perhaps a very good one, but a weapon of kinds, and then she was out of the side door and following quickly along the path through the shrubbery. She was out of breath, but completely resolute. Only when she got at last to the door, did she slacken up and take care to move softly. The door was slightly ajar. She pushed it further open and looked in . . .

ii.

At about the time when Miss Chadwick was rising from bed in search of aspirin, Ann Shapland, looking very attractive in a black dance frock, was sitting at a table in Le Nid Sauvage eating supreme of chicken and smiling at the young man opposite her. Dear Denis, thought Ann to herself, always so exactly the same. It is what I simply couldn't bear if I married him. He *is* rather a pet, all the same. Aloud she remarked:

"What fun this is, Denis. Such a glorious *change.*"

"How is the new job?" said Denis.

"Well, actually, I'm rather enjoying it."

"Doesn't seem to me quite your sort of thing."

Ann laughed. "I'd be hard put to it to say what is my sort of thing. I like variety, Denis."

"I never can see why you gave up your job with old Sir Mervyn Todhunter."

"Well, chiefly because of Sir Mervyn Todhunter. The attention he bestowed on me was beginning to annoy his wife. And it's part of my policy never to annoy wives. They can do you a lot of harm, you know."

"Jealous cats," said Denis.

"Oh, no, not really," said Ann. "I'm rather on the wives' side. Anyway I liked Lady Todhunter much better than old Mervyn. Why are you surprised at my present job?"

"Oh, a school. You're not scholastically minded at all, I should have said."

"I'd hate to *teach* in a school. I'd hate to be penned up. Herded with a lot of women. But the work as the secretary of a school like Meadowbank is rather fun. It really is a unique place, you know. And Miss Bulstrode's unique. She's really something, I can tell you. Her steel-grey eye goes through you and sees your innermost secrets. And she keeps you on your toes. I'd hate to make a mistake in any letters I'd taken down for her. Oh, yes, she's certainly something."

"I wish you'd get tired of all these jobs," said Denis. "It's quite time, you know, Ann, that you stopped all this racketing about with jobs here and jobs there and—and settled down."

"You are sweet, Denis," said Ann in a noncommittal manner.

"We could have quite fun, you know," said Denis.

"I daresay," said Ann, "but I'm not ready yet. And anyway, you know, there's my mamma."

"Yes, I was—going to talk to you about that."

"About my mamma? What were you going to say?"

"Well, Ann, you know I think you're wonderful. The way you get an interesting job and then you chuck it all up and go home to her."

"Well, I have to now and again when she gets a really bad attack."

"I know. As I say, I think it's wonderful of you. But all the same there are places, you know, very good places nowadays where—where people like your mother are well looked after and all that sort of thing. Not really loony bins."

"And which cost the earth," said Ann.

"No, no, not necessarily. Why, even under the Health Scheme . . ."

A bitter note crept into Ann's voice. "Yes, I daresay it will come to that one day. But in the meantime I've got a nice old pussy who lives with Mother and who can cope normally. Mother is quite reasonable most of the time. And when she—isn't, I come back and lend a hand."

"She's—she isn't—she's never—"

"Are you going to say violent, Denis? You've got an extraordinarily lurid imagination. No. My dear mamma is *never* violent. She just gets fuddled. She forgets where she is and who she is and wants to go for long walks, and then as like as not she'll jump into a train or a bus and take off somewhere and—well, it's all very difficult, you see. Sometimes it's too much for one person to cope with. But she's quite happy, even when she *is* fuddled. And sometimes quite funny about it. I remember her saying: 'Ann, darling, it really is very embarrassing. I knew I was going to Tibet and there I was sitting in that hotel in Dover with no idea how to get there. Then I thought why was I going to Tibet? And I thought I'd better come home. Then I couldn't remember how long ago it was when I left home. It makes it very embarrassing, dear, when you can't quite remember things.' Mummy was really very funny over it all, you know. I mean she quite sees the humorous side herself."

"I've never actually met her," Denis began.

"I don't encourage people to meet her," said Ann. "That's the one thing I think you *can* do for your own people. Protect them from—well, curiosity and pity."

"It's not curiosity, Ann."

"No, I don't think it would be with you. But it would be pity. I don't want that."

"I can see what you mean."

"But if you think I mind giving up jobs from time to time and going home for an indefinite period, I don't," said Ann. "I never meant to get embroiled in anything too deeply. Not even when I took my first post after my secretarial training. I thought the thing was to get really good at the job. Then if you're really good you can pick and choose your posts. You see different places and you see different kinds of life. At the moment I'm seeing school life. The best school in England seen from within! I shall stay there, I expect, about a year and a half."

"You never really get caught up in things, do you, Ann?"

"No," said Ann thoughtfully, "I don't think I do. I think I'm one of those people who are a born observer. More like a commentator on the radio."

"You're so detached," said Denis gloomily. "You don't really care about anything or anyone."

"I expect I shall some day," said Ann encouragingly.

"I do understand more or less how you're thinking and feeling."

"I doubt it," said Ann.

"Anyway, I don't think you'll last a year. You'll get fed up with all those women," said Denis.

"There's a very good-looking gardener," said Ann. She laughed when she saw Denis' expression. "Cheer up, I'm only trying to make you jealous."

"What's this about one of the mistresses having been killed?"

"Oh, that." Ann's face became serious and thoughtful. "That's odd, Denis. Very odd indeed. It was the games mistress. You know the type. I-am-a-plain-games-mistress. I think there's a lot more behind it than has come out yet."

"Well, don't you get mixed up in anything unpleasant."

"That's easy to say. I've never had any chance at displaying my talents as a sleuth. I think I *might* be rather good at it."

"Now, Ann."

"Darling, I'm not going to trail dangerous criminals. I'm just going to—well, make a few logical deductions. Why and who. And what for? That sort of thing. I've come across one piece of information that's rather interesting."

"Ann!"

"Don't look so agonized. Only it doesn't seem to link up with anything," said Ann thoughtfully. "Up to a point it all fits in very well. And then, suddenly, it doesn't." She added cheerfully, "Perhaps there'll be a second murder, and that will clarify things a little."

It was at exactly that moment that Miss Chadwick pushed open the Sports Pavilion door.

■
15

Murder Repeats Itself

"COME ALONG," said Inspector Kelsey, entering the room with a grim face. "There's been another."

"Another what?" Adam looked up sharply.

"Another murder," said Inspector Kelsey. He led the way out of the room and Adam followed him. They had been sitting in the latter's room drinking beer and discussing various probabilities when Kelsey had been summoned to the telephone.

"Who is it?" demanded Adam, as he followed Inspector Kelsey down the stairs.

"Another mistress—Miss Vansittart."

"Where?"

"In the Sports Pavilion."

"The Sports Pavilion again?" said Adam. "What is there about this Sports Pavilion?"

"*You'd* better give it the once-over this time," said Inspector Kelsey. "Perhaps your technique of searching may be more successful than ours has been. There must be *something* about that Sports Pavilion or why should everyone get killed there?"

He and Adam got into his car. "I expect the doctor will be there ahead of us. He hasn't so far to go."

It was, Kelsey thought, like a bad dream repeating itself, as he entered the brilliantly lighted Sports Pavilion. There, once again, was a body with the doctor kneeling beside it. Once again the doctor rose from his knees and got up.

"Killed about half an hour ago," he said. "Forty minutes at most."

"Who found her?" said Kelsey.

One of his men spoke up. "Miss Chadwick."

"That's the old one, isn't it?"

"Yes. She saw a light, came out here, and found her dead. She stumbled back to the house and more or less went into hysterics. It was the matron who telephoned, Miss Johnson."

"Right," said Kelsey. "How was she killed? Shot again?"

The doctor shook his head. "No. Slugged on the back of the head, this time. Might have been a cosh or a sandbag. Something of that kind."

A golf club with a steel head was lying near the door. It was the only thing that looked remotely disorderly in the place.

"What about that?" said Kelsey, pointing. "Could she have been hit with that?"

The doctor shook his head. "Impossible. There's no mark on her. No, it was definitely a heavy rubber cosh or a sandbag, something of that sort."

"Something—professional?"

"Probably, yes. Whoever it was, didn't mean to make any noise this time. Came up behind her and slugged her on the back of the head. She fell forward and probably never knew what hit her."

"What was she doing?"

"She was probably kneeling down," said the doctor. "Kneeling in front of this locker."

The Inspector went up to the locker and looked at it. "That's the girl's name on it, I presume," he said.

"Shaista—let me see, that's the—that's the Egyptian girl, isn't it? Her Highness Princess Shaista." He turned to Adam. "It seems to tie in, doesn't it? Wait a minute—that's the girl they reported this evening as missing?"

"That's right, sir," said the sergeant. "A car called for her here, supposed to have been sent by her uncle who's staying at Claridge's in London. She got into it and drove off."

"No reports came in?"

"Not as yet, sir. Got a network out. And the Yard is in on it."

"A nice simple way of kidnaping anyone," said Adam. "No struggle, no cries. All you've got to know is that the girl's expecting a car to fetch her and all you've got to do is to look like a high-class chauffeur and arrive there before the other car does. The girl will step in without a second thought and you can drive off without her suspecting in the least what's happening to her."

"No abandoned car found anywhere?" asked Kelsey.

"We've had no news of one," said the sergeant. "The Yard's on it now as I said," he added, "and the Special Branch."

"May mean a bit of a political schemozzle," said the Inspector. "I don't suppose for a minute they'll be able to take her out of the country."

"What do they want to kidnap her for anyway?" asked the doctor.

"Goodness knows," said Kelsey gloomily. "She told me she was afraid of being kidnaped and I'm ashamed to say I thought she was just showing off."

"I thought so, too, when you told me about it," said Adam.

"The trouble is we don't know enough," said Kelsey. "There are far too many loose ends." He looked around. "Well, there doesn't seem to be anything more that I can do here. Get on with the usual stuff—photographs, fingerprints, etc. I'd better go along to the house."

At the house he was received by Miss Johnson. She was shaken but preserved her self-control.

"It's terrible, Inspector," she said. "Two of our mistresses killed. Poor Miss Chadwick's in a dreadful state."

"I'd like to see her as soon as I can."

"The doctor gave her something and she's much calmer now. Shall I take you to her?"

"Yes, in a minute or two. First of all, just tell me what you can about the last time you saw Miss Vansittart."

"I haven't seen her at all today," said Miss Johnson. "I've been away all day. I arrived back here just before eleven and went straight up to my room. I went to bed."

"You didn't happen to look out of your window toward the Sports Pavilion?"

"No. No, I never thought of it. I'd spent the day with my sister whom I hadn't seen for some time and my mind was full of home news. I took a bath and went to bed and read a book, and I turned off the light and went to sleep. The next thing I knew was when Miss Chadwick burst in, looking as white as a sheet and shaking all over."

"Was Miss Vansittart absent today?"

"No, she was here. She was in charge. Miss Bulstrode's away."

"Who else was here?—of the mistresses, I mean."

Miss Johnson considered a moment. "Miss Vansittart, Miss Chadwick, the French mistress, Mademoiselle Blanche, Miss Rowan."

"I see. Well, I think you'd better take me to Miss Chadwick now."

Miss Chadwick was sitting in a chair in her room. Although the night was a warm one the electric fire had been turned on and a rug was wrapped round her knees. She turned a ghastly face toward Inspector Kelsey.

"She's dead—she *is* dead? There's no chance that—that she might come round?"

Kelsey shook his head slowly.

"It's so awful," said Miss Chadwick, "with Miss Bulstrode away." She burst into tears. "This will ruin the school," she said. "This will ruin Meadowbank. I can't bear it—I really can't bear it."

Kelsey sat down beside her. "I know," he said sympathetically, "I know. It's been a terrible shock to you, but I want you to be brave, Miss Chadwick, and tell me all you know. The sooner we can find out who did it, the less trouble and publicity there will be."

"Yes, yes, I can see that. You see, I—I went to bed early because I thought it would be nice for once to have a nice long night. But I couldn't go to sleep. I was worrying."

"Worrying about the school?"

"Yes. And about Shaista being missing. And then I began thinking of Miss Springer and whether—whether her murder would affect the parents, and whether perhaps they wouldn't send their girls back here next term. I was so terribly upset for Miss Bulstrode. I mean, she's *made* this place. It's been such a fine achievement."

"I know. Now go on telling me—you were worried, and you couldn't sleep?"

"No, I counted sheep and everything. And then I got up and took some aspirin and when I'd taken it I just happened to draw back the curtains from the window. I don't quite know why. I suppose because I'd been thinking about Miss Springer. Then you see, I saw—I saw a light there."

"What kind of a light?"

"Well, a sort of dancing light. I mean—I think it must have been a flashlight. It was just like the light that Miss Johnson and I saw before."

"It was just the same, was it?"

"Yes. Yes, I think so. Perhaps a little feebler, but I don't know."

"Yes. And then?"

"And then," said Miss Chadwick, her voice suddenly becoming more resonant, "I was determined that *this* time I would see who it was out there and what they were doing. So I got up and pulled on my coat and my shoes, and I rushed out of the house."

"You didn't think of calling anyone else?"

"No. No, I didn't. You see I was in such a hurry to get there. I was so afraid the person—whoever it was—would go away."

"Yes. Go on, Miss Chadwick."

"So I went as fast as I could. I went up to the door and just before I got there I went on tiptoe so that—so that I should be able to look in and nobody would hear me coming. I got there. The door was not shut—just ajar and I pushed it very slightly open. I looked round it and—and there she was. Fallen forward on her face, *dead . . .*"

She began to shake all over.

"Yes, yes, Miss Chadwick, it's all right. By the way, there was a golf club out there. Did you take it out? Or did Miss Vansittart?"

"A golf club?" said Miss Chadwick vaguely. "I can't remember. Oh, yes, I think I picked it up in the hall. I took it out with me in case—well, in case I should have to use it. When I saw Eleanor I suppose I just dropped it. Then I got back to the house somehow and I found Miss Johnson. Oh! I can't bear it. I can't bear it—this will be the end of Meadowbank—"

Miss Chadwick's voice rose hysterically. Miss Johnson came forward.

"To discover two murders is too much of a strain for anyone," said Miss Johnson. "Certainly for anyone her age. You don't want to ask her any more, do you?"

Inspector Kelsey shook his head.

As he was going downstairs, he noticed a pile of old-fashioned sandbags with buckets in an alcove. Dating from the war, perhaps, but the uneasy thought occurred to him that it needn't have been a professional with a cosh who had slugged Miss Vansittart. Someone in the building, someone who hadn't wished to risk the sound of a shot a second time, and who, very likely, had disposed of the incriminating pistol after the last murder, could have helped themselves to an innocent looking but lethal weapon—and possibly even replaced it tidily afterward!

■
16

The Riddle of the Sports Pavilion

"My head is bloody but unbowed," Adam said to himself.

He was looking at Miss Bulstrode. He had never, he thought, admired a woman more. She sat, cool and unmoved, with her lifework falling in ruins about her.

From time to time telephone calls came through announcing that yet another pupil was being removed.

Finally Miss Bulstrode had taken her decision. Excusing herself to the police officers, she summoned Ann Shapland, and dictated a brief statement. The school would be closed until the end of the term. Parents who found it inconvenient to have their children home, were welcome to leave them in her care and their education would be continued.

"You've got the list of parents' names and addresses? And their telephone numbers?"

"Yes, Miss Bulstrode."

"Then start on the telephone. After that see a typed notice goes to everyone."

"Yes, Miss Bulstrode."

On her way out, Ann Shapland paused near the door.

She flushed and her words came with a rush.

"Excuse me, Miss Bulstrode. It's not my business—but isn't it a pity to—to be premature? I mean—after the first panic, when people have had time to think—surely they won't want to take the girls away. They'll be sensible and think better of it."

Miss Bulstrode looked at her keenly.

"You think I'm accepting defeat too easily?"

Ann flushed.

"I know—you think it's cheek. But—but, well, then, yes I do."

"You're a fighter, child, I'm glad to see. But you're quite wrong. I'm not accepting defeat. I'm going on my knowledge of human nature. Urge people to take their children away, force it on them—and they won't want to nearly so much. They'll think up reasons for letting them remain. Or at the worst they'll decide to let them come back next term—if there is a next term," she added grimly.

She looked at Inspector Kelsey.

"That's up to you," she said. "Clear these murders up—catch whoever is responsible for them—and we'll be all right."

Inspector Kelsey looked unhappy. He said: "We're doing our best."

Ann Shapland went out.

"Competent girl," said Miss Bulstrode. "And loyal."

This was in the nature of a parenthesis. She pressed her attack.

"Have you absolutely *no* idea of who killed two of my mistresses in the Sports Pavilion? You ought to, by this time. And this kidnaping on top of everything else. I blame myself there. The girl talked about someone wanting to kidnap her. I thought, God forgive me, she was making herself important. I see now that there must have been something behind it. Someone must have hinted, or warned—one doesn't know which—" She broke off, resuming: "You've no news of any kind?"

"Not yet. But I don't think you need worry too much about that. It's been passed to the C.I.D. The Special Branch is on to it, too. They ought to find her within twenty-four hours, thirty-six at most. There are advantages in this being an island. All the ports, airports, etc., are alerted. And the police in every district are keeping a look-out. It's actually easy enough to kidnap anyone—it's keeping them hidden that's the problem. Oh, we'll find her."

"I hope you'll find her alive," said Miss Bulstrode grimly. "We seem to be up against someone who isn't too scrupulous about human life."

"They wouldn't have troubled to kidnap her if they'd meant to do away with her," said Adam. "They could have done that here easily enough."

He felt that the last words were unfortunate. Miss Bulstrode gave him a look.

"So it seems," she said drily.

The telephone rang. Miss Bulstrode took up the receiver.

"Yes?"

She motioned to Inspector Kelsey.

"It's for you."

Adam and Miss Bulstrode watched him as he took the call. He grunted, jotted down a note or two, said finally: "I see. Alderton Priors. That's Wallshire. Yes, we'll cooperate. Yes, Super. I'll carry on here, then."

He put down the receiver and stayed a moment lost in thought. Then he looked up.

"His Excellency got a ransom note this morning.

Typed on a new Corona. Postmark Portsmouth. Bet that's a blind."

"Where and how?" asked Adam.

"Crossroads two miles north of Alderton Priors. That's a bit of bare moorland. Envelope containing money to be put under stone behind Automobile Association box there at two A.M. tomorrow morning."

"How much?"

"Twenty thousand." He shook his head. "Sounds amateurish to me."

"What are you going to do?" asked Miss Bulstrode.

Inspector Kelsey looked at her. He was a different man. Official reticence hung about him like a cloak.

"The responsibility isn't mine, madam," he said. "We have our methods."

"I hope they're successful," said Miss Bulstrode.

"Ought to be easy," said Adam.

"Amateurish?" said Miss Bulstrode, catching at a word they had used. "I wonder . . ."

Then she said sharply:

"What about my staff? What remains of it, that is to say. Do I trust them or don't I?"

As Inspector Kelsey hesitated, she said:

"You're afraid that if you tell me who is *not* cleared, I should show it in my manner to them. You're wrong. I shouldn't."

"I don't think you would," said Kelsey. "But I can't afford to take any chances. It doesn't look, on the face of it, as though any of your staff *can* be the person we're looking for. That is, not so far as we've been able to check up on them. We've paid special attention to those who are new this term—that is Mademoiselle Blanche, Miss Springer and your secretary, Miss Shapland. Miss Shapland's past is completely corroborated. She's the daughter of a retired General, she has held the posts she says she did and her former employers vouch for her. In addition she has an alibi for last night. When Miss Vansittart was killed, Miss Shapland was with a Mr. Denis Rathbone at a night club. They're both well known there, and Mr. Rathbone has an excellent character. Mademoiselle Blanche's antecedents have also been checked. She has taught at a school in the north of England and at two schools in Germany, and has been given an excellent character. She is said to be a first-class teacher."

"Not by our standards," sniffed Miss Bulstrode.

"Her French background has also been checked. As regards Miss Springer, things are not quite so conclusive. She did her training where she says, but there have been gaps since in her periods of employment which are not fully accounted for.

"Since, however, she was killed," added the Inspector, "that seems to exonerate her."

"I agree," said Miss Bulstrode drily, "that both Miss Springer and Miss Vansittart are *hors de combat* as suspects. Let us talk sense. Is Mademoiselle Blanche, in spite of her blameless background, still a suspect merely because she is alive?"

"She *could* have done both the murders. She was here, in the building, last night," said Kelsey. "She *says* she went to bed early and slept and heard nothing until the alarm was given. There's no evidence to the contrary. We've got nothing against her. But Miss Chadwick says definitely that she's sly."

Miss Bulstrode waved that aside impatiently.

"Miss Chadwick always finds the French mistresses sly. She's got a thing about them." She looked at Adam. "What do *you* think?"

"I think she pries," said Adam slowly. "It may be just natural inquisitiveness. It may be something more. I can't make up my mind. She doesn't *look* to me like a killer, but how does one know?"

"That's just it," said Kelsey. "There *is* a killer here, a ruthless killer who has killed twice—but it's very hard to believe that it's one of the staff. Miss Johnson was with her sister last night at Limeston on Sea, and anyway she's been with you seven years. Miss Chadwick's been with you since you started. Both of them, anyway, are clear of Miss Springer's death. Miss Rich has been with you over a year and was staying last night at the Alton Grange Hotel, twenty miles away. Miss Blake was with friends at Littleport. Miss Rowan has been with you for a year and has a good background. As for your servants, frankly, I can't see any of them as murderers. They're all local, too . . ."

Miss Bulstrode nodded pleasantly.

"I quite agree with your reasoning. It doesn't leave much, does it? So—" She paused and fixed an accusing eye on Adam. "It looks really—as though it must be *you.*"

His mouth opened in astonishment.

"On the spot," she mused. "Free to come and go . . . Good story to account for your presence here. Background O.K., but you *could* be a double-crosser, you know."

Adam recovered himself.

"Really, Miss Bulstrode," he said admiringly, "I take off my hat to you. You think of *everything!*"

ii.

"Good gracious!" cried Mrs. Sutcliffe at the breakfast table. "Henry!"

She had just unfolded her newspaper.

The width of the table was between her and her husband since her week-end guests had not yet put in an appearance for the meal.

Mr. Sutcliffe, who had opened his paper to the financial page, and was absorbed in the unforeseen movements of certain shares, did not reply.

"Henry!"

The clarion call reached him. He raised a startled face.

"What's the matter, Joan?"

"The matter? Another murder! At Meadowbank! At Jennifer's school."

"What? Here, let *me* see!"

Disregarding his wife's remark that it would be in his paper, too, Mr. Sutcliffe leant across the table and snatched the sheet from his wife's grasp.

"Miss Eleanor Vansittart . . . Sports Pavilion . . . same spot where Miss Springer, the games mistress . . . hm . . . hm . . ."

"I can't believe it!" Mrs. Sutcliffe was wailing. "Meadowbank. Such an exclusive school. Royalty there and everything . . ."

Mr. Sutcliffe crumpled up the paper and threw it down on the table.

"Only one thing to be done," he said. "You get over there right away and take Jennifer out of it."

"You mean take her away—altogether?"

"That's what I mean."

"You don't think that would be a little too drastic? After Rosamund being so good about it and managing to get her in?"

"You won't be the only one taking your daughter away! Plenty of vacancies soon at your precious Meadowbank."

"Oh, Henry, do you think so?"

"Yes, I do. Something badly wrong there. Take Jennifer away today."

"Yes—of course—I suppose you're right. What shall we do with her?"

"Send her to a secondary modern somewhere handy. They don't have murders there."

"Oh, Henry, but they *do*. Don't you remember? There was a boy who shot the science master at one. It was in last week's *News of the World*."

"I don't know what England's coming to," said Mr. Sutcliffe.

Disgusted, he threw his napkin on the table and strode from the room.

iii.

Adam was alone in the Sports Pavilion . . . His deft fingers were turning over the contents of the lockers. It was unlikely that he would find anything where the police had failed but after all, one could never be sure. As Kelsey had said every department's technique varied a little.

What was there that linked this expensive modern building with sudden and violent death? The idea of a rendezvous was out. No one would choose to keep a rendezvous a second time in the same place where murder had occurred. It came back to it, then, that there was something here that someone was looking for. Hardly a cache of jewels. That seemed ruled out. There could be no secret hiding place, false drawers, spring catches, etc. And the contents of the lockers were pitifully simple.

They had their secrets, but they were the secrets of school life. Photographs of pin-up heroes, packets of cigarettes, an occasional unsuitable cheap paperback. Especially he returned to Shaista's locker. It was while bending over that that Miss Vansittart had been killed. What had Miss Vansittart expected to find there? Had she found it? Had her killer taken it from her dead hand and then slipped out of the building in the nick of time to miss being discovered by Miss Chadwick?

In that case it was no good looking. Whatever it was, was gone.

The sound of footsteps outside aroused him from his thoughts. He was on his feet lighting a cigarette in the middle of the floor when Julia Upjohn appeared in the doorway, hesitating a little.

"Anything you want, miss?" asked Adam.

"I wondered if I could have my tennis racquet."

"Don't see why not," said Adam. "Police constable left me here," he explained mendaciously. "Had to drop back to the station for something. Told me to stop here while he was away."

"To see if he came back, I suppose," said Julia.

"The police constable?"

"No, I mean the murderer. They do, don't they? Come back to the scene of the crime. They have to! It's a compulsion."

"You may be right," said Adam. He looked up at the serried rows of racquets in their presses. "Whereabouts is yours?"

"Under U," said Julia. "Right at the far end. We have our names on them," she explained, pointing out the adhesive tape as he handed the racquet to her.

"Seen some service," said Adam. "But been a good racquet once."

"Can I have Jennifer Sutcliffe's, too?" asked Julia.

"New," said Adam appreciatively, as he handed it to her.

"Brand new," said Julia. "Her aunt sent it to her only the other day."

"Lucky girl."

"She ought to have a good racquet. She's very good at

tennis. Her backhand's come on like anything this term."
She looked round. "Don't you think he *will* come back?"

Adam was a moment or two getting it.

"Oh. The murderer? No, I don't think it's really likely.
Bit risky, wouldn't it be?"

"You don't think murderers feel they *have* to?"

"Not unless they've left something behind."

"You mean a clue? I'd like to find a clue. Have the
police found one?"

"They wouldn't tell me."

"No. I suppose they wouldn't . . . Are you interested in
crime?"

She looked at him inquiringly. He returned her glance.
There was, as yet, nothing of the woman in her. She must
be of much the same age as Shaista, but her eyes held
nothing but interested inquiry.

"Well—I suppose—up to a point—we all are."

Julia nodded in agreement.

"Yes. I think so, too . . . I can think of all sorts of
solutions—but most of them are very farfetched. It's
rather fun, though."

"You weren't fond of Miss Vansittart?"

"I never really thought about her. She was all right. A
bit like the Bull—Miss Bulstrode—but not really like
her. More like an understudy in a theatre. I didn't mean
that it was fun she was dead. I'm sorry about that."

She walked out holding the two racquets.

Adam remained looking round the Pavilion.

"What the hell could there ever have been here?" he
muttered to himself.

iv.

"Good Lord," said Jennifer, allowing Julia's forehand
drive to pass her. "There's Mummy."

The two girls turned to stare at the agitated figure of
Mrs. Sutcliffe, shepherded by Miss Rich, rapidly arriving
and gesticulating as she did so.

"More fuss, I suppose," said Jennifer resignedly. "It's
the murder. You *are* lucky, Julia, that your mother's
safely on a bus in the Caucasus."

"There's still Aunt Isabel."

"Aunts don't mind in the same way.

"Hullo, Mummy," she added, as Mrs. Sutcliffe arrived.

"You must come and pack your things, Jennifer. I'm taking you back with me."

"Back home?"

"Yes."

"But—you don't mean altogether? Not for good?"

"Yes. I do."

"But you can't—really. My tennis has come on like anything. I've got a very good chance of winning the singles and Julia and I *might* win the doubles, though I don't think it's very likely."

"You're coming home with me today."

"Why?"

"Don't ask questions."

"I suppose it's because of Miss Springer and Miss Vansittart being murdered. But no one's murdered any of the girls. I'm sure they wouldn't want to. And Sports Day is in three weeks' time. I *think* I shall win the long jump and I've a good chance for the hurdling."

"Don't argue with me, Jennifer. You're coming back with me today. Your father insists."

"But, Mummy—"

Arguing persistently Jennifer moved toward the house by her mother's side.

Suddenly she broke away and ran back to the tennis court.

"Goodby, Julia. Mummy seems to have got the wind up thoroughly. Daddy, too, apparently. Sickening, isn't it? Goodby. I'll write to you."

"I'll write to you, too, and tell you all that happens."

"I hope they don't kill Chaddy next. I'd rather it was Mademoiselle Blanche, wouldn't you?"

"Yes. She's the one we could spare best. I say, did you notice how black Miss Rich was looking?"

"She hasn't said a word. She's furious at Mummy coming and taking me away."

"Perhaps she'll stop her. She's very forceful, isn't she? Not like anyone else."

"She reminds me of someone," said Jennifer.

"I don't think she's a bit like anybody. She always seems to be quite different."

"Oh, yes. She is different. I meant in appearance. But the person I knew was quite fat."

"I can't imagine Miss Rich being fat."

"Jennifer . . ." called Mrs. Sutcliffe.

"I do think parents are trying," said Jennifer crossly. "Fuss, fuss, fuss. They never stop. I do think you're lucky to—"

"I know. You said that before. But just at the moment, let me tell you, I wish Mummy were a good deal nearer, and *not* on a bus in Anatolia."

"Jennifer . . ."

"Coming . . ."

Julia walked slowly in the direction of the Sports Pavilion. Her steps grew slower and slower and finally she stopped altogether. She stood, frowning, lost in thought.

The luncheon bell sounded, but she hardly heard it. She stared down at the racquet she was holding, moved a step or two along the path, then wheeled round and marched determinedly toward the house. She went in by the front door, which was not allowed, and thereby avoided meeting any of the other girls. The hall was empty. She ran up the stairs to her small bedroom, looked round her hurriedly, then lifting the mattress on her bed, shoved the racquet flat beneath it. Then, rapidly smoothing her hair, she walked demurely downstairs to the dining room.

<hr>

■
17

Aladdin's Cave

THE GIRLS WENT up to bed that night more quietly than usual. For one thing their numbers were much depleted. At least thirty of them had gone home. The others reacted according to their several dispositions. Excitement, trepidation, a certain amount of giggling that was purely nervous in origin, and there were some again who were merely quiet and thoughtful.

Julia Upjohn went up quietly among the first wave. She went into her room and closed the door. She stood there listening to the whispers, giggles, footsteps, and goodnights. Then silence closed down—or a near silence. Faint voices echoed in the distance, and footsteps went to and fro to the bathroom.

There was no lock on the door. Julia pulled a chair against it, with the top of the chair wedged under the handle. That would give her warning if anyone should come in. But no one was likely to come in. It was strictly forbidden for the girls to go into each other's rooms, and the only mistress who did so was Miss Johnson, if one of the girls was ill or out of sorts.

Julia went to her bed, lifted up the mattress and groped under it. She brought out the tennis racquet and stood a moment holding it. She had decided to examine it now, and not later. A light in her room showing under the door might attract attention when all lights were supposed to be off. Now was the time when a light was normal for undressing and for reading in bed until half past ten if you wanted to do so.

She stood staring down at the racquet. How could there be anything hidden in a tennis racquet?

"But there must be," said Julia to herself. "There *must*. The burglary at Jennifer's home, the woman who came with that silly story about a new racquet . . .

"Only Jennifer would have believed that," thought Julia scornfully.

No, it was "new lamps for old" and that meant, like in Aladdin, that there was *something* about this particular tennis racquet. Jennifer and Julia had never mentioned to anyone that they had swopped racquets—or at least, she herself never had.

So really then, *this* was the racquet that everyone was looking for in the Sports Pavilion. And it was up to her to find out *why!* She examined it carefully. There was nothing unusual about it to look at. It was a good quality racquet, somewhat the worse for wear, but restrung and eminently usable. Jennifer had complained of the balance.

The only place you could possibly conceal anything in a tennis racquet was in the handle. You could, she supposed, hollow out the handle to make a hiding place. It sounded a little farfetched but it was possible. And if the handle had been tampered with, that probably *would* upset the balance.

There was a round of leather with lettering on it, the lettering almost worn away. That of course was only stuck on. If one removed that? Julia sat down at her dressing table and attacked it with a penknife and presently managed to pull the leather off. Inside was a round of thin wood. It didn't look quite right. There was a join all round it. Julia dug in her penknife. The blade snapped. Nail scissors were more effective. She succeeded at last in prizing it out. A mottled red and blue substance now showed. Julia poked it and enlightenment came to her. *Modeling clay!* But surely handles of tennis racquets didn't normally contain clay? She grasped the nail scissors firmly and began to dig out lumps of clay. The stuff was encasing something. Something that felt like buttons or pebbles.

She attacked the clay vigorously.

Something rolled out on the table—then another something. Presently there was quite a heap.

Julia leaned back and gasped.

She stared and stared and stared . . .

Liquid fire, red and green and deep blue and dazzling white . . .

In that moment, Julia grew up. She was no longer a child. She became a woman. A woman looking at jewels . . .

All sorts of fantastic snatches of thought raced through her brain. Aladdin's cave . . . Marguerite and her casket of jewels (they had been taken to Covent Garden to hear *Faust* last week) . . . fatal stones . . . the Hope diamond . . . romance . . . herself in a black velvet gown with a flashing necklace round her throat . . .

She sat and gloated and dreamed. She held the stones in her fingers and let them fall through in a rivulet of fire, a flashing stream of wonder and delight.

And then, some slight sound, perhaps, recalled her to herself.

She sat thinking, trying to use her common sense, deciding what she ought to do. That faint sound had alarmed her. She swept up the stones, took them to the washstand and thrust them into her sponge bag and rammed her sponge and nail brush down on top of them. Then she went back to the tennis racquet, forced the putty back inside it, replaced the wooden top and tried to gum down the leather on top again. It curled upward, but she managed to deal with that by applying adhesive tape the wrong way up in thin strips and then pressing the leather onto it.

It was done. The racquet looked and felt just as before, its weight hardly altered in feel. She looked at it and then cast it down carelessly on a chair.

She looked at her bed, neatly turned down and waiting. But she did not undress. Instead she sat listening. Was that a footstep outside?

Suddenly and unexpectedly she knew fear. Two people had been killed. If anyone knew what she had found, *she* would be killed . . .

There was a fairly heavy oak chest of drawers in the room. She managed to drag it in front of the door, wishing that it was the custom at Meadowbank to have keys in the locks. She went to the window, pulled up the top sash and bolted it. There was no tree growing near the window and no creepers. She doubted if it was possible for anyone to come in that way but she was not going to take any chances.

She looked at her small clock. Half past ten. She drew a deep breath and turned out the light. No one must notice anything unusual. She pulled back the curtain a little from the window. There was a full moon and she could see the door clearly. Then she sat down on the edge of the bed. In her hand she held the stoutest shoe she possessed.

"If anyone tries to come in," Julia said to herself, "I'll rap on the wall here as hard as I can. Mary King is next door and that will wake her up. *And* I'll scream—at the top of my voice. And then, if lots of people come, I'll say I had a nightmare. Anyone might have a nightmare after all the things that have been going on here."

She sat there and time passed. Then she heard it—a

soft step along the passage. She heard it stop outside her door. A long pause and then she saw the handle slowly turning.

Should she scream? Not yet.

The door was pushed—just a crack, but the chest of drawers held it. That must have puzzled the person outside.

Another pause, and then there was a knock, a very gentle little knock, on the door.

Julia held her breath. A pause, and then the knock came again—but still soft and muted.

"I'm asleep," said Julia to herself. "I don't hear *anything.*"

Who would come and knock on her door in the middle of the night? If it was someone who had a right to knock, they'd call out, rattle the handle, make a noise. But this person couldn't afford to make a noise . . .

For a long time Julia sat there. The knock was not repeated, the handle stayed immovable. But Julia sat tense and alert.

She sat like that for a long time. She never knew herself how long it was before sleep overcame her. The school bell finally awoke her, lying in a cramped and uncomfortable heap on the edge of her bed.

ii.

After breakfast, the girls went upstairs and made their beds, then went down to prayers in the big hall and finally dispersed to various classrooms.

It was during that last exercise, when girls were hurrying in different directions, that Julia went into one classroom, out by a further door, joined a group hurrying round the house, dived behind a rhododendron, made a series of further strategic dives and arrived finally near the wall of the grounds where a lime tree had thick growth almost down to the ground. Julia climbed the tree with ease, she had climbed trees all her life. Completely hidden in the leafy branches, she sat, glancing from time to time at her watch. She was fairly sure she would not be missed for some time. Things were disorganized, two teachers were missing, and more than half the girls had gone home. That meant that all classes would have been reorganized, so nobody would be likely to observe the absence of Julia Upjohn until lunchtime and by then . . .

Julia looked at her watch again, scrambled easily down the tree to the level of the wall, straddled it and dropped neatly on the other side. A hundred yards away was a bus stop where a bus ought to arrive in a few minutes. It duly did so, and Julia hailed and boarded it, having by now abstracted a felt hat from inside her cotton frock and clapped it on her slightly dishevelled hair. She got out at the station and took a train to London.

In her room, propped up on the washstand, she had left a note addressed to Miss Bulstrode.

> *Dear Miss Bulstrode,*
> *I have not been kidnaped or run away, so don't worry. I will come back as soon as I can.*
> *Yours very sincerely,*
> *Julia Upjohn*

iii.

At 28 Whitehouse Mansions, Georges, Hercule Poirot's immaculate valet and manservant, opened the door and contemplated with some surprise a schoolgirl with a rather dirty face.

"Can I see M. Hercule Poirot, please?"

Georges took just a shade longer than usual to reply. He found the caller unexpected.

"Mr. Poirot does not see anyone without an appointment," he said.

"I'm afraid I haven't time to wait for that. I really must see him now. It is very urgent. It's about some murders and a robbery and things like that."

"I will ascertain," said Georges, "if Mr. Poirot will see you."

He left her in the hall and withdrew to consult his master.

"A young lady, sir, who wishes to see you urgently."

"I daresay," said Hercule Poirot. "But things do not arrange themselves as easily as that."

"That is what I told her, sir."

"What kind of a young lady?"

"Well, sir, she's more of a little girl."

"A little girl? A young lady? Which do you mean, Georges? They are really not the same."

"I'm afraid you did not quite get my meaning, sir. She is, I should say, a little girl—of school age, that is to say. But though her frock is dirty and indeed torn, she is essentially a young lady."

"A social term. I see."

"And she wishes to see you about some murders and a robbery."

Poirot's eyebrows went up.

"*Some* murders, and *a* robbery. Original. Show the little girl—the young lady—in."

Julia came into the room with only the slightest trace of diffidence. She spoke politely and quite naturally.

"How do you do, M. Poirot. I am Julia Upjohn. I think you know a great friend of Mummy's, Mrs. Summerhayes. We stayed with her last summer and she talked about you a lot."

"Mrs. Summerhayes . . ." Poirot's mind went back to a village that climbed a hill and to a house on top of that hill. He recalled a charming freckled face, a sofa with broken springs, a large quantity of dogs, and other things both agreeable and disagreeable.

"Maureen Summerhayes," he said. "Ah yes."

"I call her Aunt Maureen, but she isn't really an aunt at all. She told us how wonderful you'd been and saved a man who was in prison for murder, and when I couldn't think of what to do and who to go to, I thought of you."

"I am honoured," said Poirot gravely.

He brought forward a chair for her.

"Now tell me," he said. "Georges, my servant, told me you wanted to consult me about a robbery and some murders—more than one murder, then?"

"Yes," said Julia. "Miss Springer and Miss Vansittart. And of course there's the kidnaping, too—but I don't think that's really my business."

"You bewilder me," said Poirot. "Where have all these exciting happenings taken place?"

"At my school—Meadowbank."

"Meadowbank!" exclaimed Poirot. "Ah." He stretched

out his hand to where the newspapers lay neatly folded beside him. He unfolded one and glanced over the front page, nodding his head.

"I begin to comprehend," he said. "Now tell me, Julia, tell me everything from the beginning."

Julia told him. It was quite a long story and a comprehensive one—but she told it clearly—with an occasional break as she went back over something she had forgotten.

She brought her story up to the moment when she had examined the tennis racquet in her bedroom last night.

"You see, I thought it was just like Aladdin—new lamps for old—and there must be something about that tennis racquet."

"And there was?"

"Yes."

Without any false modesty, Julia pulled up her skirt, rolled up her knicker leg nearly to her thigh and exposed what looked like a grey poultice attached by adhesive plaster to the upper part of her leg.

She tore off the strips of plaster, uttering an anguished "Ouch" as she did so, and freed the poultice which Poirot now perceived to be a packet enclosed in a portion of grey plastic sponge bag. Julia unwrapped it and without warning poured a heap of glittering stones on the table.

"*Nom d'un nom d'un nom!*" ejaculated Poirot in an awe-inspired whisper.

He picked them up, letting them run through his fingers.

"*Nom d'un nom d'un nom!* But they are *real*. Genuine."

Julia nodded.

"I think they must be. People wouldn't kill other people for them otherwise, would they? But I can understand people killing for *these!*"

And suddenly, as had happened last night, a woman looked out of the child's eyes.

Poirot looked keenly at her and nodded.

"Yes—you understand—you feel the spell. They cannot be to you just pretty coloured playthings—more is the pity."

"They're *jewels!*" said Julia, in tones of ecstasy.

"And you found them, you say, in this tennis racquet?"

Julia finished her recital.

"And you have now told me everything?"

"I think so. I may, perhaps, have exaggerated a little here and there. I do exaggerate sometimes. Now Jennifer, my great friend, she's the other way round. She can make the most exciting things sound dull." She looked again at the shining heap. "M. Poirot, who do they really belong to?"

"It is probably very difficult to say. But they do not belong to either you or to me. We have to decide now what to do next."

Julia looked at him in an expectant fashion.

"You leave yourself in my hands? Good."

Hercule Poirot closed his eyes.

Suddenly he opened them and became brisk.

"It seems that this is an occasion when I cannot, as I prefer, remain in my chair. There must be order and method, but in what you tell me, there is no order and method. That is because we have here many threads. But they all converge and meet at one place. Meadowbank. Different people, with different aims, and representing different interests—all converge at Meadowbank. So, I, too, go to Meadowbank. And as for you—where is your mother?"

"Mummy's gone in a bus to Anatolia."

"Ah, your mother has gone in a bus to Anatolia. *Il ne manquait que ça!* I perceive well that she might be a friend of Mrs. Summerhayes! Tell me, did you enjoy your visit with Mrs. Summerhayes?"

"Oh, yes, it was great fun. She's got some lovely dogs."

"The dogs, yes, I well remember."

"They come in and out through all the windows—like in a pantomime."

"You are so right! And the food? Did you enjoy the food?"

"Well, it was a bit peculiar sometimes," Julia admitted.

"Peculiar, yes, indeed."

"But Aunt Maureen makes smashing omelettes."

"She makes smashing omelettes," Poirot's voice was happy. He sighed.

"Then Hercule Poirot has not lived in vain," he said. "It was *I* who taught your Aunt Maureen to make an omelette." He picked up the telephone receiver.

"We will now reassure your good school mistress as to your safety and announce my arrival with you at Meadowbank."

"She knows I'm all right. I left a note saying I hadn't been kidnaped."

"Nevertheless, she will welcome further reassurance."

In due course he was connected, and was informed that Miss Bulstrode was on the line.

"Ah, Miss Bulstrode? My name is Hercule Poirot. I have with me here your pupil Julia Upjohn. I propose to motor down with her immediately, and for the information of the police officer in charge of the case, a certain packet of some value has been safely deposited in the bank."

He rang off and looked at Julia.

"You would like a syrup?" he suggested.

"Golden syrup?" Julia looked doubtful.

"No, a syrup of fruit juice. Black currant, raspberry, groseille—that is, red currant?"

Julia settled for red currant.

"But the jewels aren't in the bank," she pointed out.

"They will be in a very short time," said Poirot. "But for the benefit of anyone who listens in at Meadowbank, or who overhears, or who is told, it is as well to think they are already there and no longer in your possession. To obtain jewels from a bank requires time and organization. And I should very much dislike anything to happen to you, my child. I will admit that I have formed a high opinion of your courage and your resource."

Julia looked pleased but embarrassed.

18

Consultation

HERCULE POIROT had prepared himself to beat down any insular prejudice that a headmistress might have against aged foreigners with pointed patent leather shoes and large moustaches. But he was agreeably surprised. Miss Bulstrode greeted him with cosmopolitan aplomb. She also, to his gratification, knew all about him.

"It was kind of you, M. Poirot," she said, "to ring up so promptly and allay our anxiety. All the more so because that anxiety had hardly begun. You weren't missed at lunch, Julia, you know," she added, turning to the girl. "So many girls were fetched away this morning, and there were so many gaps at table, that half the school could have been missing, I think, without any apprehension being aroused. These are unusual circumstances," she said, turning back to Poirot. "I assure you we should not be so slack normally. When I received your telephone call," she went on, "I went to Julia's room and found the note she had left."

"I didn't want you to think I'd been kidnaped, Miss Bulstrode," said Julia.

"I appreciate that, but I think, Julia, that you might have told me what you were planning to do."

"I thought I'd better not," said Julia, and added unexpectedly, *"Les oreilles ennemies nous écoutent."*

"Mademoiselle Blanche doesn't seem to have done much to improve your accent yet," said Miss Bulstrode, briskly. "But I'm not scolding you, Julia." She looked from Julia to Poirot. "Now, if you please, I want to hear exactly what has happened."

"You permit?" said Hercule Poirot. He stepped across the room, opened the door and looked out. He made an exaggerated gesture of shutting it. He returned beaming.

153

"We are alone," he said mysteriously. "We can proceed."

Miss Bulstrode looked at him, then she looked at the door, then she looked at Poirot again. Her eyebrows rose. He returned her gaze steadily. Very slowly Miss Bulstrode inclined her head. Then, resuming her brisk manner, she said, "Now then, Julia, let's hear all about this."

Julia plunged into her recital. The exchange of tennis racquets, the mysterious woman. And finally her discovery of what the racquet contained. Miss Bulstrode turned to Poirot.

"Mademoiselle Julia has stated everything correctly," he said. "I took charge of what she brought me. It is safely lodged in a bank. I think therefore that you need anticipate no further developments of an unpleasant nature here."

"I see," said Miss Bulstrode. "Yes, I see . . ." She was quiet for a moment or two and then she said, "You think it wise for Julia to remain here? Or would it be better for her to go to her aunt in London?"

"Oh, please," said Julia, "do let me stay here."

"You're happy here then?" said Miss Bulstrode.

"I love it," said Julia. "And besides, there have been such exciting things going on."

"That is *not* a formal feature of Meadowbank," said Miss Bulstrode, drily.

"I think that Julia will be in no danger here now," said Hercule Poirot. He looked again toward the door.

"I think I understand," said Miss Bulstrode.

"But for all that," said Poirot, "there should be discretion. Do you understand discretion, I wonder?" he added, looking at Julia.

"M. Poirot means," said Miss Bulstrode, "that he would like you to hold your tongue about what you found. Not talk about it to the other girls. Can you hold your tongue?"

"Yes," said Julia.

"It is a very good story to tell to your friends," said Poirot. "Of what you found in a tennis racquet in the dead of night. But there are important reasons why it would be advisable that that story should not be told."

"I understand," said Julia.

"Can I trust you, Julia?" said Miss Bulstrode.

"You can trust me," said Julia. "Cross my heart."

Miss Bulstrode smiled. "I hope your mother will be home before long," she said.

"Mummy? Oh, I do hope so."

"I understand from Inspector Kelsey," said Miss Bulstrode, "that every effort is being made to get in touch with her. Unfortunately," she added, "Anatolian buses are liable to unexpected delays and do not always run to schedule."

"I can tell Mummy, can't I?" said Julia.

"Of course. Well, Julia, that's all settled. You'd better run along now."

Julia departed. She closed the door after her. Miss Bulstrode looked very hard at Poirot.

"I have understood you correctly, I think," she said. "Just now, you made a great parade of closing that door. Actually—you deliberately left it slightly open."

Poirot nodded.

"So that what we said could be overheard?"

"Yes—if there was anyone who wanted to overhear. It was a precaution of safety for the child. The news must get round that what she found is safely in a bank, and not in her possession."

Miss Bulstrode looked at him for a moment—then she pursed her lips grimly together.

"There's got to be an end to all this," she said.

ii.

"The idea is," said the Chief Constable, "that we try to pool our ideas and information. We are very glad to have you with us, M. Poirot," he added. "Inspector Kelsey remembers you well."

"It's a great many years ago," said Inspector Kelsey. "Chief Inspector Warrender was in charge of the case. I was a fairly raw sergeant knowing my place."

"The gentleman called, for convenience's sake by us, Mr. Adam Goodman, is not known to you, M. Poirot, but I believe you do know his—his—er—chief. Special Branch," he added.

"Colonel Pikeaway?" said Hercule Poirot thoughtfully.

"Ah, yes, it is some time since I have seen him. Is he still as sleepy as ever?" he asked Adam.

Adam laughed. "I see you know him all right, M. Poirot. I've never seen him wide awake. When I do, I'll know that for once he isn't paying attention to what goes on."

"You have something there, my friend. It is well observed."

"Now," said the Chief Constable, "let's get down to things. I shan't push myself forward or urge my own opinions. I'm here to listen to what the men who are actually working on the case know and think. There are a great many sides to all this, and one thing perhaps I ought to mention first of all. I'm saying this as a result of representations that have been made to me from—er—various quarters high up." He looked at Poirot. "Let's say," he said, "that a little girl—a schoolgirl—came to you with a pretty tale of something she'd found in the hollowed-out handle of a tennis racquet. Very exciting for her. A collection, shall we say, of coloured stones, paste, good imitation—something of that kind—or even semi-precious stones which often look as attractive as the other kind. Anyway let's say something that a child would be excited to find. She might even have exaggerated ideas of its value. That's quite possible, don't you think?" He looked very hard at Hercule Poirot.

"It seems to me eminently possible," said Hercule Poirot.

"Good," said the Chief Constable. "Since the person who brought these—er—coloured stones into the country did so quite unknowingly and innocently, we don't want any question of illicit smuggling to arise.

"Then there is the question of our foreign policy," he went on. "Things, I am led to understand, are rather—delicate just at present. When it comes to large interests in oil, mineral deposits, all that sort of thing, we have to deal with whatever government's in power. We don't want any awkward questions to arise. You can't keep murder out of the press, and murder hasn't been kept out of the press. But there's been no mention of anything like jewels in connection with it. For the present, at any rate, there needn't be."

"I agree," said Poirot. "One must always consider international complications."

"Exactly," said the Chief Constable. "I think I'm right in saying that the late ruler of Ramat was regarded as a friend of this country, and that the powers that be would like his wishes in respect of any property of his that *might* be in this country to be carried out. What that amounts to, I gather, nobody knows at present. If the new government of Ramat is claiming certain property which they allege belongs to them, it will be much better if we know nothing about such property being in this country. A plain refusal would be tactless."

"One does not give plain refusals in diplomacy," said Hercule Poirot. "One says instead that such a matter shall receive the utmost attention but that at the moment nothing definite is known about any little—nest egg, say— that the late ruler of Ramat may have possessed. It may still be in Ramat, it may be in the keeping of a faithful friend of the late Prince Ali Yusuf, it may have been taken out of the country by half a dozen people, it may be hidden somewhere in the city of Ramat itself." He shrugged his shoulders. "One simply does not know."

The Chief Constable heaved a sigh. "Thank you," he said. "That's just what I mean." He went on, "M. Poirot, you have friends in very high quarters in this country. They put much trust in you. Unofficially they would like to leave a certain article in your hands if you do not object."

"I do not object," said Poirot. "Let us leave it at that. We have more serious things to consider, have we not?" He looked round at them. "Or perhaps you do not think so? But after all, what is three quarters of a million or some such sum in comparison with human life?"

"You're right, M. Poirot," said the Chief Constable.

"You're right every time," said Inspector Kelsey. "What we want is a murderer. We shall be glad to have your opinion, M. Poirot," he added, "because it's largely a question of guess and guess again and your guess is as good as the next man's and sometimes better. The whole thing's like a snarl of tangled wool."

"That is excellently put," said Poirot, "one has to take

up that snarl of wool and pull out the one colour that we seek, the colour of a murderer. Is that right?"

"That's right."

"Then tell me, if it is not too tedious for you to indulge in repetition, all that is known so far."

He settled down to listen.

He listened to Inspector Kelsey, and he listened to Adam Goodman. He listened to the brief summing up of the Chief Constable. Then he leaned back, closed his eyes, and slowly nodded his head.

"Two murders," he said, "committed in the same place and roughly under the same conditions. One kidnaping. The kidnaping of a girl who might be the central figure of the plot. Let us ascertain first *why* she was kidnaped."

"I can tell you what she said herself," said Kelsey.

He did so, and Poirot listened.

"It does not make sense," he complained.

"That's what I thought at the time. As a matter of fact I thought she was just making herself important . . ."

"But the fact remains that she *was* kidnaped. Why?"

"There have been ransom demands," said Kelsey slowly, "but . . ." He paused.

"But they have been, you think, phoney? They have been sent merely to bolster up the kidnaping theory?"

"That's right. The appointments made weren't kept."

"Shaista, then, was kidnaped for some other reason. What reason?"

"So that she could be made to tell where the—er—valuables were hidden?" suggested Adam doubtfully.

Poirot shook his head.

"She did not know where they were hidden," he pointed out. "That, at least, is clear. No, there must be something . . ."

His voice tailed off. He was silent, frowning, for a moment or two. Then he sat up, and asked a question.

"Her knees," he said. "Did you ever notice her knees?"

Adam stared at him in astonishment.

"No," he said. "Why should I?"

"There are many reasons why a man notices a girl's knees," said Poirot severely. "Unfortunately, you did not."

"Was there something odd about her knees? A scar? Something of that kind? I wouldn't know. They all wear stockings most of the time, and their skirts are just below knee length."

"In the swimming pool, perhaps?" suggested Poirot hopefully.

"Never saw her go in," said Adam. "Too chilly for her, I expect. She was used to a warm climate. What are you getting at? A scar? Something of that kind?"

"No, no, that is not it at all. Ah well, a pity."

He turned to the Chief Constable.

"With your permission, I will communicate with my old friend, the Préfet, at Geneva. I think he may be able to help us."

"About something that happened when she was at school there?"

"It is possible, yes. You do permit? Good. It is just a little idea of mine." He paused and went on: "By the way, there has been nothing in the papers about the kidnaping?"

"The Emir Ibrahim was most insistent."

"But I did notice a little remark in a gossip column. About a certain foreign young lady who had departed from school very suddenly. A budding romance, the columnist suggested. To be nipped in the bud if possible!"

"That was my idea," said Adam. "It seemed a good line to take."

"Admirable. So now we pass from kidnaping to something more serious. Murder. Two murders at Meadowbank."

19

Consultation Continued

"TWO MURDERS AT Meadowbank," repeated Poirot thoughtfully.

"We've given you the facts," said Kelsey. "If you've any ideas—?"

"Why the Sports Pavilion?" said Poirot. "That was your question, wasn't it?" he said to Adam. "Well, now we have the answer. Because in the Sports Pavilion there was a tennis racquet containing a fortune in jewels. Someone knew about that racquet. Who was it? It could have been Miss Springer herself. She was, so you all say, rather peculiar about that Sports Pavilion. Disliked people coming there—unauthorized people, that is to say. She seemed to be suspicious of their motives. Particularly was that so in the case of Mademoiselle Blanche."

"Mademoiselle Blanche," said Kelsey thoughtfully.

Hercule Poirot again spoke to Adam.

"You yourself considered Mademoiselle Blanche's manner odd where it concerned the Sports Pavilion?"

"She explained," said Adam. "She explained too much. I should never have questioned her right to be there if she had not taken so much trouble to explain it away."

Poirot nodded.

"Exactly. That certainly gives one to think. But all we *know* is that Miss Springer was killed in the Sports Pavilion at one o'clock in the morning when she had no business to be there."

He turned to Kelsey.

"Where was Miss Springer before she came to Meadowbank?"

"We don't know," said the Inspector. "She left her last place of employment," he mentioned a famous school, "last summer. Where she has been since we do not know." He added drily: "There was no occasion to ask the question until she was dead. She has no near relatives, or, apparently, any close friends."

"She *could* have been in Ramat, then," said Poirot thoughtfully.

"I believe there was a party of school teachers out there at the time of the trouble," said Adam.

"Let us say, then, that she was there, that in some way she learned about the tennis racquet. Let us assume that after waiting a short time to familiarize herself with the routine at Meadowbank she went out one night to the Sports Pavilion. She got hold of the racquet and was about to remove the jewels from their hiding place when"—he paused—"when someone interrupted her. Someone who had been watching her. Following her that evening? Whoever it was had a pistol—and shot her— but had no time to prize out the jewels, or to take the racquet away, because people were approaching the Sports Pavilion who had heard the shot."

He stopped.

"You think that's what happened?" asked the Chief Constable.

"I do not know," said Poirot. "It is one possibility. The other is that that person with the pistol was there *first,* and was surprised by Miss Springer. Someone who Miss Springer was already suspicious of. She was, you have told me, that kind of woman. A noser out of secrets."

"And the other woman?" asked Adam.

Poirot looked at him. Then, slowly, he shifted his gaze to the other two men.

"*You* do not know," he said. "And *I* do not know. It could have been someone from outside . . . ?"

His voice half asked a question.

Kelsey shook his head.

"I think not. We have sifted the neighbourhood very carefully. Especially, of course, in the case of strangers. There was a Madame Kolinsky staying nearby—known to Adam here. But she could not have been concerned in either murder."

"Then it comes back to Meadowbank. And there is only one method to arrive at the truth—elimination."

Kelsey sighed.

"Yes," he said. "That's what it amounts to. For the first murder, it's a fairly open field. Almost anybody could have killed Miss Springer. The exceptions are Miss Johnson and Miss Chadwick—and a child who had the earache. But the second murder narrows things down. Miss Rich, Miss Blake and Miss Shapland are out of it. Miss Rich was staying at Alton Grange Hotel, twenty miles away, Miss Blake was at Littleport, Miss Shapland was in London at a night club, Le Nid Sauvage, with Mr. Denis Rathbone."

"And Miss Bulstrode was also away, I understand?"

Adam grinned. The Inspector and the Chief Constable looked shocked.

"Miss Bulstrode," said the Inspector severely, "was staying with the Duchess of Welsham."

"That eliminates Miss Bulstrode then," said Poirot gravely. "And leaves us—what?"

"Two members of the domestic staff who sleep in, Mrs. Gibbons and a girl called Doris Hogg. I can't consider either of them seriously. That leaves Miss Rowan and Mademoiselle Blanche."

"And the pupils, of course."

Kelsey looked startled.

"Surely you don't suspect them?"

"Frankly, no. But one must be exact."

Kelsey paid no attention to exactitude. He plodded on.

"Miss Rowan has been here about a year. She has a good record. We know nothing against her."

"So we come, then, to Mademoiselle Blanche. It is there that the journey ends."

There was a silence.

"There's no evidence," said Kelsey. "Her credentials seem genuine enough."

"They would have to be," said Poirot.

"She snooped," said Adam. "But snooping isn't evidence of murder."

"Wait a minute," said Kelsey, "there was something about a key. In our first interview with her—I'll look it up—something about the key of the Pavilion falling out of the door and she picked it up and forgot to replace it—walked out with it and Springer bawled her out."

"Whoever wanted to go out there at night and look for the racquet would have had to have a key to get in with," said Poirot. "For that, it would have been necessary to take an impression of the key."

"Surely," said Adam, "in that case she would never have mentioned the key incident to you."

"That doesn't follow," said Kelsey. "Springer might have talked about the key incident. If so, she might think it better to mention it in a casual fashion."

"It is a point to be remembered," said Poirot.

"It doesn't take us very far," said Kelsey.

He looked gloomily at Poirot.

"There would seem," said Poirot, "that is, if I have been informed correctly, one possibility. Julia Upjohn's mother, I understand, recognized someone here on the first day of term. Someone whom she was surprised to see. From the context, it would seem likely that that someone was connected with foreign espionage. If Mrs. Upjohn definitely points out Mademoiselle Blanche as the person she recognized, then I think we could proceed with some assurance."

"Easier said than done," said Kelsey. "We've been trying to get in contact with Mrs. Upjohn, but the whole thing's a headache! When the child said a bus, I thought she meant a proper coach tour, running to schedule, and a party all booked together. But that's not it at all. Seems she's just taking local buses to any place she happens to fancy! She's not done it through Cook's or a recognized travel agency. She's all on her own, wandering about. What can you do with a woman like that? She might be anywhere. There's a lot of Anatolia!"

"It makes it difficult, yes," said Poirot.

"Plenty of nice coach tours," said the Inspector in an injured voice. "All made easy for you—where you stop and what you see, and inclusive fares so that you know exactly where you are."

"But clearly, that kind of travel does not appeal to Mrs. Upjohn."

"And in the meantime, here *we* are," went on Kelsey. "Stuck! That Frenchwoman can walk out any moment she chooses. We've nothing on which we could hold her."

Poirot shook his head.

"She will not do that."

"You can't be sure."

"I am sure. If you have committed murder, you do not want to do anything out of character, that may draw attention to you. Mademoiselle Blanche will remain here quietly until the end of the term."

"I hope you're right."

"I am sure I am right. And remember, the person whom Mrs. Upjohn saw, *does not know that Mrs. Upjohn saw her*. The surprise when it comes will be complete."

Kelsey sighed.

"If that's all we've got to go on . . ."

"There are other things. Conversation, for instance."

"Conversation?"

"It is very valuable, conversation. Sooner or later, if one has something to hide, one says too much."

"Gives oneself away?" The Chief Constable sounded skeptical.

"It is not quite so simple as that. One is guarded about the thing one is trying to hide. But often one says too much about other things. And there are other uses for conversation. There are the innocent people who know things, but are unaware of the importance of what they know. And that reminds me—"

He rose to his feet.

"Excuse me, I pray. I must go and demand of Miss Bulstrode if there is someone here who can draw."

"Draw?"

"Draw."

"Well," said Adam, as Poirot went out. "First girls' knees, and now draughtsmanship! What next, I wonder!"

ii.

Miss Bulstrode answered Poirot's question without evincing any surprise.

"Miss Laurie is our visiting drawing mistress," she said briskly. "But she isn't here today. What do you want her to draw for you?" she added in a kindly manner as though to a child.

"Faces," said Poirot.

"Miss Rich is good at sketching people. She's clever at getting a likeness."

"That is exactly what I need."

Miss Bulstrode, he noted with approval, asked him no questions as to his reasons. She merely left the room and returned with Miss Rich.

After introductions, Poirot said: "You can sketch people? Quickly? With a pencil?"

Eileen Rich nodded.

"I often do. For amusement."

"Good. Please, then, sketch for me the late Miss Springer."

"That's difficult. I knew her for such a short time. I'll try."

She screwed up her eyes, then began to draw rapidly.

"Bien," said Poirot, taking it from her. "And now, if you please, Miss Bulstrode, Miss Rowan, Mademoiselle Blanche and—yes—the gardener Adam."

Eileen Rich looked at him doubtfully, then set to work. He looked at the result, and nodded appreciatively.

"You are good—you are very good. So few strokes— and yet the likeness is there. Now I will ask you to do something more difficult. Give, for example, to Miss Bulstrode a different hair arrangement. Change the shape of her eyebrows."

Eileen stared at him as though she thought he was mad.

"No," said Poirot. "I am not mad. I make an experiment, that is all. Please do as I ask."

In a moment or two she said: "Here you are."

"Excellent. Now do the same for Mademoiselle Blanche and Miss Rowan."

When she had finished he lined up the three sketches.

"Now I will show you something," he said. "Miss Bulstrode, in spite of the changes you have made, is still unmistakably Miss Bulstrode. But look at the other two. Because their features are negative, and since they have not Miss Bulstrode's personality, they appear almost different people, do they not?"

"I see what you mean," said Eileen Rich.

She looked at him as he carefully folded the sketches away.

"What are you going to do with them?" she asked.

"Use them," said Poirot.

■
20

Conversation

"WELL—I DON'T KNOW what to say," said Mrs. Sutcliffe. "Really I don't know what to say—"

She looked with definite distaste at Hercule Poirot.

"Henry, of course," she said, "is not at home."

The meaning of this pronouncement was slightly obscure, but Hercule Poirot thought that he knew what was in her mind. Henry, she was feeling, would be able to deal with this sort of thing. Henry had so many international dealings. He was always flying to the Middle East and to Ghana and to South America and to Geneva, and even occasionally, but not so often, to Paris.

"The whole thing," said Mrs. Sutcliffe, "has been *most* distressing. I was so glad to have Jennifer safely at home with me. Though, I must say," she added, with a trace of vexation, "Jennifer has really been most tiresome. After having made a great fuss about going to Meadowbank and being quite sure she wouldn't like it there, and saying it was a snobby kind of school and not the kind she wanted to go to, *now* she sulks all day long because I've taken her away. It's really too bad."

"It is undeniably a very good school," said Hercule Poirot. "Many people say the best school in England."

"It *was*, I daresay," said Mrs. Sutcliffe.

"And will be again," said Hercule Poirot.

"You think so?" Mrs. Sutcliffe looked at him doubtfully. His sympathetic manner was gradually piercing her defenses. There is nothing that eases the burden of a mother's life more than to be permitted to unburden herself of the difficulties, rebuffs and frustrations which she has in dealing with her offspring. Loyalty so often compels silent endurance. But to a foreigner like Hercule Poirot Mrs. Sutcliffe felt that this loyalty was not applicable. It was not like talking to the mother of another daughter.

"Meadowbank," said Hercule Poirot, "is just passing through an unfortunate phase."

It was the best thing he could think of to say at the moment. He felt its inadequacy and Mrs. Sutcliffe pounced upon the inadequacy immediately.

"Rather more than unfortunate!" she said. "Two murders! And a girl kidnaped. You can't send your daughter to a school where the mistresses are being murdered all the time."

It seemed a highly reasonable point of view.

"If the murders," said Poirot, "turn out to be the work of one person and that person is apprehended, that makes a difference, does it not?"

"Well—I suppose so. Yes," said Mrs. Sutcliffe doubtfully. "I mean—you mean—oh, I see, you mean like Jack the Ripper or that other man—who was it? Something to do with Devonshire. Cream? Neil Cream. Who went about killing an unfortunate type of woman. I suppose this murderer just goes about killing schoolmistresses! If once you've got him safely in prison, and hanged too, I hope, because you're only allowed one murder, aren't you?—like a dog with a bite—what was I saying? Oh, yes, if he's safely caught, well, then I suppose it *would* be different. Of course there can't be many people like that, can there?"

"One certainly hopes not," said Hercule Poirot.

"But then there's this kidnaping, too," pointed out Mrs. Sutcliffe. "You don't want to send your daughter to a school where she may be kidnaped, either, do you?"

"Assuredly not, madame. I see how clearly you have thought out the whole thing. You are so right in all you say."

Mrs. Sutcliffe looked faintly pleased. Nobody had said anything like that to her for some time. Henry had merely said things like "What did you want to send her to

Meadowbank for anyway?" and Jennifer had sulked and refused to answer.

"I *have* thought about it," she said. "A great deal."

"Then I should not let kidnaping worry you, madame. *Entre nous,* if I may speak in confidence, about Princess Shaista. It is not exactly a kidnaping—one suspects a romance."

"You mean the naughty girl just ran away to marry somebody?"

"My lips are sealed," said Hercule Poirot. "You comprehend it is not desired that there should be any scandal. This is in confidence *entre nous.* I know you will say nothing."

"Of course not," said Mrs. Sutcliffe virtuously. She looked down at the letter that Poirot had brought with him from the Chief Constable. "I don't quite understand who you are, M.—er—Poirot. Are you what they call in books—a private eye?"

"I am a consultant," said Hercule Poirot loftily.

This flavour of Harley Street encouraged Mrs. Sutcliffe a great deal.

"What do you want to talk to Jennifer about?" she demanded.

"Just to get her impressions of things," said Poirot. "She is observant—yes?"

"I'm afraid I wouldn't say that," said Mrs. Sutcliffe. "She's not what I call a noticing kind of child at all. I mean, she is always so matter of fact."

"It is better than making up things that have never happened at all," said Poirot.

"Oh, Jennifer wouldn't do *that* sort of thing," said Mrs. Sutcliffe, with certainty. She got up, went to the window and called, "Jennifer."

"I wish," she said, to Poirot, as she came back again, "that you'd try and get it into Jennifer's head that her father and I are only doing our best for her."

Jennifer came into the room with a sulky face and looked with deep suspicion at Hercule Poirot.

"How do you do?" said Poirot. "I am a very old friend of Julia Upjohn. She came to London to find me."

"Julia went to London?" said Jennifer, slightly surprised. "Why?"

"To ask my advice," said Hercule Poirot.

Jennifer looked unbelieving.

"I was able to give it to her," said Poirot. "She is now back at Meadowbank," he added.

"So her Aunt Isabel didn't take *her* away," said Jennifer, shooting an irritated look at her mother.

Poirot looked at Mrs. Sutcliffe and for some reason, perhaps because she had been in the middle of counting the laundry when Poirot arrived and perhaps because of some unexplained compulsion, she got up and left the room.

"It's a bit hard," said Jennifer, "to be out of all that's going on there. All this fuss! I told Mummy it was silly. After all, none of the *pupil*s have been killed."

"Have you any ideas of your own about the murders?" asked Poirot.

Jennifer shook her head. "Someone who's batty?" she offered. She added thoughtfully, "I suppose Miss Bulstrode will have to get some new mistresses now."

"It seems possible, yes," said Poirot. He went on, "I am interested, Mademoiselle Jennifer, in the woman who came and offered you a new racquet for your old one. Do you remember?"

"I should think I do remember," said Jennifer. "I've never found out to this day who really sent it. It wasn't Aunt Gina at all."

"What did this woman look like?" said Poirot.

"The one who brought the racquet?" Jennifer half closed her eyes as though thinking. "Well, I don't know. She had on a sort of fussy dress with a little cape, I think. Blue, and a floppy sort of hat."

"Yes?" said Poirot. "I meant perhaps not so much her clothes as her face."

"A good deal of make-up, I think," said Jennifer vaguely. "A bit too much for the country, I mean, and fair hair. I think she was an American."

"Had you ever seen her before?" asked Poirot.

"Oh, no," said Jennifer. "I don't think she lived down there. She said she'd come down for a luncheon party or a cocktail party or something."

Poirot looked at her thoughtfully. He was interested in

Jennifer's complete acceptance of everything that was said to her. He said gently:

"But she might not have been speaking the truth?"

"Oh," said Jennifer. "No, I suppose not."

"You're quite sure you hadn't seen her before? She could not have been, for instance, one of the girls dressed up? Or one of the mistresses?"

"Dressed up?" Jennifer looked puzzled.

Poirot laid before her the sketch Eileen Rich had done for him of Mademoiselle Blanche.

"This was not the woman, was it?"

Jennifer looked at it doubtfully.

"It's a little like her—but I don't think it's her."

Poirot nodded thoughtfully.

There was no sign that Jennifer recognized that this was actually a sketch of Mademoiselle Blanche.

"You see," said Jennifer, "I didn't really look at her much. She was an American and a stranger, and then she told me about the racquet . . ."

After that, it was clear, Jennifer would have had eyes for nothing but her new possession.

"I see," said Poirot. He went on, "Did you ever see at Meadowbank anyone that you'd seen out in Ramat?"

"In Ramat?" Jennifer thought. "Oh, no—at least—I don't think so."

Poirot pounced on the slight expression of doubt. "But you are not *sure*, Mademoiselle Jennifer."

"Well," Jennifer scratched her forehead with a worried expression, "I mean, you're always seeing people who look like somebody else. You can't quite remember who it is they look like. Sometimes you see people that you *have* met but you don't remember who they are. And they say to you, 'You don't remember me,' and then that's awfully awkward because really you don't. I mean, you sort of know their face but you can't remember their names or where you saw them."

"That is very true," said Poirot. "Yes, that is very true. One often has that experience." He paused a moment, then he went on, prodding gently, "Princess Shaista, for instance, you probably recognized *her* when you saw her because you must have seen her in Ramat."

"Oh, was she in Ramat?"

"Very likely," said Poirot. "After all she is a relation of the ruling house. You might have seen her there?"

"I don't think I did," said Jennifer frowning. "Anyway, she wouldn't go about with her face showing there, would she? I mean, they all wear veils and things like that. Though they take them off in Paris and Cairo, I believe. And in London, of course," she added.

"Anyway, you had no feeling of having seen anyone at Meadowbank whom you had seen before?"

"No, I'm sure I hadn't. Of course most people do look rather alike and you might have seen them anywhere. It's only when somebody's got an odd sort of face like Miss Rich, that you notice it."

"Did you think you'd seen Miss Rich somewhere before?"

"I hadn't really. It must have been someone like her. But it was someone much fatter than she was."

"Someone much fatter," said Poirot thoughtfully.

"You couldn't imagine Miss Rich being fat," said Jennifer with a giggle. "She's so frightfully thin and nobbly. And anyway Miss Rich couldn't have been in Ramat because she was away ill last term."

"And the other girls," said Poirot, "had you seen any of the girls before?"

"Only the ones I knew already," said Jennifer. "I did know one or two of them. After all, you know, I was only there three weeks and I really don't know half of the people there even by sight. I wouldn't know most of them if I met them tomorrow."

"You should notice things more," said Poirot severely.

"One can't notice everything," protested Jennifer. She went on: "If Meadowbank is carrying on I would like to go back. See if you can do anything with Mummy. Though really," she added, "I think it's Daddy who's the stumbling block. It's awful here in the country. I get *no* opportunity to improve my tennis."

"I assure you I will do what I can," said Poirot.

21

Gathering Threads

"I WANT TO TALK to you, Eileen," said Miss Bulstrode.

Eileen Rich followed Miss Bulstrode into the latter's sitting room. Meadowbank was strangely quiet. About twenty-five pupils were still there. Pupils whose parents had found it either difficult or unwelcome to fetch them. The panic-stricken rush had, as Miss Bulstrode had hoped, been checked by her own tactics. There was a general feeling that by next term everything would have been cleared up. It was much wiser of Miss Bulstrode, they felt, to close the school.

None of the staff had left. Miss Johnson fretted with too much time on her hands. A day in which there was too little to do did not in the least suit her. Miss Chadwick, looking old and miserable, wandered round in a kind of coma of misery. She was far harder hit to all appearance than Miss Bulstrode. Miss Bulstrode, indeed, managed, apparently without difficulty to be completely herself, unperturbed, and with no sign of strain or of collapse. The two younger mistresses were not averse to the extra leisure. They bathed in the swimming pool, wrote long letters to friends and relations and sent for cruise literature to study and compare. Ann Shapland had a good deal of time on her hands and did not appear to resent the fact. She spent a good deal of that time in the garden and devoted herself to gardening with quite unexpected efficiency. That she preferred to be instructed in the work by Adam rather than by old Briggs was perhaps a not unnatural phenomenon.

"Yes, Miss Bulstrode?" said Eileen Rich.

"I've been wanting to talk to you," said Miss Bulstrode. "Whether this school can continue or not I do not know. What people will feel is always fairly incalculable

172

because they will all feel differently. But the result will be that whoever feels most strongly will end by converting all the rest. So either Meadowbank is finished—"

"No," said Eileen Rich, interrupting, "not finished." She almost stamped her foot and her hair immediately began coming down. "You mustn't let it be stopped," she said. "It would be a sin—a crime."

"You speak very strongly," said Miss Bulstrode.

"I feel strongly. There are so many things that really don't seem worth while a bit, but Meadowbank does seem worth while. It seemed worth while to me the first moment I came here."

"You're a fighter," said Miss Bulstrode. "I like fighters, and I assure you that I don't intend to give in tamely. In a way I'm going to enjoy the fight. You know, when everything's too easy and things go too well one gets—I don't know the exact word I mean—complacent? Bored? A kind of hybrid of the two. But I'm not bored now and I'm not complacent and I'm going to fight with every ounce of strength I've got, and with every penny I've got, too. Now what I want to say to you is this: If Meadowbank continues, will you come in on a partnership basis?"

"Me?" Eileen Rich stared at her. "Me?"

"Yes, my dear," said Miss Bulstrode. "You."

"I couldn't," said Eileen Rich. "I don't know enough. I'm too young. Why, I haven't got the experience, the knowledge that you'd want."

"You must leave it to me to know what I want," said Miss Bulstrode. "Mind you, this isn't, at the present moment of talking, a good offer. You'd probably do better for yourself elsewhere. But I want to tell you this, and you've got to believe me. I had already decided before Miss Vansittart's unfortunate death, that you were the person I wanted to carry on this school."

"You thought so then?" Eileen Rich stared at her. "But I thought—we all thought—that Miss Vansittart . . ."

"There was no arrangement made with Miss Vansittart," said Miss Bulstrode. "I had her in mind, I will confess. I've had her in mind for the last two years. But something's always held me back from saying anything definite to her about it. I daresay everyone assumed that she'd be my successor. She may have thought so herself. I myself thought so until very recently. And then I decided that she was not what I wanted."

"But she was so suitable in every way," said Eileen Rich. "She would have carried out things in exactly your ways, in exactly your ideas."

"Yes," said Miss Bulstrode, "and that's just what would have been wrong. You can't hold on to the past. A certain amount of tradition is good but never too much. A school is for the children of *today*. It's not for the children of fifty years ago or even of thirty years ago. There are some schools in which tradition is more important than others, but Meadowbank is not one of those. It's not a school with a long tradition behind it. It's a creation, if I may say it, of one woman. Myself. I've tried certain ideas and carried them out to the best of my ability, though occasionally I've had to modify them when they haven't produced the results I'd expected. It's not been a conventional school, but it has not prided itself on being an unconventional school either. It's a school that tries to make the best of both worlds—the past and the future, but the real stress is on the present. That's how it's going to go on, how it ought to go on. Run by someone with ideas—ideas of the present day. Keeping what is wise from the past, looking forward toward the future. You're very much the age I was when I started here but you've got what I no longer can have. You'll find it written in the Bible. *Their old men dream dreams and their young men have visions.* We don't need dreams here, we need vision. I believe you to have vision and that's why I decided that you were the person and not Eleanor Vansittart."

"It would have been wonderful," said Eileen Rich. "Wonderful. The thing I should have liked above all."

Miss Bulstrode was faintly surprised by the tense, although she did not show it. Instead she agreed promptly.

"Yes," she said, "it would have been wonderful. But it isn't wonderful now? Well, I suppose I understand that."

"No, no, I don't mean that at all," said Eileen Rich. "Not at all. I—I can't go into details very well, but if you had—if you had asked me, spoken to me like this a week or a fortnight ago I should have said at once that I couldn't, that it would have been quite impossible. The only reason why it—why it might be possible now is because—well, because it *is* a case of fighting—of taking on things. May I—may I think it over, Miss Bulstrode? I don't know what to say now."

"Of course," said Miss Bulstrode. She was still surprised. One never really knew, she thought, about anybody.

ii.

"There goes Rich with her hair coming down again," said Ann Shapland as she straightened herself up from a flower bed. "If she can't control it I can't think why she doesn't get it cut off. She's got a good shaped head and she would look better."

"You ought to tell her so," said Adam.

"We're not on those terms," said Ann Shapland. She went on, "D'you think this place will be able to carry on?"

"That's a very doubtful question," said Adam, "and who am I to judge?"

"You could tell as well as another I should think," said Ann Shapland. "It might, you know. The old Bull, as the girls call her, has got what it takes. A hypnotizing effect on parents to begin with. How long is it since the beginning of term—only a month? It seems like a year. I shall be glad when it comes to an end."

"Will you come back if the school goes on?"

"No," said Ann with emphasis, "no indeed. I've had enough of schools to last me a lifetime. I'm not cut out for being cooped up with a lot of women anyway. And, frankly, I don't like murder. It's the sort of thing that's fun to read about in the paper or to read yourself to sleep with in the way of a nice book. But the real thing isn't so good. I think," added Ann thoughtfully, "that when I leave here at the end of the term I shall marry Denis and settle down."

"Denis?" said Adam. "That's the one you mentioned to me, wasn't it? As far as I remember his work takes him to Burma and Malaya and Singapore and Japan and places like that. It won't be exactly settling down, will it, if you marry him?"

Ann laughed suddenly. "No, no, I suppose it won't. Not in the physical, geographical sense."

"I think you can do better than Denis," said Adam.

"Are you making me an offer?" said Ann.

"Certainly not," said Adam. "You're an ambitious girl, you wouldn't like to marry a humble jobbing gardener."

"I was wondering about marrying into the C.I.D.," said Ann.

"I'm not in the C.I.D.," said Adam.

"No, no, of course not," said Ann. "Let's preserve the niceties of speech. You're not in the C.I.D. Shaista wasn't kidnaped, everything in the garden's lovely. It is rather," she added, looking round. "All the same," she said after a moment or two, "I don't understand in the least about Shaista turning up in Geneva or whatever the story is. How did she get there? All you people must be very slack to allow her to be taken out of this country."

"My lips are sealed," said Adam.

"I don't think you know the first thing about it," said Ann.

"I will admit," said Adam, "that we have to thank Monsieur Hercule Poirot for having had a bright idea."

"What, the funny little man who brought Julia back and came to see Miss Bulstrode?"

"Yes. He calls himself," said Adam, "a consultant detective."

"I think he's pretty much of a has-been," said Ann.

"I don't understand what he's up to at all," said Adam. "He even went to see my mother—or some friend of his did."

"Your mother?" said Ann. "Why?"

"I've no idea. He seems to have a kind of morbid interest in mothers. He went to see Jennifer's mother too."

"Did he go and see Miss Rich's mother, and Chaddy's?"

"I gather Miss Rich hasn't got a mother," said Adam. "Otherwise, no doubt, he would have gone to see her."

"Miss Chadwick's got a mother in Cheltenham, she told me," said Ann, "but she's about eighty-odd, I be-

lieve. Poor Miss Chadwick, she looks about eighty herself. She's coming to talk to us now."

Adam looked up. "Yes," he said, "she's aged a lot in
the last week."

"Because she really loves the school," said Ann. "It's
her whole life. She can't bear to see it go downhill."

Miss Chadwick indeed looked ten years older than she
had done on the day of the opening of term. Her step had
lost its brisk efficiency. She no longer trotted about, happy and bustling. She came up to them now, her steps
dragging a little.

"Will you please come to Miss Bulstrode," she said to
Adam. "She has some instruction about the garden."

"I'll have to clean up a bit first," said Adam. He laid
down his tools and moved off in the direction of the
potting shed.

Ann and Miss Chadwick walked together toward the
house.

"It does seem quiet, doesn't it," said Ann, looking
round. "Like an empty house at the theatre," she added
thoughtfully, "with people spaced out by the box office as
tactfully as possible to make them look like an audience."

"It's dreadful," said Miss Chadwick, "dreadful! Dreadful to think that Meadowbank has come to *this*. I can't
get over it. I can't sleep at night. Everything in ruins. All
the years of work, of building up something really fine."

"It may get all right again," said Ann cheerfully. "People have got very short memories, you know."

"Not as short as all that," said Miss Chadwick grimly.

Ann did not answer. In her heart she rather agreed
with Miss Chadwick.

iii.

Mademoiselle Blanche came out of the classroom where
she had been teaching French literature.

She glanced at her watch. Yes, there would be plenty
of time for what she intended to do. With so few pupils
there was always plenty of time these days.

She went upstairs to her room and put on her hat. She
was not one of those who went about hatless. She studied

her appearance in the mirror with dissatisfaction. Not a personality to be noticed! Well, there could be advantages in that! She smiled to herself. It had made it easy for her to use her sister's testimonials. Even the passport photograph had gone unchallenged. It would have been a thousand pities to waste those excellent credentials when Angele had died. Angele had really enjoyed teaching. For herself, it was unutterable boredom. But the pay was excellent. Far above what she herself had ever been able to earn. And besides, things had turned out unbelievably well. The future was going to be very different. Oh, yes, very different. The drab Mademoiselle Blanche would be transformed. She saw it all in her mind's eye. The Riviera. Herself smartly dressed, suitably made up. All one needed in this world was money. Oh, yes, things were going to be very pleasant indeed. It was worth having come to this detestable English school.

She picked up her handbag, went out of her room and along the corridor. Her eyes dropped to the kneeling woman who was busy there. A new daily help. A police spy, of course. How simple they were—to think that one would not know!

A contemptuous smile on her lips, she went out of the house and down the drive to the front gate. The bus stop was almost opposite. She stood at it, waiting. The bus should be here in a moment or two.

There were very few people about in this quiet country road. A car, with a man bending over the open hood. A bicycle leaning against a hedge. A man also waiting for the bus.

One or other of the three would, no doubt, follow her. It would be skilfully done, not obviously. She was quite alive to the fact, and it did not worry her. Her "shadow" was welcome to see where she went and what she did.

The bus came. She got in. A quarter of an hour later, she got out in the main square of the town. She did not trouble to look behind her. She crossed to where the show windows of a fairly large department store showed their display of new model gowns. Poor stuff, for provincial tastes, she thought, with a curling lip. But she stood looking at them as though much attracted.

Presently she went inside, made one or two trivial

purchases, then went up to the first floor and entered the ladies' rest room. There was a writing table there, some easy chairs, and a telephone box. She went into the box, put the necessary coins in, dialled the number she wanted, waiting to hear if the right voice answered.

She nodded in approval, and spoke.

"This is the Maison Blanche. You understand me, the Maison *Blanche?* I have to speak of an account that is owed. You have until tomorrow evening. Tomorrow evening. To pay into the account of the Maison Blanche at the Crédit National in London, Ledbury St. branch, the sum that I tell you."

She named the sum.

"If that money is not paid in, then it will be necessary for me to report in the proper quarters what I observed on the night of the twelfth. The reference—pay attention —is to Miss Springer. You have a little over twenty-four hours."

She hung up and emerged into the rest room. A woman had just come in from outside. Another customer of the shop, perhaps, or again perhaps not. But if the latter, it was too late for anything to be overheard.

Mademoiselle Blanche freshened herself up in the adjoining cloak room, then she went out into the street again, smiling to herself. She looked into a bookshop, and then caught a bus back to Meadowbank.

She was smiling to herself as she walked up the drive. She had arranged matters very well. The sum she had demanded had not been too large—not impossible to raise at short notice. And it would do very well to go on with. Because, of course, in the future, there would be further demands . . .

Yes, a very pretty little source of income this was going to be. She had no qualms of conscience. She did not consider it in any way her duty to report what she knew and had seen to the police. That Springer had been a detestable woman, rude, *mal elevée.* Prying into what was no business of hers. Ah, well, she had got her deserts.

Mademoiselle Blanche stayed for a while by the swimming pool. She watched Eileen Rich diving. Then Ann

Shapland, too, climbed up and dived—very well, too. There was laughing, and squeals from the girls.

A bell rang, and Mademoiselle Blanche went in to take her junior class. They were inattentive and tiresome, but Mademoiselle Blanche hardly noticed. She would soon have done with teaching forever.

She went up to her room to tidy herself for supper. Vaguely, without really noticing, she saw that, contrary to her usual practice, she had thrown her garden coat across a chair in the corner instead of hanging it up as usual.

She leaned forward, studying her face in the glass. She applied powder, lipstick.

The movement was so quick that it took her completely by surprise. Noiseless! Professional. The coat on the chair seemed to gather itself together, drop to the ground and in an instant behind Mademoiselle Blanche a hand with a sandbag rose and, as she opened her lips to scream, fell, dully, on the back of her neck.

■
22

Incident in Anatolia

MRS. UPJOHN was sitting by the side of the road overlooking a deep ravine. She was talking partly in French and partly with gestures to a large and solid-looking Turkish woman who was telling her with as much detail as possible under these difficulties of communications all about her last miscarriage. Nine children she had had, she explained. Eight of them boys, and five miscarriages. She seemed as pleased at the miscarriages as she did at the births.

"And you?" she poked Mrs. Upjohn amiably in the ribs. "*Combien—garçons—filles—combien?*" She held up her hands ready to indicate on the fingers.

"*Une fille,*" said Mrs. Upjohn.

"Et garçons?"

Seeing that she was about to fall in the Turkish woman's estimation, Mrs. Upjohn in a surge of nationalism proceeded to perjure herself. She held up five fingers of her right hand.

"Cinq," she said.

"Cinq garçons? Très bien!"

The Turkish woman nodded with approbation and respect. She added that if only her cousin who spoke French really fluently were here they could understand each other a great deal better. She then resumed the story of her last miscarriage.

The other passengers were sprawled about near them, eating odd bits of food from the baskets they carried with them. The bus, looking slightly the worse for wear, was drawn up against an overhanging rock, and the driver and another man were busy inside the hood. Mrs. Upjohn had lost complete count of time. Floods had blocked two of the roads, detours had been necessary and they had once stuck for seven hours until the river they were fording subsided. Ankara lay in the not impossible future and that was all she knew. She listened to her friend's eager and incoherent conversation, trying to gauge when to nod admiringly, when to shake her head in sympathy.

A voice cut into her thoughts, a voice highly incongruous with her present surroundings.

"Mrs. Upjohn, I believe," said the voice.

Mrs. Upjohn looked up. A little way away a car had driven up. The man standing opposite her had undoubtedly alighted from it. His face was unmistakably British, as was his voice. He was impeccably dressed in a grey flannel suit.

"Good heavens," said Mrs. Upjohn. "Dr. Livingstone?"

"It must seem rather like that," said the stranger pleasantly. "My name's Atkinson. I'm from the Consulate in Ankara. We've been trying to get in touch with you for two or three days, but the roads have been cut."

"You wanted to get in touch with me? Why?" Suddenly Mrs. Upjohn rose to her feet. All traces of the gay traveller had disappeared. She was all mother, every inch of her. "Julia?" she said sharply. "Has something happened to Julia?"

"No, no," Mr. Atkinson reassured her. "Julia's quite all right. It's not that at all. There's been a spot of trouble at Meadowbank and we want to get you home there as soon as possible. I'll drive you back to Ankara, and you can get on a plane in about an hour's time."

Mrs. Upjohn opened her mouth and then shut it again. Then she rose and said, "You'll have to get my bag off the top of that bus. It's the dark blue one." She turned, shook hands with her Turkish companion, said: "I'm sorry, I have to go home now," waved to the rest of the busload with the utmost friendliness, called out a Turkish farewell greeting which was part of her small stock of Turkish, and prepared to follow Mr. Atkinson immediately without asking any further questions. It occurred to him as it had occurred to many other people that Mrs. Upjohn was a very sensible woman.

■

23

Showdown

IN ONE OF THE smaller classrooms Miss Bulstrode looked at the assembled people. All the members of her staff were there: Miss Chadwick, Miss Johnson, Miss Rich and the two younger mistresses. Ann Shapland sat with her pad and pencil in case Miss Bulstrode wanted her to take notes. Beside Miss Bulstrode sat Inspector Kelsey and beyond him, Hercule Poirot. Adam Goodman sat in a no man's land of his own halfway between the staff and what he called to himself, the executive body. Miss Bulstrode rose and spoke in her practiced, decisive voice.

"I feel it is due to you all," she said, "as members of my staff, and interested in the fortunes of the school, to know exactly to what point this inquiry has progressed. I have been informed by Inspector Kelsey of several facts. M. Hercule Poirot, who has international connections, has obtained valuable assistance from Switzerland and will report himself on that particular matter. We have not yet come to the end of the inquiry, I am sorry to say, but certain minor matters have been cleared up and I thought it would be a relief to you all to know how matters stand at the present moment." Miss Bulstrode looked toward Inspector Kelsey, and he rose.

"Officially," he said, "I am not in a position to disclose all that I know. I can only reassure you to the extent of saying that we are making progress and we are beginning to have a good idea who is responsible for the three crimes that have been committed on the premises. Beyond that I will not go. My friend, M. Hercule Poirot, who is not bound by official secrecy and is at perfect liberty to give you his own ideas, will disclose to you certain information which he himself has been instrumental in procuring. I am sure you are all loyal to Meadowbank and to Miss Bulstrode and will keep to yourselves various matters upon which M. Poirot is going to touch and which are not of any public interest. The less gossip or speculation about them the better, so I will ask you to keep the facts that you will learn here today to yourselves. Is that understood?"

"Of course," said Miss Chadwick, speaking first and with emphasis. "Of course we're all loyal to Meadowbank, I should hope."

"Naturally," said Miss Johnson.

"Oh, yes," said the two younger mistresses.

"I agree," said Eileen Rich.

"Then perhaps, M. Poirot?"

Hercule Poirot rose to his feet, beamed on his audience and carefully twisted his moustaches. The two younger mistresses had a sudden desire to giggle, and looked away from each other pursing their lips together.

"It has been a difficult and anxious time for you all," he said. "I want you to know first that I do appreciate that. It has naturally been worst of all for Miss Bulstrode herself, but you have all suffered. You have suffered first the loss of three of your colleagues, one of whom has been here for a considerable period of time. I refer to Miss Vansittart. Miss Springer and Mademoiselle Blanche were, of course, newcomers but I do not doubt that their deaths were a great shock to you and a distressing happening. You must also have suffered a good deal of apprehension yourselves, for it must have seemed as though there were a kind of vendetta aimed against the mistresses of Meadowbank school. That I can assure you, and Inspector Kelsey will assure you also, is not so. Meadowbank by a fortuitous series of chances became the centre for the attentions of various undesirable interests. There has been, shall we say, a cat among the pigeons. There have been three murders here and also a kidnaping. I will deal first with the kidnaping, for all through this business the difficulty has been to clear out of the way extraneous matters which, though criminal in themselves, obscure the most important thread—the thread of a ruthless and determined killer in your midst."

He took from his pocket a photograph.

"First, I will pass round this photograph."

Kelsey took it, handed it to Miss Bulstrode and she in turn handed it to the staff. It was returned to Poirot. He looked at their faces, which were quite blank.

"I ask you, all of you, do you recognize the girl in that photograph?"

One and all they shook their heads.

"You should do so," said Poirot. "Since that is a photograph obtained by me from Geneva of Princess Shaista."

"But it's not Shaista at all," cried Miss Chadwick.

"Exactly," said Poirot. "The threads of all this business start in Ramat where, as you know, a revolutionary *coup d'état* took place about three months ago. The ruler, Prince Ali Yusuf, managed to escape, flown out by his own private pilot. Their plane, however, crashed in the mountains north of Ramat and was not discovered until later in the year. A certain article of great value which was always carried on Prince Ali's person, was missing. It was not found in the wreck and there were rumours that it had been brought to this country. Several groups of people were anxious to get hold of this very valuable article. One of their leads to it was Prince Ali Yusuf's only remaining relation, his first cousin, a girl who was then at a school in Switzerland. It seemed likely that if the precious article had been safely got out of Ramat it would be brought to Princess Shaista or to her relatives and guardians. Certain agents were detailed to keep an eye on her uncle, the Emir Ibrahim, and others to keep an eye on the Princess herself. It was known that she was due to come to this school, Meadowbank, this term. Therefore it would have been only natural that someone should be detailed to obtain employment here and to keep a close watch on anyone who approached the Princess, her letters, and any telephone messages. But an even simpler and more efficacious idea was evolved, that of kidnaping Shaista and sending one of their own number to the school as Princess Shaista herself. This could be done successfully since the Emir Ibrahim was in Egypt and did not propose to visit England until late summer. Miss Bulstrode herself had not seen the girl and all arrangements that she had made concerning her reception had been made with the Embassy in London.

"The plan was simple in the extreme. The real Shaista left Switzerland accompanied by a representative from the Embassy in London. Or so it was supposed. Actually, the Embassy in London was informed that a representative from the Swiss school would accompany the girl to London. The real Shaista was taken to a very pleasant chalet in Switzerland where she has been ever since, and an entirely different girl arrived in London, was met there by a representative of the Embassy and subsequently brought to this school. This substitute, of course, was necessarily much older than the real Shaista. But that would hardly attract attention since Eastern girls noticeably look much more mature than their age. A young French actress who specializes in playing schoolgirl parts was the agent chosen.

"I did ask," said Hercule Poirot, in a thoughtful voice, "as to whether anyone had noticed Shaista's knees. Knees are a very good indication of age. The knees of a woman of twenty-three or twenty-four can never really be mistaken for the knees of a girl of fourteen or fifteen. Nobody, alas, had noticed her knees.

"The plan was hardly as successful as had been hoped. Nobody attempted to get in touch with Shaista, no letters or telephone calls of significance arrived for her and as time went on an added anxiety arose. The Emir Ibrahim might arrive in England ahead of schedule. He was not a man who announced his plans ahead. He was in the habit, I understand, of saying one evening 'Tomorrow I go to London' and thereupon to go.

"The false Shaista, then, was aware that at any moment someone who knew the real Shaista might arrive. Especially was this so after the murder and therefore she began to prepare the way for a kidnaping by talking about it to Inspector Kelsey. Of course, the actual kidnaping was nothing of the kind. As soon as she learned that her uncle was coming to take her out the following morning, she sent a brief message by telephone, and half an hour earlier than the genuine car, a showy car with false *Corps Diplomatique* plates on it arrived and Shaista was officially 'kidnaped.' Actually, of course, she was set down by the car in the first large town where she at once resumed her own personality. An amateurish ransom note was sent just to keep up the fiction."

Hercule Poirot paused, then said, "It was, as you can see, merely the trick of the conjuror. Misdirection. You focus the eyes on the kidnaping *here* and it does not occur to anyone that the kidnaping *really* occurred three weeks earlier in Switzerland."

What Poirot really meant, but was too polite to say, was that it had not occurred to anyone but himself!

"We pass now," he said, "to something far more serious than kidnaping—murder.

"The false Shaista could, of course, have killed Miss Springer but she could not have killed Miss Vansittart or Mademoiselle Blanche, and would have had no motive to kill anybody, nor was such a thing required of her. Her role was simply to receive a valuable packet if, as seemed likely, it should be brought to her; or, alternatively, to receive news of it.

"Let us go back now to Ramat where all this started. It was widely rumoured in Ramat that Prince Ali Yusuf had given this valuable packet to Bob Rawlinson, his private pilot, and that Bob Rawlinson had arranged for its dispatch to England. On the day in question Rawlinson went to Ramat's principal hotel where his sister Mrs. Sutcliffe and her daughter Jennifer were staying. Mrs. Sutcliffe and Jennifer were out, but Bob Rawlinson went up to their room where he remained for at least twenty minutes. That is rather a long time under the circumstances. He might of course have been writing a long letter to his sister. But that was not so. He merely left a short note which he could have scribbled in a couple of minutes.

"It was a very fair inference then, inferred by several separate parties, that during his time in her room he had placed this object among his sister's effects and that she had brought it back to England. Now we come to what I may call the dividing of two separate threads. One set of interests, or possibly more than one set, assumed that Mrs. Sutcliffe had brought this article back to England and in consequence her house in the country was ransacked and a thorough search made. This showed that whoever was searching *did not know where exactly the article was hidden*. Only that it was probably *somewhere* in Mrs. Sutcliffe's possession.

"But somebody else knew very definitely exactly where that article was, and I think that by now it will do no harm for me to tell you where, in fact, Bob Rawlinson did conceal it. He concealed it in the handle of a tennis racquet, hollowing the handle out and afterward piecing it together again so skilfully that it was difficult to see what had been done.

"The tennis racquet belonged, not to his sister, but to her daughter Jennifer. Someone who knew exactly where the cache was, went out to the Sports Pavilion one night, having previously taken an impression of the key and got a key cut. At that time of night everyone should have been in bed and asleep. But that was not so. Miss Springer saw the light of a flashlight in the Sports Pavilion from the house, and went out to investigate. She was a tough hefty young woman and had no doubts of her own ability to cope with anything she might find. The person in question was probably sorting through the tennis racquets to find the right one. Discovered and recognized by Miss Springer, there was no hesitation. The searcher was a killer, and shot Miss Springer dead. Afterward, however, the killer had to act fast. The shot had been heard, people were approaching. At all costs the killer must get out of the Sports Pavilion unseen. The racquet must be left where it was for the moment.

"Within a few days another method was tried. A strange woman with a faked American accent waylaid Jennifer Sutcliffe as she was coming from the tennis courts, and told her a plausible story about a relative of hers having sent her down a new tennis racquet. Jennifer unsuspiciously accepted this story and gladly exchanged the racquet she was carrying for the new expensive one the stranger had brought. But a circumstance had arisen which the woman with the American accent knew nothing about. That was that a few days previously Jennifer Sutcliffe and Julia Upjohn had exchanged racquets so that what the strange woman took away with her was in actual fact Julia Upjohn's old racquet, though the identifying tape on it bore Jennifer's name.

"We come now to the second tragedy. Miss Vansittart for some unknown reason, but possibly connected with the kidnaping of Shaista which had taken place that afternoon, took a flashlight and went out to the Sports Pavilion after everybody had gone to bed. Somebody who had followed her there, struck her down with a cosh or a sandbag, as she was stooping down by Shaista's locker. Again the crime was discovered almost immediately. Miss Chadwick saw a light in the Sports Pavilion and hurried out there.

"The police once more took charge at the Sports Pavilion, and again the killer was debarred from searching and examining the tennis racquets there. But by now, Julia Upjohn, an intelligent child, had thought things over and had come to the logical conclusion that the racquet she possessed and which had originally belonged to Jennifer, was in some way important. She investigated on her own behalf, found that she was correct in her surmise, and brought the contents of the racquet to me.

"These are now," said Hercule Poirot, "in safe custody and need concern us here no longer." He paused and then went on, "It remains to consider the third tragedy.

"What Mademoiselle Blanche knew or suspected we shall never know. She may have seen someone leaving the house on the night of Miss Springer's murder. Whatever it was that she knew or suspected, she knew the identity of the murderer. And she kept that knowledge to herself. She planned to obtain money in return for her silence.

"There is nothing," said Hercule Poirot, with feeling, "more dangerous than levying blackmail on a person who has killed perhaps twice already. Mademoiselle Blanche may have taken her own precautions but whatever they were, they were inadequate. She made an appointment with the murderer and she was killed."

He paused again.

"So there," he said, looking round at them, "you have the account of this whole affair."

They were all staring at him. Their faces which at first had reflected interest, surprise, excitement, seemed now frozen into a uniform calm. It was as though they were terrified to display any emotion. Hercule Poirot nodded at them.

"Yes," he said, "I know how you feel. It has come, has it not, very near home? That is why, you see, I and Inspector Kelsey and Mr. Adam Goodman have been making the inquiries. We have to know, you see, if there is still a cat among the pigeons! You understand what I mean? Is there still someone here who is masquerading under false colours?"

There was a slight ripple passing through those who listened to him, a brief almost furtive sidelong glance as though they wished to look at each other, but did not dare do so.

"I am happy to reassure you," said Poirot. "All of you here at this moment *are exactly who you say you are*. Miss Chadwick, for instance, is Miss Chadwick—that is certainly not open to doubt, she has been here as long as Meadowbank itself! Miss Johnson, too, is unmistakably Miss Johnson. Miss Rich is Miss Rich. Miss Shapland is Miss Shapland. Miss Rowan and Miss Blake are Miss Rowan and Miss Blake. To go further," said Poirot, turning his head, "Adam Goodman who works here in the garden, is, if not precisely Adam Goodman, at any rate the person whose name is on his credentials. So then, where are we? We must seek not for someone masquerading as someone else, but for someone who is, in his or her proper identity, a murderer."

The room was very still now. There was menace in the air.

Poirot went on.

"We want, primarily, *someone who was in Ramat three months ago*. Knowledge that the prize was concealed in the tennis racquet could only have been acquired in one way. Someone must have *seen* it put there by Bob Rawlinson. It is as simple as that. Who then, of all of you present here, was in Ramat three months ago? Miss Chadwick was here, Miss Johnson was here." His eyes went on to the two junior mistresses. "Miss Rowan and Miss Blake were here."

His finger went out pointing.

"But Miss Rich—Miss Rich was not here last term, was she?"

"I—no. I was ill." She spoke hurriedly. "I was away for a term."

"That is the thing that we did not know," said Hercule Poirot, "until a few days ago somebody mentioned it casually. When questioned by the police originally, you merely said that you had been at Meadowbank for a year and a half. That in itself is true enough. But you were absent last term. You could have been in Ramat—I think you were in Ramat. Be careful. It can be verified, you know, from your passport."

There was a moment's silence, then Eileen Rich looked up.

"Yes," she said quietly. "I was in Ramat. Why not?"

"Why did you go to Ramat, Miss Rich?"

"You already know. I had been ill. I was advised to take a rest—to go abroad. I wrote to Miss Bulstrode and explained that I must take a term off. She quite understood."

"That is so," said Miss Bulstrode. "A doctor's certificate was enclosed which said that it would be unwise for Miss Rich to resume her duties until the following term."

"So—you went to Ramat?" said Hercule Poirot.

"Why shouldn't I go to Ramat?" said Eileen Rich. Her voice trembled slightly. "There are cheap fares offered to school teachers. I wanted a rest. I wanted sunshine. I went out to Ramat. I spent two months there. *Why not? Why not, I say?*"

"You have never mentioned that you were in Ramat at the time of the revolution."

"Why should I? What has it got to do with anyone here? I haven't killed anyone, I tell you. I haven't killed anyone."

"You were recognized, you know," said Hercule Poirot. "Not recognized definitely, but indefinitely. The child Jennifer was very vague. She said she thought she'd seen you in Ramat but concluded it couldn't be you because, she said, the person she had seen was *fat,* not thin." He leaned forward, his eyes boring into Eileen Rich's face.

"What have you to say, Miss Rich?"

She wheeled round. "I know what you're trying to make out!" she cried. "You're trying to make out that it wasn't a secret agent or anything of that kind who did these murders. That it was someone who just *happened* to be there, someone who *happened* to see this treasure hidden in a tennis racquet. Someone who realized that the child was coming to Meadowbank and that she'd have an opportunity to take for herself this hidden thing. But I tell you it isn't *true!*"

"I think that is what happened. Yes," said Poirot. "Someone saw the jewels being hidden and forgot all other duties or interests in the determination to possess them!"

"It isn't true, I tell you. I saw nothing—"

"Inspector Kelsey," Poirot turned his head.

Inspector Kelsey nodded—went to the door, opened it, and Mrs. Upjohn walked into the room.

ii.

"How do you do, Miss Bulstrode," said Mrs. Upjohn, looking rather embarrassed. "I'm sorry I'm looking rather untidy, but I was somewhere near Ankara yesterday and I've just flown home. I'm in a terrible mess and I really haven't had time to clean myself up or do *anything.*"

"That does not matter," said Hercule Poirot. "We want to ask you something."

"Mrs. Upjohn," said Kelsey, "when you came here to bring your daughter to the school and you were in Miss

Bulstrode's sitting room, you looked out of the window—the window which gives on the front drive—and you uttered an exclamation as though you recognized someone you saw there. That is so, is it not?"

Mrs. Upjohn stared at him. "When I was in Miss Bulstrode's sitting room? I looked—oh, yes, of *course!* Yes, I did see someone."

"Someone you were surprised to see?"

"Well, I was rather . . . You see, it had all been such years ago."

"You mean the days when you were working in Intelligence toward the end of the war?"

"Yes. It was about fifteen years ago. Of course, she looked much older, but I recognized her at once. And I wondered what on earth she could be doing *here*."

"Mrs. Upjohn, will you look round this room and tell me if you see that person here now?"

"Yes, of course," said Mrs. Upjohn. "I saw her as soon as I came in. That's her."

She stretched out a pointing finger. Inspector Kelsey was quick and so was Adam, but they were not quick enough. Ann Shapland had sprung to her feet. In her hand was a small wicked-looking automatic and it pointed straight at Mrs. Upjohn. Miss Bulstrode, quicker than the two men, moved sharply forward, but swifter still was Miss Chadwick. It was not Mrs. Upjohn that she was trying to shield—it was the woman who was standing between Ann Shapland and Mrs. Upjohn.

"No, you shan't," cried Chaddy, and flung herself on Miss Bulstrode just as the small automatic went off.

Miss Chadwick staggered, then slowly crumpled down. Miss Johnson ran to her. Adam and Kelsey had got hold of Ann Shapland now. She was struggling like a cat, but they wrested the small automatic from her.

Mrs. Upjohn said breathlessly:

"They said then that she was a killer. Although she was so young. One of the most dangerous agents they had. Angelica was her code name."

"You lying bitch!" Ann Shapland fairly spat out the words.

Hercule Poirot said:

"She does not lie. You are dangerous. You have always led a dangerous life. Up to now, you have never been suspected in your own identity. All the jobs you have taken in your own name have been perfectly genuine jobs, efficiently performed—but they have all been jobs with a purpose, and that purpose has been the gaining of information. You have worked with an oil company, with an archaeologist whose work took him to a certain part of the globe, with an actress whose protector was an eminent politician. Ever since you were seventeen you have worked as an agent—though for many different masters. Your services have been for hire and have been highly paid. You have played a dual role. Most of your assignments have been carried out in your own name, but there were certain jobs for which you assumed different identities. Those were the times when ostensibly you had to go home and be with your mother.

"But I strongly suspect, Miss Shapland, that the elderly woman I visited who lives in a small village with a nurse-companion to look after her, an elderly woman who is genuinely a mental patient with a confused mind, is not your mother at all. She has been your excuse for retiring from employment and from the circle of your friends. The three months this winter that you spent with your 'mother' who had one of her 'bad turns,' covers the time when you went out to Ramat. Not as Ann Shapland but as Angelica da Toredo, a Spanish, or near-Spanish, cabaret dancer. You occupied the room in the hotel next to that of Mrs. Sutcliffe and somehow you managed to see Bob Rawlinson conceal the jewels in the racquet. You had no opportunity of taking the racquet then for there was the sudden evacuation of all British people, but you had read the labels on their luggage and it was easy to find out something about them. To obtain a secretarial post here was not difficult. I have made some inquiries. You paid a substantial sum to Miss Bulstrode's former secretary to vacate her post on the plea of a 'breakdown.' And you had quite a plausible story. You had been commissioned to write a series of articles on a famous girls' school 'from within.'

"It all seemed quite easy, did it not? If a child's racquet was missing, what of it? Simpler still, you would go out at night to the Sports Pavilion, and abstract the jewels. But you had not reckoned with Miss Springer. Perhaps she had already seen you examining the racquets. Perhaps she just happened to wake that night. She followed you out there and you shot her. Later, Mademoiselle Blanche tried to blackmail you, and you killed her. It comes natural to you, does it not, to kill?"

He stopped. In a monotonous official voice, Inspector Kelsey cautioned his prisoner.

She did not listen. Turning toward Hercule Poirot, she burst out in a low-pitched flood of invective that startled everyone in the room.

"Whew!" said Adam, as Kelsey took her away. "And I thought she was a nice girl!"

Miss Johnson had been kneeling by Miss Chadwick.

"I'm afraid she's badly hurt," she said. "She'd better not be moved until the doctor comes."

■

24

Poirot Explains

MRS. UPJOHN, wandering through the corridors of Meadowbank school, forgot the exciting scene she had just been through. She was for the moment merely a mother seeking her young. She found her in a deserted classroom. Julia was bending over a desk, her tongue protruding slightly, absorbed in the agonies of composition.

She looked up and stared. Then flung herself across the room and hugged her mother.

"Mummy!"

Then, with the self-consciousness of her age, ashamed of her unrestrained emotion, she detached herself and spoke in a carefully casual tone—indeed almost accusingly.

"Aren't you back rather *soon,* Mummy?"

"I flew back," said Mrs. Upjohn, almost apologetically, "from Ankara."

"Oh," said Julia. "Well—I'm glad you're back."

"Yes," said Mrs. Upjohn, "I am very glad too."

They looked at each other, embarrassed. "What are you doing?" said Mrs. Upjohn, advancing a little closer.

"I'm writing a composition for Miss Rich," said Julia. "She really does set the most exciting subjects."

"What's this one?" said Mrs. Upjohn. She bent over.

The subject was written at the top of the page. Some nine or ten lines of writing in Julia's uneven and sprawling handwriting came below. "Contrast the Attitudes of Macbeth and Lady Macbeth to Murder," read Mrs. Upjohn.

"Well," she said doubtfully, "you can't say that the subject isn't topical!"

She read the start of her daughter's essay. "Macbeth," Julia had written, "liked the idea of murder and had been thinking of it a lot, but he needed a push to get him started. Once he'd got started he enjoyed murdering people and had no more qualms or fears. Lady Macbeth was just greedy and ambitious. She thought she didn't mind what she did to get what she wanted. But once she'd done it she found she didn't like it after all."

"Your language isn't very elegant," said Mrs. Upjohn. "I think you'll have to polish it up a bit, but you've certainly got something there."

ii.

Inspector Kelsey was speaking in a slightly complaining tone.

"It's all very well for you, Poirot," he said. "You can say and do a lot of things we can't; and I'll admit the whole thing was well stage-managed. Got her off her guard, made her think we were after Rich, and then Mrs. Upjohn's sudden appearance made her lose her head. Thank the Lord she kept that automatic after shooting Springer. If the bullet corresponds—"

"It will, *mon ami,* it will," said Poirot.

"Then we've got her cold for the murder of Springer. And I gather Miss Chadwick's in a bad way. But look here, Poirot, I still can't see how she can possibly have killed Miss Vansittart. It's physically impossible. She's got a cast-iron alibi—unless young Rathbone and the whole staff of Le Nid Sauvage are in it with her."

Poirot shook his head. "Oh, no," he said. "Her alibi is perfectly good. She killed Miss Springer and Mademoiselle Blanche. But Miss Vansittart—" He hesitated for a moment, his eyes going to where Miss Bulstrode sat listening to them. "Miss Vansittart was killed by Miss Chadwick."

"Miss Chadwick?" exclaimed Miss Bulstrode and Kelsey together.

Poirot nodded. "I am sure of it."

"But—why?"

"I think," said Poirot, "Miss Chadwick loved Meadowbank too much . . ." His eyes went across to Miss Bulstrode.

"I see . . ." said Miss Bulstrode. "Yes, yes, I see . . . I ought to have known." She paused. "You mean that she—"

"I mean," said Poirot, "that she started here with you, that all along she has regarded Meadowbank as a joint venture between you both."

"Which in one sense it was," said Miss Bulstrode.

"Quite so," said Poirot. "But that was merely the financial aspect. When you began to talk of retiring she regarded herself as the person who would take over."

"But she's far too old," objected Miss Bulstrode.

"Yes," said Poirot, "she is too old and she is not suited to be a headmistress. But she herself did not think so. She thought that when you went she would be headmistress of Meadowbank as a matter of course. And then she found that was not so. That you were considering someone else, that you had fastened upon Eleanor Vansittart. And she loved Meadowbank. She loved the school and she did not like Eleanor Vansittart. I think in the end she hated her."

"She might have done," said Miss Bulstrode. "Yes, Eleanor Vansittart was—how shall I put it—she was always very complacent, very superior about everything. That would be hard to bear if you were jealous. That's what you mean, isn't it? Chaddy was jealous."

"Yes," said Poirot. "She was jealous of Meadowbank

and jealous of Eleanor Vansittart. She couldn't bear the thought of the school and Miss Vansittart together. And then perhaps something in your manner led her to think that you were weakening."

"I did weaken," said Miss Bulstrode. "But I didn't weaken in the way that perhaps Chaddy thought I would weaken. Actually I thought of someone younger still than Miss Vansittart. I thought it over and then I said, Not enough experience. Chaddy was with me then, I remember."

"And she thought," said Poirot, "that you were referring to Miss Vansittart. That you were saying Miss Vansittart was too young. She thoroughly agreed. She thought that experience and wisdom such as she had got were far more important things. But then, after all, you returned to your original decision. You chose Eleanor Vansittart as the right person and left her in charge of the school that week end. This is what I think happened. On that Sunday night Miss Chadwick was restless; she got up and saw the light in the squash court. She went out there exactly as she says she went. There is only one thing different in her story from what she said. It wasn't a golf club she took with her. She picked up one of the sandbags from the pile in the hall. She went out there all ready to deal with a burglar, with someone who for a second time had broken into the Sports Pavilion. She had the sandbag ready in her hand to defend herself if attacked. And what did she find? She found Eleanor Vansittart kneeling down looking in a locker, and she thought, it may be—for I am good," said Hercule Poirot in a parenthesis, "at putting myself into other people's minds—she thought, '*If* I were a marauder, a burglar, I would come up behind her and strike her down.' And as the thought came into her mind, only half conscious of what she was doing, she raised the sandbag and struck. And there was Eleanor Vansittart dead, out of her way. She was appalled then, I think, at what she had done. It has preyed on her ever since—for she is not a natural killer, Miss Chadwick. She was driven, as some are driven, by jealousy and by obsession. The obsession of love for Meadowbank. Now that Eleanor Vansittart was dead she was quite sure that she would succeed you at Meadowbank. So she didn't confess. She told her story to the police exactly as it had occurred but for the one vital fact, that it was *she* who had struck the blow. But when she was asked about the golf club which presumably Miss Vansittart took with her, being nervous after all that had occurred, Miss Chadwick said quickly that she had taken it out there. She didn't want you to think even for a moment that she had handled the sandbag."

"Why did Ann Shapland also choose a sandbag to kill Mademoiselle Blanche?" asked Miss Bulstrode.

"For one thing, she could not risk a pistol shot in the school building, and for another she is a very clever young woman. She wanted to tie up this third murder with the second one, for which she had an alibi."

"I don't really understand what Eleanor Vansittart was doing herself in the Sports Pavilion," said Miss Bulstrode.

"I think one could make a guess. She was probably far more concerned over the disappearance of Shaista than she allowed to appear on the surface. She was as upset as Miss Chadwick was. In a way it was worse for her, because she had been left by you in charge—and the kidnaping had happened while she was responsible. Moreover she had pooh-poohed it as long as possible through an unwillingness to face unpleasant facts squarely."

"So there was weakness behind the façade," mused Miss Bulstrode. "I sometimes suspected it."

"She, too, I think, was unable to sleep. And I think she went out quietly to the Sports Pavilion to make an examination of Shaista's locker in case there might be some clue there to the girl's disappearance."

"You seem to have explanations for everything, M. Poirot."

"That's his specialty," said Inspector Kelsey with slight malice.

"And what was the point of getting Eileen Rich to sketch various members of my staff?"

"I wanted to test the child Jennifer's ability to recognize a face. I soon satisfied myself that Jennifer was so entirely preoccupied by her own affairs, that she gave outsiders at most a cursory glance, taking in only the external details of their appearance. She did not recognize a sketch of Mademoiselle Blanche with a different hairdo. Still less, then, would she have recognized Ann Shapland who, as your secretary, she seldom saw at close quarters."

"You think that the woman with the racquet was Ann Shapland herself."

"Yes. It has been a one-woman job all through. You remember that day you rang for her to take a message to Julia but in the end, as the buzzer went unanswered, sent a girl to find Julia? Ann was accustomed to quick disguise. A fair wig, differently pencilled eyebrows, a 'fussy' dress and hat. She need only be absent from her typewriter for about twenty minutes. I saw from Miss Rich's clever sketches how easy it is for a woman to alter her appearance by purely external matters."

"Miss Rich—I wonder . . ." Miss Bulstrode looked thoughtful.

Poirot gave Inspector Kelsey a look and the Inspector said he must be getting along.

"Miss Rich?" said Miss Bulstrode again.

"Send for her," said Poirot. "It is the best way."

Eileen Rich appeared. She was white-faced and slightly defiant.

"You want to know," she said to Miss Bulstrode, "what I was doing in Ramat?"

"I think I have an idea," said Miss Bulstrode.

"Just so," said Poirot. "Children nowadays know all the facts of life—but their eyes often retain innocence."

He added that he, too, must be getting along, and slipped out.

"That was it, wasn't it?" said Miss Bulstrode. Her voice was brisk and businesslike. "Jennifer merely described it as fat. She didn't realize it was a pregnant woman she had seen."

"Yes," said Eileen Rich. "That was it. I was going to have a child. I didn't want to give up my job here. I carried on all right through the autumn, but after that, it was beginning to show. I got a doctor's certificate that I wasn't fit to carry on, and I pleaded illness. I went abroad to a remote spot where I thought I wasn't likely to meet anyone who knew me. I came back to this country and the child was born—dead. I came back this term and

I hoped that no one would ever know. But you understand now, don't you, why I said I should have had to refuse your offer of a partnership if you'd made it? Only now, with the school in such a disaster, I thought that, after all, I might be able to accept."

She paused and said in a matter-of-fact voice,

"Would you like me to leave now? Or wait until the end of term?"

"You'll stay till the end of the term," said Miss Bulstrode, "and if there is a new term, which I still hope, you'll come back."

"Come back?" said Eileen Rich. "Do you mean you still want me?"

"Of course I want you," said Miss Bulstrode. "You haven't murdered anyone, have you? Not gone mad over jewels and planned to kill to get them? I'll tell you what you've done. You've probably denied your instincts too long. There was a man, you fell in love with him, you had a child. I suppose you couldn't marry."

"There was never any question of marriage," said Eileen Rich. "I knew that. He isn't to blame."

"Very well, then," said Miss Bulstrode. "You had a love affair and a child. You wanted to have that child?"

"Yes," said Eileen Rich. "Yes, I wanted to have it."

"So that's that," said Miss Bulstrode. "Now I'm going to tell you something. I believe that in spite of this love affair, your real vocation in life is teaching. I think your profession means more to you than any normal woman's life with a husband and children would mean."

"Oh, yes," said Eileen Rich. "I'm sure of that. I've known that all along. That's what I really want to do—that's the real passion of my life."

"Then don't be a fool," said Miss Bulstrode. "I'm making you a very good offer. If, that is, things come right. We'll spend two or three years together putting Meadowbank back on the map. You'll have different ideas as to how that should be done from the ideas that I have. I'll listen to your ideas. Maybe I'll even give in to some of them. You want things to be different, I suppose, at Meadowbank?"

"I do in some ways, yes," said Eileen Rich. "I won't

pretend. I want more emphasis on getting girls that really matter."

"Ah," said Miss Bulstrode, "I see. It's the snob element that you don't like, is that it?"

"Yes," said Eileen, "it seems to me to spoil things."

"What you don't realize," said Miss Bulstrode, "is that to get the kind of girl you want you've *got* to have that snob element. It's quite a small element really, you know. A few foreign royalties, a few great names and everybody, all the silly parents all over this country and other countries want their girls to come to Meadowbank. Fall over themselves to get their girls admitted to Meadowbank. What's the result? An enormous waiting list, and I look at the girls and I see the girls and I choose! You get your pick, do you see? I choose my girls. I choose them very carefully, some for character, some for brains, some for pure academic intellect. Some because I think they haven't had a chance but are capable of being made something of that's worth while. You're young, Eileen. You're full of ideals—it's the teaching that matters to you and the ethical side of it. Your vision's quite right. It's the girls that matter, but if you want to make a success of anything, you know, you've got to be a good tradesman as well. Ideas are like everything else. They've got to be marketed. We'll have to do some pretty slick work in future to get Meadowbank going again. I'll have to get my hooks into a few people, former pupils, bully them, plead with them, get them to send their daughters here. And then the others will come. You let me be up to my tricks, and then you shall have your way. Meadowbank will go on and it'll be a fine school."

"It'll be the finest school in England," said Eileen Rich enthusiastically.

"Good," said Miss Bulstrode, "and Eileen, I should go and get your hair properly cut and shaped. You don't seem able to manage that bun. And now," she said, her voice changing, "I must go to Chaddy."

She went in and came up to the bed. Miss Chadwick was lying very still and white. The blood had all gone from her face and she looked drained of life. A policeman with a notebook sat nearby and Miss Johnson sat on the other side of the bed. She looked at Miss Bulstrode and shook her head gently.

"Hallo, Chaddy," said Miss Bulstrode. She took up the limp hand in hers. Miss Chadwick's eyes opened.

"I want to tell you," she said, "Honoria—it was—it was me."

"Yes, dear, I know," said Miss Bulstrode.

"Jealous," said Chaddy. "I wanted—"

"I know," said Miss Bulstrode.

Tears rolled very slowly down Miss Chadwick's cheeks. "It's so awful . . . I didn't mean—I don't know how I came to do such a thing!"

"Don't think about it any more," said Miss Bulstrode.

"But I can't—you'll never—I'll never forgive my-self—"

Miss Bulstrode held the hand a little more tightly in hers.

"Listen, dear," she said. "You saved my life, you know. My life and the life of that nice woman, Mrs. Upjohn. That counts for something, doesn't it?"

"I only wish," said Miss Chadwick, "I could have given *my* life for you both. That would have made it all right . . ."

Miss Bulstrode looked at her with great pity. Miss Chadwick took a great breath, smiled, then, moving her head very slightly to one side, she died.

"You *did* give your life, my dear," said Miss Bulstrode softly. "I hope you realize that—now."

25

Legacy

"A MR. ROBINSON has called to see you, sir."

"Ah!" said Hercule Poirot. He stretched out his hand and picked up a letter from the desk in front of him. He looked down on it thoughtfully.

He said: "Show him in, Georges."

The letter was only a few lines:

Dear Poirot,

A Mr. Robinson may call upon you in the near future. You may already know something about him. Quite a prominent figure in certain circles. There is a demand for such men in our modern world. I believe, if I may so put it, that he is, in this particular matter, on the side of the angels. This is just a recommendation, if you should be in doubt. Of course, and I underline this, we have no idea as to the matter on which he wishes to consult you.

Ha ha! and likewise ho ho!

Yours ever,
Ephraim Pikeaway

Poirot laid down the letter and rose as Mr. Robinson came into the room. He bowed, shook hands, indicated a chair.

Mr. Robinson sat, pulled out a handkerchief and wiped his large yellow face. He observed that it was a warm day.

"You have not, I hope, walked here in this heat?"

Poirot looked horrified at the idea. By a natural association of ideas, his fingers went to his moustaches. He was reassured. There was no limpness.

Mr. Robinson looked equally horrified.

"No, no, indeed. I came in my Rolls. But these traffic blocks. One sits for half an hour sometimes."

Poirot nodded sympathetically.

There was a pause—the pause that ensues on part one of a conversation before entering upon part two.

"I was interested to hear—of course one hears so many things—most of them quite untrue—that you had been concerning yourself with the affairs of a girls' school."

"Ah," said Poirot. "That!"

He leaned back in his chair.

"Meadowbank," said Mr. Robinson thoughtfully. "Quite one of the premier schools of England."

"It is a fine school."

"Is? Or was?"

"I hope the former."

"I hope so, too," said Mr. Robinson. "I fear it may be touch and go. Ah well, one must do what one can. A little financial backing to tide over a certain inevitable period of depression. A few carefully chosen new pupils. I am not without influence in European circles."

"I, too, have applied persuasion in certain quarters. If, as you say, we can tide things over. Mercifully, memories are short."

"That is what one hopes. But one must admit that events have taken place there that might well shake the nerves of fond mammas—and papas also. The games mistress, the French mistress, and yet another mistress—all murdered."

"As you say."

"I hear," said Mr. Robinson, "one hears so many things, that the unfortunate young woman responsible has suffered from a phobia about schoolmistresses since her youth. An unhappy childhood at school. Psychiatrists will make a good deal of this. They will try at least for a verdict of diminished responsibility, as they call it nowadays."

"That line would seem to be the best choice," said Poirot. "You will pardon me for saying that I hope it will not succeed."

"I agree with you entirely. A most cold-blooded killer. But they will make much of her excellent character, her work as secretary to various well-known people, her war record—quite distinguished, I believe—counterespionage . . ."

He let the last words out with a certain significance—a hint of a question in his voice.

"She was very good, I believe," he said more briskly. "So young—but quite brilliant, of great use—to both sides. That was her métier—she should have stuck to it. But I can understand the temptation—to play a lone hand, and gain a big prize." He added softly, "A very big prize."

Poirot nodded.

Mr. Robinson leaned forward.

"Where are they, M. Poirot?"

"I think you know where they are."

"Well, frankly, yes, Banks are such useful institutions, are they not?"

Poirot smiled.

"We needn't beat about the bush really, need we, my dear fellow? What are you going to do about them?"

"I have been waiting."

"Waiting for what?"

"Shall we say—for suggestions?"

"Yes—I see."

"You understand they do not belong to me. I would like to hand them over to the person they do belong to. But that, if I appraise the position correctly, is not so simple."

"Governments are in such a difficult position," said Mr. Robinson. "Vulnerable, so to speak. What with oil, and steel, and uranium, and cobalt and all the rest of it, foreign relations are a matter of the utmost delicacy. The great thing is to be able to say that Her Majesty's Government has absolutely *no* information on the subject."

"But I cannot keep this important deposit at my bank indefinitely."

"Exactly. That is why I have come to propose that you should hand it over to me."

"Ah," said Poirot. "Why?"

"I can give you some excellent reasons. These jewels—mercifully we are not official, we can call things by their right names—were unquestionably the personal property of the late Prince Ali Yusuf."

"I understand that is so."

"His Highness handed them over to Squadron Leader Robert Rawlinson with certain instructions. They were to be got out of Ramat, and they were to be delivered to *me*."

"Have you proof of that?"

"Certainly."

Mr. Robinson drew a long envelope from his pocket. Out of it he took several papers. He laid them before Poirot on the desk.

Poirot bent over them and studied them carefully.

"It seems to be as you say."

"Well, then?"

"Do you mind if I ask a question?"

"Not at all."

"What do you, personally, get out of this?"

Mr. Robinson looked surprised.

"My dear fellow. Money, of course. Quite a lot of money."

Poirot looked at him thoughtfully.

"It is a very old trade," said Mr. Robinson. "And a lucrative one. There are quite a lot of us, a network all over the globe. We are, how shall I put it, the arrangers behind the scenes. For kings, for presidents, for politicians, for all those, in fact, upon whom the fierce light beats, as a poet has put it. We work in with one another, and remember this: we keep faith. Our profits are large but we are honest. Our services are costly—but we do render service."

"I see," said Poirot. *"Eh bien!* I agree to what you ask."

"I can assure you that that decision will please everyone." Mr. Robinson's eyes just rested for a moment on Colonel Pikeaway's letter where it lay at Poirot's right hand.

"But just one little moment. I am human. I have curiosity. What are you going to do with these jewels?"

Mr. Robinson looked at him. Then his large yellow face creased into a smile. He leaned forward.

"I shall tell you."
He told him.

ii.

Children were playing up and down the street. Their
raucous cries filled the air. Mr. Robinson, alighting pon-
derously from his Rolls, was cannoned into by one of
them.

Mr. Robinson put the child aside with a not unkindly
hand and peered up at the number of the house.

No. 15. This was right. He pushed open the gate and
went up the three steps to the front door. Neat white
curtains at the windows, he noted, and a well polished
brass knocker. An insignificant little house in an insignificant street in an insignificant part of London, but it was
well kept. It had self-respect.

The door opened. A girl of about twenty-five, pleasant
looking, with a kind of fair, chocolate-box prettiness,
welcomed him with a smile.

"Mr. Robinson? Come in."

She took him into the small sitting room. A television
set, cretonnes of a Jacobean pattern, a cottage piano
against the wall. She had on a dark skirt and a grey
pullover.

"You'll have some tea? I've got the kettle on."

"Thank you, but no. I never drink tea. And I can only
stay a short time. I have only come to bring you what I
wrote to you about."

"From Ali?"

"Yes."

"There isn't—there couldn't be any hope? I mean—
it's really true—that he was killed? There couldn't be any
mistake?"

"I'm afraid there was no mistake," said Mr. Robinson
gently.

"No—no, I suppose not. Anyway, I never expected
. . . When he went back there I didn't think really I'd
ever see him again. I don't mean I thought he was going
to be killed or that there would be a revolution. I just
mean—well, you know—he'd have to carry on, do his

stuff—what was expected of him. Marry one of his own people—all that."

Mr. Robinson drew out a package and laid it down on the table.

"Open it, please."

Her fingers fumbled a little as she tore the wrappings off and then unfolded the final covering . . .

She drew her breath in sharply.

Red, blue, green, white, all sparkling with fire, with life, turning the dim little room into Aladdin's cave.

Mr. Robinson watched her. He had seen so many women look at jewels.

She said at last in a breathless voice:

"Are they—they can't be—*real?*"

"They are real."

"But they must be worth—they must be worth . . ."

Her imagination failed.

Mr. Robinson nodded.

"If you wish to dispose of them, you can probably get at least half a million pounds for them."

"No—no, it's not possible."

Suddenly she scooped them up in her hands and rewrapped them with shaking fingers.

"I'm scared," she said. "They frighten me. What am I to do with them?"

The door burst open. A small boy rushed in.

"Mum, I got a smashing tank off Billy. He—"

He stopped, staring at Mr. Robinson.

An olive-skinned, dark-eyed boy.

His mother said:

"Go in the kitchen, Allen, your tea's all ready. Milk and biscuits and there's a bit of gingerbread."

"Oh, good." He departed noisily.

"You call him Allen?" said Mr. Robinson.

She flushed.

"It was the nearest name to Ali. I couldn't call him Ali—too difficult for him and the neighbours and all."

She went on, her face clouding over again.

"What am I to do?"

"First, have you got your marriage certificate? I have to be sure you're the person you say you are."

She stared a moment, then went over to a small desk.

From one of the drawers she brought out an envelope, extracted a paper from it and brought it to him.

"Hm . . . yes . . . Registrar of Edmondstow . . . Ali Yusuf, student . . . Alice Calder, spinster. Yes, all in order."

"Oh, it's legal all right—as far as it goes. And no one ever tumbled to who he was. There's so many of these foreign Moslem students, you see. We knew it didn't mean anything really. He was a Moslem and he could have more than one wife, and he knew he'd have to go back and do just that. We talked about it. But Allen was on the way, you see, and he said this would make it all right for him—we were married all right in this country and Allen would be legitimate. It was the best he could do for me. He really did love me, you know. He really did."

"Yes," said Mr. Robinson. "I am sure he did."

He went on briskly, "Now, supposing that you put yourself in my hands. I will see to the selling of these stones. And I will give you the address of a lawyer, a really good and reliable solicitor. He will advise you, I expect, to put most of the money in a trust fund. And there will be other things, education for your son, and a new way of life for you. You'll want social education and guidance. You're going to be a very rich woman and all the sharks and the confidence tricksters and the rest of them will be after you. Your life's not going to be easy except in the purely material sense. Rich people don't have an easy time in life, I can tell you—I've seen too many of them to have that illusion. But you've got character. I think you'll come through. And that boy of yours may be a happier man than his father ever was."

He paused. "You agree?"

"Yes. Take them." She pushed them toward him, then said suddenly: "That schoolgirl—the one who found them —I'd like her to have one of them—which—what colour do you think she'd like?"

Mr. Robinson reflected. "An emerald, I think—green for mystery. A good idea of yours. She will find that very thrilling."

He rose to his feet.

"I shall charge you for my services, you know," said

Mr. Robinson. "And my charges are pretty high. But I shan't cheat you."

She gave him a level glance.

"No, I don't think you will. And I need someone who knows about business, because I don't."

"You seem a very sensible woman if I may say so. Now then, I'm to take these? You don't want to keep—just one—say?"

He watched her with curiosity, the sudden flicker of excitement, the hungry covetous eyes—and then the flicker died.

"No," said Alice. "I won't keep—even one." She flushed. "Oh, I daresay that seems daft to you—not to keep just one big ruby or an emerald—just as a keepsake. But you see, he and I—he was a Moslem but he let me read bits now and again out of the Bible. And we read that bit—about a woman whose price was above rubies. And so—I won't have any jewels. I'd rather not."

"A most unusual woman," said Mr. Robinson to himself as he walked down the path and into his waiting Rolls.

He repeated to himself:

"A most unusual woman."

Agatha Christie

Baffling Tales of Murder, Mystery and Mayhem!

Available at bookstores everywhere, or order direct from publisher.   AC 78B